Summer to Fall

Albert Waitt

ACKNOWELDGEMENTS

There are many people I am indebted to upon the completion of this novel. Thanks to my readers, Ray Bartlett, Dan Healy, and especially Rob O'Regan, who also served time as editor. I'd like to thank my parents, Al and Angie. My wife Kim also deserves much credit, as her patience is tested on a daily basis when I choose writing over mowing the lawn and other household chores. Sydney and Aaron, thanks for making me want to do better. Thanks to Dave Allen and Kati Gaulkin, "the Art Department." Thanks to Doug "the Bug" Quintal, my former band mate and songwriting partner, who now offers guidance in other areas. Thanks to Fred Pahl, who was there to give me a kick in the pants when I needed one. And my gratitude goes out to Tom Bailey and Leslie Epstein, the right teachers at the right times.

PART ONE

CHAPTER ONE

Gravel shot out behind the pickup as Cam Preston gunned it onto the dirt road that led to Nate Horton's place. He was only ten minutes late but working for Brinkley he knew he'd hear about it. On his left lay the backside of Laurel Harbor. The tidal pool was flooded, the water flat and still, reflecting the sun into his eyes. All but one of the lobster boats that moored there were out; the rumble of their grinding engines drifted in from beyond the jetty. Horton liked to brag about the number of painters he kicked off his property: Across the cove, the abandoned, gray bait shed at the near end of the pier looked postcard Maine. The rotting bait fish it once held, however, had curdled many a stomach.

Cam parked at the end of the driveway. Warren Brinkley stood next to his van drinking a Dunkin Donuts coffee. He was staring at the garage they were going to tear down and then rebuild to three times its size, adding an in-law apartment, two horse stalls, and a pottery studio for Horton's wife. The single-story, two-bay hovel listed to the right like a torpedoed ship. Its cedar shingles bowed out and the weather vane on the rotting cupola indicated that the sky was north and the ground south. The garage doors hung on rusted hinges, and they, too, were uneven. Brinkley, with a body like a beer keg, could have thrown himself at it and toppled the thing. He looked ready to do so.

"This is not going to become a habit, right?" Brinkley said as soon as Cam stepped out of his truck. In his Harley shirt, Brinkley's stomach looked as hard as his biceps. White, frizzled hair that normally hung to his shoulders instead struck out in every direction from under a faded Red Sox cap.

"I know. I was on my way out the door when these friends of my parents called about building them a doghouse, if you can believe that."

"That'd be about right for your skills."

"Hey, you're the one who taught me."

"Take a look," Brinkley said, lifting and walking open one of the doors. He leaned it against the front of the garage so it wouldn't fall. "Going to be a long few months, my friend."

The inside of the building, which Horton assured them would be cleared out, looked like a junk store: rusted bikes, wooden lobster traps with torn twine and busted lathes, three-legged chairs and tables, shovels, toothless rakes, a wheel barrow, a variety of cardboard boxes, and a considerable assortment of scrap lumber. A refrigerator stood in the far corner next to two retired washing machines. There wasn't a square foot of free floor space.

"There's about five tons of bundled newspapers in the loft, too," Brinkley said, pointing his wide, flat nose up at the sagging ceiling. "Could probably find out who won the Civil War if you wanted to."

"What an ass."

"You expect something different?" Brinkley smiled and the sun highlighted the faded pen-line scar that ran from the corner of his mouth to his chin. It was unseasonably warm: seventy-five degrees in the beginning of April, a welcome tease.

"I guess not." Cam shrugged.

"We might as well get started."

"You're the boss."

"No shit."

Cam shook his head and wheeled a Schwinn Stingray onto the driveway. It squeaked. Brinkley grunted and grabbed a ten speed.

They had a shoulder-high stack of frayed beach chairs sprawled next to the bicycles when they noticed Horton was halfway across the lawn and headed their way. Cam stopped, assuming they would no doubt be receiving specific instructions on where and how to arrange the garbage. Horton had bought the place six years earlier when the house was as run down as the garage. Charlie Sarofian had done the renovation; Brinkley had been his foreman. Cam had spent that summer, between his sophomore and junior years in college, as Sarofian's gopher.

"What's up guys?" Horton said, rubbing his chin. A red Fidelity Investments t-shirt didn't quite cover his ten-pin shape. His gray sweatpants stretched down to his feet, where he wore his topsiders squished at the heels like sandals.

"Lot of shit you got in there, Nate," Brinkley said, throwing a Yago Sangria beach umbrella onto the pile.

"Don't I know it," he said shaking his head. He laughed. "It all came with the place, no extra charge. Morning, Cam."

"Nate."

"We can get a dumpster here this afternoon if that's the way you want to go," Brinkley said, not bothering to mention that this was already supposed to have been taken care of. "I wouldn't worry about finding any of that PBS buried treasure."

"That's what I wanted to talk to you guys about."

Cam smirked at Brinkley. This was going to be a job of extras. People were never satisfied with their original plans:

"While you're here doing the deck do you think you could fashion a stall for the outdoor shower?" Then they went brain dead when they got their bill. "I didn't know I was going to get charged for it. Wasn't it part of the job?" Right from the start you had to explain things to clients as if they were fifth graders. If there was a point of contention, to maintain the relationship—and get paid—it was the contractor who compromised and that cost money. Sarofian never let anyone get away with anything. As far as Cam could see, that's about the only thing he had over Brinkley. Still, if Nate threw cash around here the way he bought drinks at the Dockside, they'd do very well. Brinkley just had to lay out the ground rules and get out his pen.

Horton looked down at his feet and then up at the sparse clouds lining the sky like contrails. He exhaled.

"I've got to postpone the job."

Cam laughed. Only a hardass like Brinkley would start something like this on a Friday. They weren't about to get rid of all this trash in a day and Horton didn't want to spend the weekend gazing at it. Some of his cronies were probably headed up from Boston—the bank directors and Vice Presidents he liked to parade around Laurel. It wouldn't be too impressive to have a miniature version of the town dump on the front lawn.

"I guess we can come back Monday," Brinkley said.

"Actually, Brink, I was thinking more like next spring."

"You're kidding, right?" Cam asked, an edge to his voice.

"Sorry." Horton's eyes were glued to the ground.

"What's going on?" Brinkley asked.

"I'm sure you guys are aware of how the market's been. Last year at this time I had the money to build a goddamn Taj Mahal. But a couple of months ago I got a few margin calls— totally bullshit, out of nowhere—and they sucked up the funds I had earmarked for this. Believe me, I'm not happy about it. But honestly, there's nothing I can do."

Brinkley's black pupils dilated. The skin around his jaw tightened. "You're just telling us today?"

"I knew how much this job meant to you, and I had some things in play that could have put me right back in the game. Unfortunately, they didn't fall the way we needed them to. You guys watch the news, right? Things are pretty fucked up nationally, economically speaking."

"Well, this sure fucks us up, locally, economically speaking," Cam said.

"I know you guys are the best." Nate's round, hairless face had turned white. "That's why I hired you. You'll probably have voice mails trying to snatch you up before you get home."

"Thanks for the kind words," Cam said. "I feel so much goddamn better now."

"Cam, zip it." Brinkley's face shaded a light crimson.

"Don't misunderstand me," Horton said. "You guys still have the job. I can practically guarantee that by next April, maybe even this winter, we'll be back on track here. This is your gig, Brink."

"You haven't done us any favors by waiting," Brinkley said. He kicked a stone loose from the gravel. "The kid's right to be mad. You should have given us a heads up when you started having doubts."

"I thought I explained that. I'm sorry guys. I really am." Horton straightened up to his full five-foot eight. His stomach bloated and fell with each breath. "A lot of people would have let you get going and then just not paid. You hear a lot about that kind of thing."

"Where?" Cam asked. "In your office? 'Oh, the Dow dipped a hundred points today. I guess I'll stiff the guys who redid my kitchen?'"

"Come on, I didn't do anything like that. But I can't start this project right now."

Cam looked up at Horton's house. A thirty-by-sixty Cape with two-story wings on each side. It had cost three hundred thousand to build and now had to be worth five times that. A Volvo and BMW were parked in front of it. Horton sure didn't look cash poor, which was the exact state Cam would now inhabit. This was supposed to have taken them through the summer; their next job was scheduled for October. Those who wanted beach houses renovated didn't want to lose the place during the only months they used them. Now he'd have to spend the weekend building a doghouse, not because it might be amusing, but because he could use the money. He'd also look like an ass calling back the Silvas to tell them he'd do it.

The three of them stood there for a full minute, Horton staring at the driveway, the seagulls, and his lawn.

"I guess we'll see you later, then," Brinkley said.

"Hell, I'll see you at the Dockside, same as always." He placed a hand on Brinkley's shoulder. Brinkley looked up and Horton removed it. "I really feel awful about this. I tell you what I'm going to do; I'm going to swing by there and talk to Riley about setting up a tab for you two for tonight. You guys can probably use a drink after this. It's not much, but it's the least I can do."

"That's the truth," Cam said.

"Guys, consider this project money in the bank. It'll happen."

"Maybe you could put that in writing and I'll pass it along to Ford Motor Credit," Cam said.

"I'm a victim here, too." Horton sighed. "I'll take care of you at the Dock. It'll be a good time. And seeing as how I'm willing to do that, could you gentlemen do me a small favor and shove these bikes and stuff back in there? I'd do it myself but I've got a conference call in another minute." He looked down at his wrist; he wasn't wearing a watch.

"You've got some balls, Nate," Brinkley said.

"You know what? Leave them." Horton forced a laugh, nodding as if he were a bobble head. "What the hell, they can't get any more rust on them, can they?"

"Good enough," Brinkley said.

They watched Horton waddle back up to the house. Cam went over to his truck and flipped down the tailgate. He sat down and dangled his legs. Brinkley stood across from him.

"I'll buy you a couple drinks if you put the junk back," Cam said. "Would you like a golden shower with that?"

"He's a dick, all right."

"I can't believe you took it."

"What the hell was I supposed to do? He can afford to be a punk. We can't."

"Him playing golf with Schilling. Him having lunch with Belichick. On the set of that movie with Nicholson and Matt Damon. My ass."

"Well, if he does get the money up, we'll be the ones he hires, right? Then again, he might never do it and we keep stuffing shit down the throat. But we've got to hedge our bet."

"It's not right, Brink. Look at that place."

"I know."

"Are you going to be able to move anything up?" Cam asked. "I can't afford to do nothing for a month."

"Don't start crying. You can always build that doghouse."

"I'm going to have to."

"Let's throw this crap back in the garage and get out of here."

"Like hell."

"It's fifteen minutes," Brinkley said.

"If he wants to build this winter, I'll come back and do it on Christmas."

"Suit yourself."

Cam knew that Brinkley wouldn't blame him for walking off, the same way he couldn't rag Brinkley for keeping his head. He was being a good businessman, and it wasn't his fault that Cam couldn't afford to have a job like this vanish. Now that he'd decided to move on his grandmother's house, he needed every dollar he could get. Cam grabbed the Stingray and heaved it into the garage as far as it would go.

CHAPTER TWO

Cam drove back to Gray Gull Beach. It was a quiet spot, five miles north of town off of Route 9. Tidal rivers marked its north and south ends, and ninety percent of the area between them was saltwater marsh. The houses built on the remaining lands were not crammed together as in York and Old Orchard, where they left barely enough room for a dandelion. Whether an old cottage on blocks or a contemporary behemoth, every place had something that could be called a yard, with grass and flowers and shrubs. A general store and inn marked the extent of commercialization, and they only opened from June to September. Not even the new money had changed that.

His grandmother's New Englander, his home for the past four years, sat on a short rise between the road and the beach. The front porch was shaded by the oaks of King's Highway, and the windows of the living room and upstairs bedrooms faced the Atlantic. With a year-old paint job and a new roof, the house itself appeared unyielding. The interior, however, could not hide its age. Wind whistled through the casings, and the worn hardwood of the floors creaked with every step. Each August, a bat would find its way in through the eaves and dive bomb dinner. With what his family let him spend, Cam took care of it as best he could. It didn't have to be a showplace to be appreciated. All he had to do was ignore the "For Sale" sign knifed into the front lawn.

When his grandmother had died in January, Cam knew things would change. What he hadn't expected was his mother and her brother Dan putting the house on the market just two weeks later. As he had stood in the kitchen numbed by shock, his father had tried to explain. His uncle Dan lived in Los Angeles and was lucky if he saw the place once a year. To him, it was an asset to be cashed in. While his parents enjoyed visiting Laurel, spending long weekends and most of their summer there, as teachers, even if they wanted to they weren't in any position to buy out Dan's share. Though the house itself was tired, the land it sat on was gold. They'd set the asking price at one-point-four million. If Cam had been sitting in on a case study from a finance class, he could have accepted the reasoning.

But he'd spent every summer of his life there and moved in for good upon graduating from college. When he'd decided that he was going to remain in Laurel and make a go of his summer construction job, his grandmother had made him an offer: He loved it at the beach, so why didn't he just stay with her? She had turned eighty-three and they all agreed that having someone around might not be a bad thing. It had worked out better than the two of them had hoped. He gladly fulfilled the few responsibilities that she gave him. She wrote the grocery list, he did and paid for the shopping. If she needed to go somewhere, he drove her. If he wasn't coming home for dinner, he called. No girls would be overnight guests unless previously arranged, and they would sleep in the downstairs bedroom with no midnight crossings. Otherwise, he was on his own.

Unlike his mother, Gram did not attempt to manage his life. She didn't require an itinerary every time he went out the door, nor did she provide a breakfast table report of what time he came in the previous night. Gram didn't ask if he was ever going to use his degree or if he wanted to reconsider taking the LSAT's. Instead, they swore in unison when a Sox reliever gave up a home run and discovered that they'd both been feeding the feral cat living under the neighbor's porch. Late on Sunday afternoons, they would open a beer out on the deck and watch the sun dissolve over their ocean. They'd grin at each other and she'd clink her glass against his bottle.

"Are we the only ones who get it?" he'd say.

"Hard to believe," she'd reply.

When she began to occasionally call him Martin, his father's name, two summers after he moved in, he didn't think much of it. She was, after all, eighty-five, and in season everyone, including his parents, tended to come and go at dizzying rates. But in September, he came home from work one night and discovered her missing. A frantic search found her a mile away on the bridge over the Little River, eyes glued to the water, shivering and unable to explain how she'd gotten there. It was an event that began to repeat itself. Gram begged him not tell his mother about the episodes. But winter lay ahead and things weren't going to get better on their own. He could either chance her wandering off and freezing to death or get her some help—and by doing so, potentially condemn her to what she feared would be a roach-infested old folks home. His stomach roiling with acid, he called his mother, Sherri. When Francine's condition was diagnosed as the onset of Alzheimer's-related dementia, Sherri deemed the situation too much for Cam to handle alone. She mandated that Francine be moved three hours south to an assisted living residence in Londonderry, New Hampshire, where his parents would be five minutes away and his sister Kiernan close by in Massachusetts. Gram made it four months there. Then it was the full-care nursing facility.

While his grandmother lived out her days strapped to a

metal bed under the glow of a sickly television, Cam woke with the Atlantic Ocean filling his windows. He'd had the house to himself for the past two years, save for the occasional weekend and his parents' summer vacations. He had often felt more like a thief than a caretaker.

When he arrived home, he called the Silvas and asked if they were still interested in having him build the doghouse. They were. He grabbed a legal pad and had them repeat the details they'd started to give him that morning when he'd had no intention of taking the job. They wanted it to be an exact replica of their own house, a Cape, complete with shingled siding, windows, and a central dormer. The sleeping area would have to be four-by-four, but they wanted the structure to be proportional, even if the extra space wasn't usable. That meant he'd have to build it eight feet wide. Cam wanted to tell them they'd be better off buying a small shed and throwing some hay in it. They were disappointed to hear that he couldn't purchase pre-weathered cedar shingles and that it would take a few years before the shade of the houses matched. Cam figured that Ralph, a gigantic Leonberger, wouldn't care either way.

Cam gave them a price based on a slightly surcharged square footage rate for a regular house, adding in a combined loss-of-dignity and combat pay boost, as the possibility existed that the dog might actually eat him while he was working. Ralph looked like the star of a psychedelic remake of the Hound of the Baskervilles; he was big, long-haired, brown-black-and-white, and drooled like a leaking faucet. All Cam could do was shake his head when Jim Silva said that the amount seemed fair.

He grabbed the book he'd been reading, *The Big Sleep*, and went out onto the deck. He'd built it himself on the Labor

Day weekend after his first summer as a carpenter. Its noticeable pitch and lack of aesthetic detail were entirely unintentional. His grandmother had liked it anyway, and it drove him crazy that she wouldn't let him redo it. After she'd left, he'd considered ripping it up and starting over, but as far as he had been concerned, it was still her place. He wasn't about to touch it now, either, not with them trying to sell it out from under him. He read for a few hours, with Horton's idiocy preventing him from enjoying either the story or the view.

The house stood at the midpoint of the three-mile beach, just off its apex, where the shore reached out in quarter moons on each flank. A thick lawn stretched fifty feet to the seawall; a wooden staircase led over the rocks down to the white sand. To Cam's left was the public beach, where Pine Knoll Island sat a half-mile away protecting the coast. When the tide was out, men, women, children, and dogs journeyed over a sand bar to poke around the rocks, brush, and hundred-yard cluster of trees, which was all they found there. Opposite the island, a staggered series of shoals started directly in front of the cottage and stretched right along the private end. They would be spreading his grandmother's ashes on the ocean side of those black rocks the following weekend. That, too, was something he tried not to think about.

It being early for the Dockside, Cam decided he might as well draw up a framing plan for the doghouse. He didn't have anything else to do, and if he had a blueprint, maybe he wouldn't have to blow every minute of the weekend. He started by sketching a design. It was a project that he probably could have done in his head; that's how Brinkley would have run it. But Brinkley had been building for almost as long as Cam had been alive. According to his boss, it was all about the details and he did not want to screw up a doghouse. He mapped out the specs, including how to fit in his dormer and the two windows, and then called the lumber yard to place his

order. He was pleased—and somewhat surprised—that his
quote had been a good one.

His family considered his profession nothing more than an
extended summer job, generating beer money and killing time
until he determined what he really wanted to do. His mother
still expected him to wake up one morning and say he was
ready to follow Kiernan to law school. His father frequently
reminded him that since he already had his bachelor's in
English, he could start a Masters in Education program and be
teaching in a year.   Cam had given up trying to explain
himself. He figured he made as much as either of his parents,
and his income was only going to go up. That was what would
enable him to buy his grandmother's house, an idea that had
come to him a week earlier as he had sat alone on his cockeyed
deck layered in sweatshirts on a Sunday afternoon, sipping a
Budweiser.

Since he was a teenager, Cam knew that once he had a
choice he would live in Laurel. But he'd been realistic about it.
Even after settling in with his grandmother, he accepted that
he wouldn't be able to stay there forever. He'd always thought
that when he went to buy his own place, he'd have to go inland
where there was plenty of reasonably priced woodland. He
would grab ten acres off of the Fox Farm road, clear it, and
build. He wouldn't have a view of the ocean, but he'd have
some space and he'd be in Laurel. Gram had even helped him
along. While she had left her children the house, she'd
bequeathed he, Kiernan, and his cousin Miles, thirty thousand
each—money he never knew she had. Cam swore not to
touch it until he was making a down payment. Only recently
did he realize it could be used for the house he lived in now.

Holly James, the real estate agent, had warned his parents
that if they wanted to get full value, as opposed to just
dumping the property, the sale might not take place overnight.
Setting the price so high was the only good thing that had
happened since his grandmother had died. Cam knew of four

or five places on Laurel Shore Drive in the same range, all built in the last decade, that had been sitting on the market for three years. Anyone spending that kind of money wouldn't be happy shelling out for an interior that hadn't been touched since the eighties. Additional investment would be required, cutting down the pool of potential buyers even further. If he were going to acquire the place himself, Cam needed time. He was confident he would have it.

Cam also planned on going out on his own as a builder. His summers with Sarofian were his apprenticeship, his time with Brinkley graduate school. He watched closely how they approached construction, as well as aspects of the business that went along with it. In addition, he'd taken civil technology courses at the University of Southern Maine when things slowed down in the winter. He had expected that when he hit thirty, he'd be ready to run his own crew. But as he contemplated the opportunity in front of him, he asked, "Why not sooner?" With another year of seasoning he'd be close enough. Instead of merely working for Brinkley, he'd be a younger, hungrier version of the man. Brinkley was good enough to cherry-pick his jobs, but many that he turned down would be money-makers for someone like Cam, who while not Brinkley, would be much better than the remaining alternatives. There'd be plenty of work, and once Cam started taking it on, the ability to carry a place like his grandmother's would come with it.

For the rest, he'd need some luck. After the house sat for a few years, his parents and Dan would have to be willing to drop the price, which they'd hopefully bring down further for him—once they saw that he had the means to pull it off. They were family, after all, and letting him stay there "as is" for the cost of the property taxes and utilities. Of course, he was going to need a huge down payment, much more than he could put together now. Dropping six figures into their laps would show them that this wasn't some pipe dream.

Everything he made from here on out would be banked. There'd be no ski weekends at Sugarloaf or trips to California or Cancun.   No new truck, no boat. With enough cash up front, he could leave the banks out of it and convince his parents and Dan to hold the paper themselves. If he fell on his ass, they'd be no worse off than they were before. He just needed to get his shit together. That's why he'd spend the weekend building a high class shack for a drooling canine.

As for his immediate future, Cam had made it to five o'clock. He'd have money coming in tomorrow. He could go out for a drink with a clear conscience.

CHAPTER THREE
"Senator" Grimes

Those who live here wait for this day, when the sun gives us its first taste of summer. Donning shorts and T-shirts pulled from the back of dresser drawers, the inhabitants of Laurel have migrated to the outdoor bar at the Dockside. We have spent the winter huddled at the Port Tavern, where the sight of each other's faces under direct lighting had begun to illicit a distinct nausea. But now smiles emerge and laughter escapes. Life is wonderful. It will be weeks before the tourists arrive to make every evening a Saturday night. For the moment, however, this is all we could have asked for and more than enough.

From my table at the Dockside, one gazes upon lobster boats and scattered pleasure craft being nudged downriver by the incoming tide. Across the way, the Monastery, enormous and white, is being primed and preened from roots to roof by an army of worker ants. Captain Pete hoses down the whale-watching Proud Mary at his marina. But my eyes fall to the two college girls who stroll up to the bar and inquire as to whether the Dockside will be hiring for the upcoming season. It's almost time for the coeds to descend from upstate to fill their pockets with tip money and their bellies with beer. Dreadful Zora tells them that they will need to return at five, in another hour, to talk to Jeremy Riley, the bar manager. Zora ignores my wave from the water's edge. Her eyes dart away so that she can later say she didn't see me offer to buy the pair a drink. It is a shame that she refuses to age gracefully.

Today those girls will not experience the pleasure of a Gosling's Black Seal rum and tonic at the best table in the place, under a clear sky with a gentle breeze. It is something to be savored, not unlike a Matisse or one of Beethoven's symphonies. They thank Dreadful Zora, and their Maui Jim's come off their hair and return to hide their bright eyes. I want to call out and tell them to be sure to return. Jeremy will recognize their energy and vitality. The boy will look at those skirts and picture the tight, young asses beneath them, and they will be given jobs. It's human nature. In a matter of weeks, they will be delivering drinks to this very table, at the least.

Less than five minutes after they leave, Jeremy emerges from the rear entrance of the restaurant. He has been in town just ten years, yet is one of our most appreciated citizens. He and the Dockside are a perfect match of personality and place. Even with Dreadful Zora tending bar with the warmth of a storm trooper, this unassuming spot on the river under a heaven-blue canopy is a favorite of townspeople and visitors alike. A refugee from Connecticut coursing our streets at fifteen miles an hour can make one want to pull his 30-06 from the cabinet, but when that same fellow is seated next to you here chatting amiably and complimenting the nature of Laurel, he becomes enjoyable.

Jeremy is a six-four, sandy blond-haired, blue-eyed former basketball player. He converses restaurants and chefs with foodies the same way he talks Red Sox outfielders and batting averages with the fanatics. He can direct people to every landmark in a hundred-mile radius. Out-of-state customers return to see him year after year. While they may all look like

John's and Mary's, he remembers them, offering names and hometowns. Once he has established his connection, he will regale them with stories of his being the twelfth man on a Holy Cross team bounced from the NCAA tournament in the first round, his work as a soap opera extra, and his prowess at Texas Hold'em. Invariably, someone will mention that he should have his own place. He will nod in response, as it is his dream.

Jeremy's bar is often packed. Young women, in particular, worship him. In the past he has readily ignored their affections, as he was spoken for. This was somewhat of a boon for the rest of us, at least those who did not spend our summer days knee-deep in fish or spreading manure over emerald lawns. I am almost ashamed to admit that by being a friendly, normal looking man of forty-eight, there can be easy pickings here in July and August. People truly want to connect.

Jeremy speaks to Zora, nods, and a frown comes to his face. Even the gods are wrought with weakness. He retreats to the restaurant and reappears with a coffee in his hand. It is admirable that he has not drunk his way to the bottom of a bottle as a result of his heartbreak. If I were experiencing the turmoil he has been facing over Sophia Harding, I don't know that I could have been so strong. Of course, that the little ferret could illicit such emotion is perhaps the most surprising aspect of the whole affair.

He walks over to my table and sits down.

"Hello, Senator," he says.

"A pleasure as always, Jeremy."

"The first busy day of the year, don't you think?"

"Summer can't be stopped now. Time again for happy hours to be happy."

"I'm not there yet. Sophia just called to ask if I minded if she still came in, this being the spot it is and all."

"And you told her?"

"That it's a free country."

"But you're king here," I say.

"Who gives a shit?"

"Apparently you do."

"Ahh." He shakes his head and empties the coffee from his cup.

"What you need to do tonight is pick out a woman with low moral character, take her home, and go at it like a pair of hormone-filled lab monkeys. With the weather as it is after that bear of a winter, it's a scenario that you can certainly bring to fruition. It will do you a world of good."

Jeremy doesn't laugh. He sighs and adjusts the sleeves of his polo shirt with the stitched logo of the dock and a passing sailboat. He then leans back in his deck chair, closes his eyes, and begins to massage his temples. As long as he looks good, he can soldier on.

Over his shoulder the Popeye-muscled Warren Brinkley walks onto the deck. It is early for him. Zora reaches into the ice well and hands him a Budweiser. She actually smiles, the bitch. Brinkley heads this way.

I am a steward of this town of three thousand and my table often serves as its hub. While my esteemed, deceased father was a United States Senator, the position I have held for the past twenty years is that of Selectman. It is the only post I have ever aspired to. Workingmen, shop owners, and summer people all stop by to converse with me, providing the insight I need to stay on top of things. Laurel does not prosper by accident, and my work here is appreciated. I have been bestowed the title of "Senator" by my friends and fellow citizens. Admittedly, the moniker is a poke in the ribs, but it is one I must endure for the sake of the town.

Even grimmer than Jeremy's face is Brinkley's. He sits down and takes a long pull on his beer.

"What's up?" Jeremy says. "You start at Horton's?"

"We finished there." Brinkley shrugs.

We wait for the explanation. He shakes his head and says, "He called off the job." Jeremy's eyes roll.

"Beautiful day," I remind them.

Brinkley coughs.

"Am I wrong?" I ask.

"Are you ever wrong?" he says.

"You know I am not a braggart."

"Then spare me the rhetoric."

We look at each other, just short of collective laughter.

"How do you like the new shirts, guys?" Jeremy asks. An eager expression appears. Why he asks us for fashion opinions, I don't know. I live in khakis and button downs, stylish yet comfortable. My carpenter friend sports nothing but tees or flannels, depending on the season, and jeans.

"They look the same to me," Brinkley says.

"No," Jeremy replies. "They're a darker blue this year. Same color as my eyes, in fact. Sophia's idea."

"Bittersweet, I'm sure," I say. Brinkley's lip twitches.

"Sometimes you just can't win," Jeremy says.

"Did Horton talk to you?" Cameron Preston asks Jeremy, as he sinks into the chair next to mine.

"Yeah, he ordered a gin and tonic and then told me not to make it," Jeremy says, smirking.

"Zora didn't know anything, either," Preston says to Brinkley. "This is bullshit."

"What did you expect?" Brinkley says.

"He could at least do something he says he's going to do."

"He can't take your beer away," Brinkley says, grinning. "Be grateful for that."

I am soon regaled with the story of how that fat bastard Horton has screwed these simple working men, Brinkley scowling as Preston's tirade provides the details. Forgive me if I fail to offer my shoulder. For Horton will talk to anyone and tell them what they want to hear, a sure indication that he cannot be trusted. As for the carpenters themselves, they are good people. But they gripe of too much work when they are busy. In the lean times, the complaints are obvious and unceasing. Spare me the sob stories. One must be willing to accept the way the world is. The one thing that it is not, is fair.

CHAPTER FOUR

Cam and Brinkley moved to the bar to wait for Miranda. All Cam needed was for her to show up and see him sitting with the Senator, who gave her the creeps. He wanted to ask Brinkley what he was going to do about Horton, but Brink was draped over the bar trying to talk to Zora. Cam checked his watch and sighed. Apparently, everyone else had known that Horton wouldn't show; the Senator and Jeremy had nodded along as if there were no doubt about it. Maybe Brinkley was right and Cam needed to wise up.

He did notice, however, that Jeremy looked more miserable than either he or Brinkley. It had been months since the Ferret had dumped him, but he still moped as if it had happened yesterday. How great could a girl be who so closely resembled a member of the weasel family? She was friendly enough, but Cam couldn't take more than five minutes of her one-thought-behind, off-kilter conversation without readying excuses for retreat. Maybe he was missing something there, too, but that one baffled even Brinkley.

As Cam contemplated what possible sexual charms Sophia Harding could possess to cause such distress, her Nike-ed feet strolled onto the deck. Shiny blond hair bounced on her shoulders as she said hello, her white ferret teeth revealed in smile.

He said, "Hi,'" and wondered why Jeremy didn't tell her to stay out of his bar. The breeze on the deck died.

Sophia scooted in behind him and grabbed a bar stool. She ordered a Planter's Punch from Jeremy as if she were just another customer. Cam watched Jeremy's jaw clench as he turned to make it. When he handed her the drink and said, "It's on me," his game face was back. Cam's eyes rolled.

Cam checked his cell phone for a message that wasn't there. Maybe Miranda could tell him why he was so obtuse. She might even enjoy it, but for once in her life she was late. In the meantime, there was nothing to do but order another beer.

"I hope that isn't going to break you," Brinkley said, joining him.

"It's the principle, Brink."

"Don't worry. We'll be working next week."

"It won't be like Horton's, though, will it?" It would have been a great payday with the bonus structure that Brinkley threw in for their more substantial projects.

"You never know. Do you need cash?"

"I do," Zora said. "Three dollars."

"No, I'm okay," Cam said to Brinkley. He dropped four ones on the bar and slid them over.

"You sure?"

"I'm going to build that doghouse this weekend."

"Really?" Brinkley's face broke into a wide grin.

"Oh, yeah. It's a dream project. The dog, Ralph, weighs about two hundred pounds and looks at me like I'm dinner. His people want his house to be a replica of their own."

"Dignity versus dollars," Zora said. "Myself, I've got to lose fifteen to fit into my money-making shorts before the Fourth."

"The owners were crushed when I told them that cedar

shingles don't come pre-weathered. They wanted the shades to be an exact match."

"It's too bad Horton shut us down," Brinkley said. "Plenty of gray, beat-to-shit shingles there. I think they were what was holding up the garage."

"I wouldn't need them if we had that fucking job."

"I'm just saying," Brinkley said.

"Screw that." Cam put down his beer. All he had to do was wait until dark and then take what he needed. "I'll just go over there tonight and strip some off. Horton won't know the difference. He'll probably think we did it before he dragged his fat ass out to fire us."

Brinkley shook his head. "Don't."

"Why not?" Cam said.

"He might actually have us build that garage at some date."

"Really?" Cam asked.

"Have you learned nothing today?" Brinkley said, shaking his head.

"Why don't you offer to buy them from him?" Sophia asked. Cam went to respond, but hesitated. Either her forehead was enormous or her hair didn't start until halfway back on her scalp. He didn't know how Jeremy could not have pondered that every morning over his coffee.

"The thing is," Cam said, "they're attached to the garage. I don't think he's quite ready to part with them."

"Then you might as well steal them," she said. The setting sun gave her blue-silver eyes an orange sheen. "How else would you get them?"

"He doesn't need you encouraging him," Brinkley said.

"I could probably charge double for authentic distressed shingles," Cam said. "Maybe I can make a go of this and put custom doghouses up and down the coast."

"There's a market for that?" Sophia asked.

"Why not? Mini-Versailles for poodles, hunting lodges for Labs and Goldens, French provincials for Brittany Spaniels."

Sophia snorted a laugh.

Cam was grateful when his phone buzzed. He stepped out of their circle and listened to Miranda tell him that she might be stuck in the city for the whole weekend. A marketing plan for Mr. Chicken's eight outlets in greater Boston was hanging in the balance. They had to present on Monday and her boss wasn't letting any of them leave until the campaign was done. Cam didn't bother telling her his news. At least one of them was having a career.

He asked Brinkley if he wanted to go to the Sea Squall for dinner, not Brinkley's favorite due to the twelve-dollar hamburger. Cam wasn't surprised when he turned him down. It looked like a sandwich, the Sox game on television, and a six pack. Which is probably what his father, a high school geometry teacher, had on his agenda. Pathetic.

Cam drove a half-mile into the center of town, a square of storefronts, galleries, and restaurants. Weeks earlier most had been boarded shut; in a few months they'd be teeming. A string of empty parking spaces in front of the Squall caught his eye and he jumped on the brakes. Dinner at the bar would leave him momentarily satisfied, even if he shouldn't have been spending the money. He went in and sipped another beer, letting his eyes rest on the volume-less pre-game show. Then he felt her next to him, familiar, and he turned, his stomach fluttering that Miranda had sandbagged him. When he saw Sophia looking at him with her animal eyes, Cam forced himself to smile. Although he wasn't sure he believed in God, he could only attribute the Ferret's presence to some sort of divine retribution. As much as he was feeling sorry for himself, he deserved it.

"You don't mind if I take this chair, do you?" she asked. It was a shame she was so vapid, he decided, because one thing

Cam did like about her was her voice. It had a smoky, *Body Heat* quality.

"Of course not," he lied.

"I love it here," she said. "Freddy's the greatest."

"Sure," Cam said. Freddy Forbes flailed in front of them, wrestling open a martini shaker. The guy never remembered a name, including Cam's, or a drink. If he had more than three customers, lines of sweat trickled down his temples. He'd go through stacks of cocktail napkins patting himself dry.

"Kidding," Sophia said. "You looked like you were about to pop."

"I might be reaching my limit of being jerked around."

Sophia clicked her short nails on the mahogany. Tiny lines rose at the corners of her eyes. Across a room she could have appeared twenty; up close it was clear those days were behind her. Now that she'd pulled her hair into a ponytail, the forehead became borderline disturbing. She ordered a rum and Coke.

"Does that help you on your morning run?" he asked. He'd seen her countless times doing a last call shot, and then he'd be headed to work the next day wondering how he was going to survive, and she'd come striding over a hill in her shorts and jog bra.

She shrugged.

"You're out there all the time," he said.

"I haven't missed a day in nine months."

"I used to run in high school," he said.

"Really?" Her surprise was no doubt a result of the softness around his stomach, which he feared would develop into a gut when he hit thirty.

"Sprints," Cam said. "I was never good enough to be serious."

"Maybe you weren't serious enough to be good."

"I'm pretty sure it was the other way around."

"You were there." She took a long sip through the thick

black straw.

"Every spring I take up jogging," he said, "and I hate it. I've already given up on this year."

"You don't know what you're missing."

"Pain?"

"It doesn't hurt when you're in shape. You've got to get there, though. Then it's relaxing."

"The thought of running in the morning makes the idea of getting up and pounding nails seem like fun."

"You shouldn't close yourself off to a world of greater possibilities."

He wanted to ask from whose E-network celebrity profile that emanated from, but didn't see the point. He'd known her for three years, but had never bothered to get her story. The Hardings had money; they lived on Shore Road north of the Grimes estate. When she first came to Laurel, he remembered her waitressing at the Brewery for a month or two, but he had no idea what she'd done since. Cam decided that he would be pleasant, wolf down his burger, and get out of there before the conversation drove him into shots of fourteen-dollar bourbon.

"What do you do after you run?" he asked.

"I take a shower," she said.

"No, really."

"I've got some things going on. It's not like I'm counting the minutes to Happy Hour."

"What's wrong with that?" he said.

"If that's what you do all day, maybe you're in the wrong business."

"I like what I'm doing, when I can do it. No thanks to fucking Horton."

"You should love your work."

"I'll take something I can stand and be happy. It's only work."

"You almost make settling sound okay." She stared at the tiny bubbles working to the surface of his glass.

"I could be doing worse. At least I'm not a suit. Two of my friends from school are lawyers. Another guy is in finance. One sells insurance. One accountant. They all bury me on the misery scale."

Freddy delivered Cam's burger, placing it in front of Sophia. She slid it over to him and ordered her own dinner. The hanging pendulum light illuminated her forehead.

"You haven't answered my question," Cam said.

"Oh, that," she replied. "I do some painting."

"Houses? Interiors?"

"Not quite."

"Do you mean you're an artist?"

"Trying."

"Do you make any money?"

"Some," she said, picking at the corners of the napkin her drink sat on.

"Enough to live on?"

"I don't really need it, right?"

"What kind of alternate universe are you existing in?" he asked.

"I'm from the planet Trust Fund. I thought everyone knew that."

"And you told me not to settle."

"I'll do something," she said. "Maybe open a gallery here in town. Maybe a restaurant with Jeremy."

"I didn't know his plans included a partner."

"It's another avenue of expression, and we each have our strengths."

"Wouldn't it be kind of hard working together when he can't even be in the same room with you?" Cam winced as soon as he said it.

"What are you talking about?"

"Well, you've split up, right? Isn't that what happens?"

"We've remained close," she said, looking him in the eye.

"You'll be okay then." Cam bit off a mouthful of ground

sirloin so he'd be forced to shut up. It was small comfort that he wasn't the only clueless person in town. She shifted in her chair and watched him. When she started comparing his looks to Jeremy's, she'd stop at plain. He had brown hair that was buzzed short, green eyes, a pointed jaw, and a hawk's nose—somewhere between handsome and hideous.

"So are you really going to steal those shingles tonight?" she asked.

"Yes, I am, unless you're planning on notifying the police or warning Horton."

"I'll keep quiet," she said. "If you'll do something for me."

"What would that be?" He was not about to become a go-between for the star-crossed lovers, not for anything, never mind siding for a doghouse. He didn't like either of them enough for that.

"Take me with you," she said.

"Why would you want to be involved in a senseless act of vandalism?"

"If I were that dog, I'd want an aesthetically pleasing house."

"You'd risk the pound for it?"

"Anything for art's sake."

"That sounds like bullshit."

"You don't know many artists, do you?" she said.

"No. But I know a lot of liars."

He had a snifter of Baker's and then another—on Sophia's tab—while she ate her dinner. He'd stopped checking his phone. By the time he was following Sophia the Ferret's Jeep up Main Street, it was dark, although too early at nine o'clock for the mission. They were going to her place first so she could change out of her sundress. She took the long way, east, back past the white lobsterman statue in the square, and then a right on Ocean Avenue. He could just picture the Senator or Brinkley standing on the sidewalk, noticing the procession.

They passed the Oarsman, which if it were anywhere but

on the river in this town would have been a forty-dollar-a-night motel, and then by a number of gingerbread-house bed-and-breakfasts. After turning at the Harbor Head Hotel, the road ran along the coast past the Grimes estate on its small peninsula. Further north, the homes were hidden behind hedges or thick bands of oak, ash, pines, and poplars. He'd passed this stretch hundreds of times from the ocean. The houses sprawled above the sea, walls of windows glittering in the sun from the tops of granite cliffs. From the road, the only signs of habitation were the nondescript mailboxes and beginnings of driveways, just like the ranches on bug-infested clearings in the woods across town.

Sophia turned onto a gravel drive that wrapped back on itself behind a row of Christmas pines. A two-story Federal with a widow's walk at its peak stood in silhouette against the moonlit sky. Ground lighting illuminated the white clapboards and glossy black shutters. A separate beam shone on a carved silver eagle over the portico. The windows were dark. He wondered how many times had Jeremy pictured his forty year-old self as the man of the house.

"Not bad," he said.

"The summer place," she said. Instead of walking up the cobblestones leading to the door, Sophia headed to the garage.

"We're not going to do this sober are we?" she asked.

"I hadn't planned on it. I've been drinking since five."

"Come on," she said. "I live in the caretaker's apartment."

They climbed the outside stairs to the second floor. The door was unlocked. She flipped on a light. Windows looked out to the main house, the ocean glimmering just beyond. An L-shaped couch, a black marble coffee table, and a stereo system took up the space in front of a breakfast bar. Two oversized windows framed with a tropical hardwood opened onto the woods to the south as if they were a movie screen. An easel with a four-foot canvas draped in a cloth stood in front of them. Cam's eyes went to the paintings on the walls.

Soft blues, reds, and yellows formed hazy coastal scenes.

"So that's what you do," he said, motioning to the paintings.

"Do you drink wine?" she asked, pulling a bottle from her stainless steel refrigerator.

"As a last resort," he said.

"Chardonnay, it is," she said, searching around in a kitchen drawer. "Do you know the reason I'm up here, instead of over there?"

"No."

"My father wouldn't allow Jeremy in the house." She walked over with the bottle and two glasses, handing him one.

"Because he was a bartender?" Cam gladly dismissed the thought that she'd brought him up here expecting something to happen. He stopped circling the room and settled into a chair at the breakfast bar.

"Please. That was a plus; it meant he had *character*. But then Pop found that Jeremy had too much of it. Jeremy didn't like the way my father spoke to me—it's how we talk in this family—and he made a pissing contest out of it. So, Pop told him to get the fuck out of his house. I went with him. The next day I moved in here."

"That's not exactly running away."

"It is for us. My brother lives in a closet, if you know what I mean."

"What were you telling me a few hours ago about people making choices?"

She disappeared into what he guessed was the bedroom. She came out wearing jeans and a paint-splattered black sweatshirt.

"Ready for action?" she asked.

"Sure," he said. "But I've got reason to be."

They stopped at the beginning of Horton's driveway. Cam should have been more excited, as Horton deserved this. He just hoped that Brinkley was right, and he wasn't about to ruin their chance of ever rebuilding the garage. Sophia, sitting in the passenger seat with a wine bottle between her legs, also worried him. She took a sip and replaced the cork. There was no telling what she might do. He couldn't even figure out why she had wanted to come. Whatever the reason, she'd avoided saying. As flighty as she seemed, it was possible that she actually thought it would be fun. He turned off the headlights and eased ahead. The tires crunched rocks into the dirt. When they reached the garage, he did a three-point turn to face the truck toward the road in case they needed to leave in a hurry.

The only lights that appeared on at the house were the small yellow lanterns flanking the front door. Cam reasoned that even if someone were awake, they'd be in the back where the living and master bedrooms looked out over the bay and the harbor's black wharf. In whispers, he told Sophia his plan.

It would be impossible to strip enough shingles in one night to side Ralph's entire home. The nails would need to be pulled slowly and evenly, so as not to crack the cedar. He'd take enough to cover the front, street side of the doghouse. Those passing the Silva's would at least see matching facades. It was the best he could do. Jim and Jane would be happy, his own ideals would be satisfied, and the missing four-by-eight patch of his garage would confuse and anger Horton more than the stock market.

He and Sophia climbed out of the truck. He opened the tool bay in the back and took out his framing hammer, flat bar, and flashlight. They snuck around to the rear of the garage. The way the building sat diagonally to the house, Horton couldn't have seen them even if he were standing on his porch. It wasn't like they had to worry about passing traffic, either.

Sophia stood to his left and aimed the light. He had to pull one row of shingles off to get at the top of the next so he could start removing them in one piece. As soon as he pried the first nail, he heard the flaw in his plan. The metal whined as it was yanked through the wood. Although it wasn't loud, the thin sound managed to echo across the harbor. He needed to work quickly and hope the Hortons were out cold.

"This isn't very exciting," Sophia said, after he had removed two rows of boards. He was cracking one of five and it had taken him ten minutes.

"You're surprised?" he said.

"It could be a lot better."

"How?" Only concentration prevented his voice from rising.

"This just isn't about the doghouse," she said.

"Of course not," he said.

"Then stop." Sophia turned off the flashlight.

"What?" He turned to face her, grinding his teeth.

"It would be better to take them from the side facing the house."

"The thing is," Cam said, "over here we don't get caught."

"Do you trust me?"

"Should I?" His hands dropped to his thighs. "You only blackmailed me to bring you along."

"I've got an idea of which boards to take. If you let me direct you, we can really make a statement."

"The plan is to get the wood and scram."

"If you're satisfied with mediocrity when you can have triumph, then go ahead. I'll keep doing my part." She clicked the flashlight back on.

"You have some experience with this kind of thing?"

"No, but I have clarity of vision."

"Fine," he said, wishing that he could stomach her wine. She had just ripped the edge off of his calm. He couldn't believe he was saying it: "What do you want me to do?"

Sophia led him around to the other side of the garage. He waited as she moved back, one step at a time, until she was halfway to the house. With the flashlight off, she stared at the building. He had a death grip on the flat bar when she finally trotted back in next to him.

"Do you have a ladder?" she asked.

"We're not after the roof."

"Anything to stand on?"

"There's a five-gallon bucket in the truck."

"Go get it." He did as he was told and when he returned, she pointed the beam at a shingle just under the eave. "Start with that one," she said.

"Take it down?" he asked.

"Do you have a problem giving up control?"

"Not if the person knows what they're doing."

"Then take down that board."

When he had it removed, she slid the beam over one tile. "Right there," she said. She worked him four across and then down, widening the run when he was halfway to the ground.

"What are you doing?" he asked. She had moved him out and down, until finally she narrowed the path back toward center.

"That one," she said, moving the light.

"We've got enough now," he said.   There was a sizeable stack of shingles behind him.

"We're not finished."

Three feet from the bottom she worked him across in a slightly upturned arc. His pants were wet from kneeling on the dewed grass to pull the final pieces. Sophia walked over and took his arm. She told him to look at his feet and led him back toward the house. When they reached her spot, she spun him around. Even without the light, he could see the pattern they'd left on the weathered plywood: A hand with a raised middle finger. Tapered and staggered shingles contoured each digit and knuckle, and the curve of the hand. It was unmistakable.

"Wow," he said.

"It will look even better with the sun on it. Horton will get it."

"What do you have against him?" He looked down into her eyes. She blinked.

"Not too much."

"I thought he was a friend of Jeremy's."

"He is."

"Let's throw the shingles in the truck and get out of here," Cam said. He slipped from her and bolted for the pile of cedar. As he hauled the shingles to the pickup, Sophia sat on the lawn and stared at the raised finger of a listing drunk etched into the wall. Even in the muted glow of a half moon, it couldn't be ignored. Before they hopped in the cab, Cam took a lap to make sure they hadn't left anything.

"Wouldn't you love to see him come stumbling out in his bathrobe," she said as they motored out, "his coffee cup dropping to the ground?"

"I wouldn't want to see him any other way than fully clothed."

"Yuk," she said, taking a pull from the wine bottle.

"That's some talent you have," he said. "You could be the Warhol of vandalism art."

"I only wanted that poor dog to have a proper home."

"Right," he said, wondering if he wanted to ask her why she had really wanted to come with him.

They hadn't said a word from Pier Road to the stop sign on Woodman Avenue. He brought the truck to a complete halt, not taking a chance that one of the town's two cruisers would happen by. He glanced across the cab and found Sophia smiling at him.

"What?" he said.

Her hand reached over to his chin and guided his face to hers. His eyes closed. Their lips met, and tongues pressed and swirled. His hand slid around her waist. She pulled back at the same instant he let go. He looked at her, head tilted, and then returned his eyes to the road. Two minutes later, they were in front of her garage.

"Want to come up for a night cap?" she asked. He had left the truck running.

"Are you sure?" He gazed out his window at the eagle over the doorway of the main house. His luck had been pushed far that evening, and he was no idiot.

"When I say drink," she said, "I mean wine. Were you thinking of something else?"

"Didn't you just kiss me back there?"

"Yes."

"Then you can see where I might have another, apparently mistaken, impression." His eyes dropped down to examine the steering wheel.

"Sometimes a kiss is a kiss, not an invitation."

"Sure," he said. "If you say so."

"Do you know the last time I kissed someone other than Jeremy?"

"No."

"Neither do I," she said. "That might explain why I need another drink."

He turned the key off, but didn't move. She stepped out of the truck and stood holding the open door.

"Well, are you coming?"

"I don't think so."

"Because you're not going to get laid?"

"I'm not convinced of that."

"If you were, we'd have a lot less clothes on."

"Is that how it works?"

"I've heard," she said.

"Thanks for your help tonight," he said.

"You know I'm going to want to see the doghouse when it's done."

"It'll be at the south end of Gray Gull, second to last house on the shore side. It will undoubtedly replace Sutton Island Light as the area's greatest attraction."

"It won't top the look on Horton's face when he steps out his front door tomorrow. I just might get my binoculars and head to the pier."

"That would be something to see."

"Why don't you meet me there?" she said. "Around seven o'clock. An artist should see how their work is received."

"Okay," he said.

"Well, goodnight," she said, shutting the door.

"Night," he said, throwing her the "I know you well enough that I've got to acknowledge you" wave he used when he saw her running. He watched her walk up the stairs, wondering what the hell he'd just done. As soon as she disappeared into her apartment, he started the truck.

.

CHAPTER FIVE

Four metallic rings of his grandmother's thirty year-old phone and he was awake. Cam's first thought was that he was late and Brinkley was calling to chew him out. Then he remembered it was Saturday. All he had to do today was build that goddamn doghouse. He closed his eyes, but then his own phone started buzzing. He reached for the nightstand. The Silvas were probably wondering why there were shingles stacked on their front lawn. He hadn't taken any chances by leaving them in the Ranger.

"What the fuck did you do last night?" Cam could hear Brinkley's nose whistling, which happened when he was worked up and breathing rapidly. Cam looked at the clock, eight-fifteen.

"What?" Cam replied, trying to sound clueless.

"Don't bullshit me."

"Hunh?" His head hurt.

"Asshole." Brinkley hung up. Apparently, Horton had discovered his late night project. Cam craved a Gatorade, but downstairs seemed a great distance. He probably shouldn't have hit the scotch when he sat down to watch the midnight replay of the Sox game, of which he'd now seen the first five innings twice. But it was more than boredom that contributed to digging for the Glenlivet his father kept under the sink. Kissing the Ferret had made him shifty. He wondered if she had gone to the pier to watch for Horton. He didn't have her cell number so he didn't have to worry about calling her. She probably hadn't bothered, either. He'd run into her soon enough. His head landed back on the pillow.

He was woken again when the screen door slapped shut. It wasn't Brinkley because there was no stomping across the linoleum. Horton wouldn't have the balls, even if he knew where Cam lived. His parents would be talking, at least one of them complaining that he was still in bed. Finally, Miranda called out for him. He yelled back and listened for her feet on the stairs.

She appeared in the doorway in a wrinkled gray suit. Her black hair was matted down and her eyes were red.

"Don't say it," she said, kicking her shoes off. "We just finished two hours ago."

"You drove straight here?"

"If I went home, I wouldn't have woken up until Sunday." She flipped her jacket to the chair where his jeans lay twisted. Her shirt went over her head. Her softball-round breasts were unencumbered by a bra.

"No wonder you had to work so late. None of the guys could concentrate."

"I took it off in the car, jackass."

She slipped her panties down her leg and then stepped out of her skirt. He flipped back the covers and she slid in. Her skin was warm and sticky. She nuzzled up into his neck. Her hair smelled like cigarettes and he wondered if she'd started up again. She began to nibble on his ear and he became hard. His phone went off.

"I probably need to get this," he said. "There might be a situation." She groaned and ran her tongue from his neck to his collarbone.

"You better get your ass over to Horton's." Cam could picture the spit flying out of Brinkley's mouth.

"I didn't think we had that job anymore," he said.

"Don't fuck with me, Preston."

"Are we back on?"

"What the hell did you do over there? He's called me three times. I don't need this shit."

"What are you talking about?"

"Some asshole carved a goddamn bird into his garage. He happens to think it was me and you."

"What? Like a crow or something?"

"You realize he'll never give us this job now."

"You're the one who said it would never happen."

"It's lucky we've already got something for next week and I need you, or I'd come over there and kick your ass." The phone slammed down again. If Brinkley actually went to Horton's to check it out, he'd be impressed. Cam wouldn't deserve the credit, though he'd be the one taking the blame. He could live with that.

"A situation?" Miranda asked, resting her head on his chest. "Did the Dockside run out of Bud or something?"

"Horton cancelled our job. You know, big money, nice place, bonus, something that would look good in a portfolio. None of that's happening."

"I'm sorry."

His hand slid down her back and over her ass. She scissored her legs around his waist and pressed into him. He started at her neck, and traced her jaw with his tongue. It was a game they played. She licked his face. The inside of her thighs tightened as his fingers glided over, and he found her wet. She lay back and waited for him, then put her knees up. He kissed her neck and wondered if there could be a scent of the Ferret's tongue on his. He entered her and she bucked once hard and then settled into her slow, steady rhythm. They were still working it when he came. She had her hands on his hips and pulled him higher. Her closed eyes opened briefly to smile. She was asleep before he slid out of her.

He lay back and drifted from Ralph the hound to Horton to the Ferret, to what this house would look like when as its owner he had the chance to renovate it. He could see Miranda on a bedroom balcony, older, but not so different. She snored softly. He got up and went for the shower. The doghouse would need to get finished this weekend if he and Brinkley were back at it on Monday.

He brewed a pot of coffee and while it dripped, wrote a note telling Miranda where she could find him. His first stop would be the lumberyard. A ten-thirty start wasn't bad, all things considered.

The Silva's Cape was nestled in a sparse pocket of pines across from the beach. The doghouse would sit in front of the trees so that Ralph would be out of the sun in the afternoon. Jim and Jane weren't home, but the dog watched him closely, drooling at the picture window. The warm weather had lingered and Cam worked in shorts and a T-shirt, the evening's alcohol sweating out of him. He had the house framed and the plywood floor down when it occurred to him that he'd missed lunch. But now that he had a rhythm going, he wasn't about to stop. When he reached into the cooler for his third Gatorade, he noticed the Jeep at the end of the driveway. She couldn't have been there long; at least he hoped not. He wondered what she expected him to do. He took a drink and waved. Sophia left the car on the side of the road and walked over.

"You are building it, aren't you?" Sophia shielded her eyes from the sun and looked over what there was of the structure.

"Who would joke about this kind of thing?"

"It was lonely out on the pier this morning." Her voice was soft. "Where were you?"

"I stayed up and watched a replay of the Sox game. I must have slept through my alarm. Did I miss anything?"

"Certainly. I had a life-altering epiphany."

"You saw Horton without his clothes on?"

"Thankfully, no," she said.

"Something must have happened. Brinkley called to scream at me."

"Oh, Horton was right there on the lawn in his bathrobe, which was better than nakedness, but no treat. He came out around eight. He'd take a few steps, talk into his cell phone and point at the garage with his other hand. Then he'd stop and take another look, followed by a few more steps and more pointing. It was like watching a sea elephant attempting modern dance."

"Brinkley must have been on the other end. Horton thought that he and I were the culprits. Naturally, Brinkley assumed it was me."

"And you said?"

"My sister and brother-in-law are both lawyers. He's good, and he tells his clients to deny everything, which is exactly what I did."

"What could Horton do anyway?" she asked.

"Call the cops, from what Brinkley said."

"Nobody knows anything?"

"Just you and me."

"Someone will figure it out," she said.

"If we keep our mouths shut, no one can prove a thing. They'll assume it was me, but your part will remain a mystery. That is, unless you can't stand me being given credit for your work, or you want to use this as a steppingstone to the world of punk art."

"No, I'm quite content laughing in private. Besides, I have something that you can actually help me with, clandestinely, as

well. We'll be even." She raised her thin eyebrows, which
seemed to barely move on that forehead.

"Okay," he said, mentally bracing himself.

"You haven't asked what my moment of grace was on the
pier this morning."

He was afraid to find out. As preposterous as it seemed
that this would involve some coupling of the two of them,
that's where his mind went. What else could it be? And why
at this instant was Miranda's Toyota pulling into the driveway?

"That's my girlfriend," he said.

Miranda started up the walk, her flats clacking on the
stones. She had ditched her suit for a jean skirt and a fitted
white tee. Cam waited for her to reach them. He feared his
headache would reignite. Miranda glanced over at Sophia, first
with a perplexed look on her face, then a hint of recognition.
Cam stood there mute.

"I thought that note was a joke," Miranda said. "But you
are building a doghouse."

Cam nodded to Ralph in the window and Miranda's jaw
dropped when she saw the expanse of his panting mouth.

"Wow," she said.

"I need the money," he said. "Did you sleep okay?"

"Until your parents got here."

"My parents are here?"

"That's what I just said. Luckily, I was under the covers
when your mother snuck into your room like she does. I'm
fairly certain she must have been standing on my ..." She
looked over at Sophia and frowned. "Well, it wasn't pretty."

"Sorry," he said. "I didn't know they were coming."

"Surprise inspection?" Sophia asked.

"You could call it that," he said.

"So, just how big is your dog?" Miranda asked Sophia.

"Oh, this isn't my house," Sophia said. "Cam's going to be
assisting me on another project."

"I feel like I'm standing in the middle of Trump Plaza with

all this business going on," Miranda said. "What are you up to?"

"Top secret," Sophia said.

"I don't even know," said Cam.

"You used to live here, didn't you?" Sophia said.

"I waitressed at the Squall summers while I was in school."

"That's right."

"I've served you many a drink," Miranda said.

"I'm sure I was grateful."

"Yes, you were." Miranda forced out a half-smile that told Cam she wasn't.

Sophia smiled back and said that she needed to get going and that she'd talk to Cam later. He grinned at Miranda as they watched Sophia drive off.

"Thank god," Miranda said. "No matter how many drinks you served the Ferret, or how much they cost, she never tipped more than a dollar a round. Cheap bitch."

"That's all behind you now."

"When did you start hanging out with her?"

"Let me tell you about yesterday." As he measured and lined the plywood that would form the walls of Ralph's house, he gave her the story from start to finish, naturally omitting his bitterness and Sophia's flirtation. She laughed as the story climaxed with Brinkley's phone calls.

"What does the Ferret have against Horton?" she asked.

"I asked the same question. She said, 'Not much.'"

"It must be something."

"Maybe she wanted to see his reaction to her work. She's an artist."

"Give me a fucking break," Miranda said.

He shrugged.

"Well, when are you going to be done here?" she asked.

"Tomorrow."

"You're kidding, right?"

"I've at least got to get these windows in and the roof up," he said. "That leaves the siding for Sunday."

"What am I supposed to do?"

"Go back to the house and go the beach?"

"Great, so your mother can play twenty-thousand questions with me? I don't think so."

"Why don't you call one of your friends?"

"They're all in Boston." She exhaled and stared tapping her foot. "We graduated, remember?"

"What about Zora?"

"I didn't drive two hours to hear about the new string of men who are in love with her."

"Last night you weren't coming at all."

"If you had told me that you were going to spend the whole weekend working, I wouldn't have."

"You can stay here and help me."

"That sounds like fun."

"Go get a lawn chair from the house and grab a book or something."

"I need lunch."

"My mother didn't feed you?"

"She tried."

"She doesn't have a secret agenda."

"If she drives you crazy, what do you think she does to me?"

It was spelled out for him. If he took her to the Clam Basket for a lobster roll, she'd be happy. Then he could swing by the house, say hello to his folks, grab a lounge chair, and send her to the beach here. It didn't matter that he had things to do. Even if she had told him she was coming, he would've had to work anyway. He didn't have time to drive Miranda into town, but that was what she wanted him to do. Of course, he didn't have five dollars in his pocket, either.

"I'll make you a deal," he said. "If you get us lunch from the Basket, I'll go home and get you a beach chair, which you can plant across the way and watch the waves—and I'll take you to dinner tonight."

"Your mother is expecting you—us—for dinner."

"I'll let her know that we won't be attending."

"I pay for lunch. You pay for dinner?"

"Deal," he said.

Cam considered leaving the Ranger in the street and sneaking Miranda's chair from the shed, but wound up parking behind the Taurus. He found his parents seated at the kitchen table reading the Coast Star.

"What?" he asked. "They don't have newspapers and coffee in Derry?"

"Look, Sherri," his father said, putting down the sports page and looking up over his half-glasses. "Hefner has returned to the Playboy mansion."

"Excuse me?" Cam said.

"Your mother was quite shocked to find an unmarried young woman sleeping in your bed. She thinks the aforementioned female might have been naked, as well."

"Martin, be quiet," his mother said.

"I don't know anything about that," Cam said. "I came home right after midnight Bible class and fell asleep on the couch."

"Cut it out," Sherri Preston said. "This is your house when you're here. We told you that. I wouldn't have said anything about it. Although Miranda can hang her clothes in the closet, if she likes. She doesn't need to leave them on the floor."

"Did she do that? I couldn't see them from the living room."

"So virtuous," Martin Preston said. "You've raised him well, Sherri."

"I can imagine where he learned to lie like this." She shook her head and sighed loudly to make sure he got the joke. Cam feared she would always think of him as a high-schooler.

"I would love to stay and chat, but I'm in the middle of a very important job for your friends, the Silvas. I'm building Ralph a doghouse. Thank you for recommending me."

"I thought you and Warren had some sort of great project," Sherri said.

"That fell through yesterday when we showed up. So, now I'm doing this."

"At least you're keeping busy."

"Speaking of which, I need to get back to work so the Hound of the Baskervilles can have accommodations worthy of his bloodline."

"You don't sound too thrilled."

"It's a doghouse, Dad," he said. His father nodded.

"Where's Miranda?" his mother asked.

"She's out getting lunch for us."

"I offered to make something for her here."

"Well," Martin said, "if you were a young lady, would you rather have lunch with us or him?"

"It wouldn't kill her to talk to us. We are her boyfriend's parents. She is staying in our house."

"Speaking of that," Cam said. "She and I are going out to dinner tonight."

"Why would you do that? I was going to go down to Bradley's and get a roast."

"Mom, the girl works her ass off. She needs to relax."

"As do you," his father said. "While you're young."

Cam started to leave.

"Will she be here next weekend?" Sherri asked. Miranda had missed his grandmother's service in January, having been at Disney World, of all places, at an advertising seminar. Although they had planned for only family being present when they spread his grandmother's ashes outside the shoals, she had instructed Cam to tell Miranda that she was welcome.

"She's coming," Cam said. "I'll see you later."

He could hear her to his father: "It wouldn't hurt him to talk to us, you know."

After having had the obligatory cocktail with Martin and Sherri on the deck, Cam and Miranda were tucked into a table in the back corner of the Break Point Inn. A candle in a frosted white glass flickered between them. She had wanted to go to the Sea Squall and he had suggested the Port Tavern. This was a compromise. It didn't really matter, he reasoned, as long as they were out of the house. They were enjoying their second round of gin and tonics.

"Do you recognize our waitress?" Miranda asked.

"She's young."

"I think she and her sister used to work at the Brewery."

"Suzanne?"

"That's it," Miranda said. Suzanne leaned on the rail in the service area while the bartender made martinis for another table. "I don't miss the late nights."

"You had a great time up here."

"That's all it was though, time. I worked for three summers and never saved shit."

"Whose fault is that?"

"My own," she said, rolling her eyes. "I'm just saying."

"I don't know," he said. "I couldn't imagine spending eight-plus hours a day in an office."

"Believe me, chaining yourself to a cube is not the most glorious way to live. But at least I'm using my mind creatively."

"There's a lot of satisfaction in selling wings for Mr. Chicken?"

"My '*More Cluck for Your Buck*' is going to be all over that city in a few weeks. It'll be plastered on the T, cab caps, and a billboard over the Mass Pike. More people are going to read that than the Globe on a daily basis. So, yeah, that makes me happy."

"Great," he said. "You're the Stephen King of the fried poultry industry."

"Don't take it out on me because your Holy Grail got cancelled."

"I wasn't aware that I was doing that," he said, picking up his menu.

"Why do you even bother?" she said.

"What?"

"Looking at that," she said. "You always have the steak."

"I can't explain it, but I've suddenly developed a taste for fried chicken." He sucked the drink from his glass to its bitter end.

"We sound like an old married couple," she said.

"That's not funny."

They looked across the table at each other, and then both searched the room for their waitress. Outside of her, they were the youngest people there. Cam rearranged his silverware. Miranda picked lint from the white linen napkin off of her black sweater. He finally caught Suzanne's eye and ordered another round of drinks.

"The doghouse is coming out nice," she said. "All kidding aside."

"Great," he said. "So how did you come up with 'More Cluck for your Buck?'"

He watched her rise up. Her hands flew from her lap as she began to tell the story. The account manager, Eddie Deperna, had tried to ignore her tag line, even though the account's goal was to promote their price point. He wanted to go with his own, "Chicken that's Kick'n." She had to fight to even get her slogan on the board. When the President, Franklin Quigley, saw the line, he jumped on it and had her and their team come up with the rest of the collateral package. Cam nodded along politely until she mentioned that on their way out, Deperna invited her over to the Four Seasons for breakfast.

"What a dick," Cam said.

"You're missing the real point. I haven't even been there a year and I'm a player. It's the accomplishment."

"Life as a responsible adult," he said.

"Maybe you should try it," she said, obviously straining to keep from sounding critical.

"What the hell am I doing now?"

"Year-round summer?"

"Please," he said. "I'm going to tell you something that I haven't told anyone yet. I've just finished working out the details, but I think you're going to be impressed."

"Don't tell me you're going to go to law school."

"I'm going to buy my grandmother's house."

Miranda spit tonic out of her nose as she began to laugh. "For one-point-four-million? Are you high?"

"Thanks for the vote of confidence," Cam said. "I know I'm not the type who can come up with catchy rhymes to sell fried chicken, but I can manage this."

"Please explain." Miranda put down her drink, sat back, and folded her arms across her chest. He explained every feature of his plan, from time passing and the price dropping, and dropping further for him, to his going out on his own as a contractor. He stated how many jobs Brinkley turned down in a year, and how that would form his market.

"What does Brinkley think of your chances?" she asked.

"I haven't told anyone, I said."

"Wouldn't he have a good idea of your chance for success?"

"He also might not be too happy about me planning to jump ship. Sometimes you never know with him."

"You're sure this will play out the way you think?" she asked, her features committed to neither enthusiasm nor scorn.

"I could be doing my own work now, building decks and

additions and two car garages until my arms rigged up. But any decent house you come across in this town, Brinkley's had a hand in it. Another year of learning and building a portfolio will pay off. Instead of putting up ranches out on the back roads, I'll be rehabbing and rebuilding on the water. That's where the real money is."

"You still have to convince your family of the rest and hope nobody buys the house in the meantime."

"Do you know anyone who would pay that much for the place? It's a wreck."

"Okay," she said, raising her hands in surrender. "Maybe you do have a plan."

"You don't think it will work?"

"Can you honestly expect to make that much money?"

"You've seen Brinkley's house, and his boat, and his Harley, et cetera…" He exhaled. "Well?"

Miranda smiled.

"So, when you start doing your own work, will you put a silhouette of a raised finger on all your garages?" she asked.

"What do you think of that as a logo, professionally speaking?"

"It would fit your personality."

"With that kind of an attitude, you might wind up in the guest house, which may not be any better than what I'm building for Ralph."

Thirty minutes later Suzanne returned and placed an enormous lobster in front of Miranda. Of course, it was the most expensive item on the menu. Cam couldn't say that she didn't deserve it.

CHAPTER SIX

On Monday morning, Cam and Brinkley stood in a heavy mist looking at a sketch the client had left for them. Scrawled in pencil on a sheet of notepaper, its proportions in no way matched the space presented. They were supposed to build an enclosure for an outdoor shower. The house was a fifty year-old Cape on a back road behind Gray Gull, its best feature being a nearly walk-able one-mile distance to the beach. The place needed paint or at least someone to scrape off the green mold that started at its foundation and rose to the windows. One end of the gutter hung a foot below the roof. As the house was enclosed by oaks and pines—which a hearty gale might have allowed to put the place out of its misery—no light from a gray sky filtered down to them.

"Brinkley, this sucks," Cam said.

"I thought you were bringing the coffee," Brinkley said. "Honest mistake on my part."

"It's not that."

"You aren't going to piss and moan about the Horton thing all summer. Let me tell you that right now. And what the fuck were you thinking, doing that to his garage?"

"I don't know what you're talking about."

"Bullshit."

"You saw it?" Cam asked.

"I don't care about that nonsense," Brinkley said. "Figure out what we're going to need here. I'll call the owner and tell him how much it's going to cost to lipstick this pig. Then I'll run for coffee."

"Fine," Cam said. It wasn't always easy working for Brinkley. He was exacting. But that's what made him good, and that's what was making Cam good.

They had completed the deck and had begun to build the stall when Cam's phone went off. The ID read Sophia Harding, and he was tempted to slip it back in his pocket. He couldn't figure out why she'd showed up at the Silva's. No one could actually care enough about a dog house to drive across town to see it. And she couldn't have any kind of interest in him, personally. Seconds after kissing him, she'd been the one to claim it was nothing, and then she'd met Miranda the next day. It had to be that she'd let something slip about Horton's. He took the call, wondering how she'd gotten his number.

"Hey," she said. "Meet me at the pier?"

"You didn't say anything to anyone did you?"

"No. Can you come out here?"

"I'm working," he said.

"You can't sneak off?"

"There's only me and Brinkley. It would be kind of tough."

"Oh. How about after?"

"It's raining."

"It's supposed to stop, and I really need you to do something for me."

"What?"

"I can't talk about it over the phone."

Before she had to remind him that he'd already agreed to help her, he gave in and told her he'd be there at five-thirty. He was better off getting it over with. He let out a deep breath and hung up.

"Whose wife are you banging?" Brinkley asked.

"I wish," Cam said. "You don't want to know."

"Then I won't ask."

Sophia waved from the time he crested the hill until he parked next to her Jeep in the fishermen's lot. She was waiting in front of the pilot house in the center of the pier. The running jacket she wore was zipped to the neck. Boats crowded the harbor behind her, and lobster traps were piled on rafts at the water's edge. No one else was around, the crews having long since left. Cam took his time getting out of the truck and going over to her.

"Come on," she said, grabbing his arm and dragging him to the old bait shed at the south end of the pier. Horton's house stood across the bay. Now it made sense. He hadn't seen their project in daylight. He waited for her to pull out binoculars.

"What would it cost to turn this into a restaurant?" she asked, touching the rough gray boards of the building in front of them, a twenty-five-by-forty saltbox.

"Aren't they going to tear it down," he asked, "now that they have the new one?" He pointed to a year-old steel structure at the opposite end of the pier past the pilot house. It was twice the size of the original.

"I've asked around and no one knows anything. But this is the perfect spot for a restaurant. People drive out here to look at the boats and the lighthouse. They'd certainly come to eat, especially if the food was good, which it would be."

"Look at this place," he said. "John Paul Jones used to

dock here."

"The guy from Led Zeppelin?"

"No." He sighed. "Is this building even inhabitable? There's been nothing inside but decomposing fish, wet rope, and empty beer bottles for years. If there's any rot, you'd probably have to start from scratch. I guess it's sturdy enough or they'd have already razed it, but who knows?"

"Trouper said they only built the new one because they needed more space."

"Have you tried to get in?" he asked, and walked over to the door. It was locked. Plywood covered the one window facing the parking lot. He knew there were service doors around back over the water. He motioned for her to follow as he circled the building.

"The first thing is to find out if it's structurally sound," he said. "You might have to get an engineer to survey that."

"Can't you just look at it and tell?"

"I can guess, with a poor chance of accuracy."

"So, guess."

He couldn't see any outward signs of decay, but there was no telling about its framing. The bay doors facing the harbor were padlocked. The two small harbor-side windows were also boarded shut. This side of the restaurant would have to be all glass for it to make any sense.

"You're probably talking about doing the whole building over," he said. "Inside and out."

"So it can be done?"

"If there's enough money."

"How much is that?"

Cam figured that for a house this size, a nice one, three hundred thousand. Triple that for a restaurant, he guessed, with the kitchen, exhaust hoods, plumbing, tables, bar. Maybe more.

"You've got a million dollars lying around?" he asked.

"Is knowing where to get it the same as having it?"

"I'd say no, but my financial wherewithal is limited to what the ATM will spit out on a given day."

"Well, my bank machine might be a little bigger than yours," she said, hugging him. She bounced on her toes as she looked at the hovel. She must have been seeing something that he couldn't imagine. "Thank you."

"I don't know how I helped."

"I just needed to know that it's possible." The smile she'd been wearing vanished. "You can't mention this to anyone. Not Brinkley, not the Senator, not your inquisitive parents, not Mariel."

"Who is Mariel?" he asked.

"Your girlfriend."

"Miranda," he said.

"Sorry. But especially don't say anything to Jeremy. I want to surprise him with it myself."

"Fine by me." As he imagined how ugly that scene might play out, the sun slipped from under the clouds, bathing them in light.

"It's a sign," she said, shielding her eyes and gazing up.

He waited for the grin to cross her face indicating a joke. It didn't come.

"I need a beer," he said.

"Let's go to the Dockside," she said. "I'll buy you one, payment for your efforts."

"I don't know," he said.

"I thought you wanted a drink."

"I do."

"Well?"

"Okay."

He walked in two steps behind her. All he needed was to have Jeremy see them come in together and assume that something was going on. Cam wouldn't be able to get served that entire summer, and as feeble as it sounded, the Dockside was not something he was ready to give up. It was ridiculous, he knew, but he was relieved to see Zora behind the bar.

Sophia ordered and started talking to Holly James, his parents' real estate agent. She was an old friend of his sister's who had a smile and two minute conversation for anyone who might possibly buy or sell a piece of property. As a nine year old, he'd seen her getting felt up by Bobby Perino on the front porch of the beach house. He was just a little brat to her then, and he didn't imagine reminding her of that incident would improve her opinion of him. When she and Sophia started discussing the new *Real World* cast, a show he hadn't seen, he listened politely for a minute and then mentioned that he needed to talk to Brinkley, who was over at the Senator's table.

Cam sat down next to Brinkley. Across from them were Lenny Perkins and Trouper Frosty.

"Doghouse?" Lenny asked.

"I'm going to build them up and down the coast," Cam said. "High-end, custom jobs. Why? You need work?"

"I'll stick to humans," he said, twirling the handlebars of his moustache. He had a shaved head and a face as thin as a flounder. "They might not be much more intelligent, but they don't pay in Milk Bones."

"You get paid for the shit you put up?" Cam said.

"If it lasts until the check clears." Perkins aimed his bottle at Trouper. "You should hear his scheme for this summer. He's going to get people to pay to watch him work."

"Pornography will never be the same," the Senator said.

"I'll be a gentleman farmer of the sea." Trouper's head was as big and square as a milk crate.

"He's going to install benches on the deck of the Lady M and offer scenic lobster cruises. This fruitcake thinks people will pay twenty-five bucks to watch him do an hour's work."

"Why not?" Trouper said. His black hair was waxed into a

flat top. "They pay big money and travel all day to see whales. I motor in and out of the coves, cruise around the Senator's spread and the grand homes along the coast, give a speech about the life of a lobsterman, and then pull some traps. I'll let a few brave souls help me and while I got them there, sell 'em some to take to the folks back home."

"I think, historically, the whale is a slightly more compelling figure than the lobster," the Senator said.

"People don't think of Maine whale," Trouper said. "It's Maine lobster."

"You just need an angle," Cam said. "Maybe you could get an eye patch and a peg leg. Pirates are big these days."

"That's not a bad idea," Trouper said.

Brinkley shook his head. "You people are complete morons."

"Aren't you ever happy, you rich fuck?" Perkins asked him.

"Let me buy you a drink, Lenny, because when you have a beer in your mouth it not only makes you happy, it prevents you from making an ass out of yourself, which makes us happy."

"Don't take it out on me because that dough boy didn't deem me worthy of not building his palace," Perkins said, pointing to the bar.

Cam turned around. Nathan Horton and a friend were ordering drinks. Cam exhaled and looked to Brinkley. Why was Horton here on a weekday?

"You must be one smart son of a bitch, Lenny," Brinkley said.

"Fooled you all these years, didn't I," Perkins said. A chipped front tooth gave his grin a crooked quality.

"There is nothing that warms a spring afternoon such as a pissing contest," said the Senator.

"It wouldn't hurt you to do a day's work, your Excellency," Trouper said, "so as to find out what the rest of us are talking about."

"This town is my life's project, as you know. Maintaining its character, purity, and integrity is a full time job."

"With a bar as your de facto office," Brinkley said.

"Hello gentlemen," Horton said, approaching them. "This is Byron Eberle, one of my associates." Horton's friend's angular frame leaned over and then he straightened himself. Their faces were flushed. They pulled chairs to the end of the table and Horton introduced them one by one. Cam braced for an accusation with his, but it did not come. That made sense. Horton canceling the project must have been a source of embarrassment and nothing he wanted to discuss in public. It was one thing if people thought you were full of shit and another to prove it.

"This is not a martini glass," Eberle said when Sandy Wolf placed their drinks on the table. He blinked rapidly and rubbed his chin with his hand. Sandy was a short woman with a tired face, but her breasts swung out in front of her, and her ass and legs were sculpted by hours of cycling. She usually wore half the clothing of the other waitresses and, according to Jeremy, made twice the money. Everyone in Laurel knew she was hands off. Her boyfriend was Police Chief Rey Turkington.

"Just drink it," Horton said. "He's upset because I took a C-note off him at Webhannet with a birdie on eighteen."

"Hey," Eberle repeated to Sandy, who was headed back to the bar. "This isn't a goddamn martini glass." She stopped and spun around.

"No, but that thing in your glass *is* a martini. Enjoy."

"As I'm paying for it, I'd like a proper glass. I know you have them. I've had dinner here."

"You see, we're outside now," Sandy said, waving from the tables to the river behind them. "Nobody has a real glass. All plastic."

"Would it be possible to perhaps go in and get one?" He pushed a sculpted wave of salt-and-pepper hair off his forehead. His eyes dropped to her chest and returned to her face.

Sandy exhaled. "You're not one of those guys who like to be seen standing around pretending you're Hugh Grant, are you?"

"I get the point, sweetie. Grab your broom and fly off."

"With pleasure, sport."

"Enjoying the local color, Byron?" the Senator asked.

"There's enough of it."

"He had the pleasure of seeing this guy's handiwork this morning," Horton said, looking at Cam.

"What's that?" Cam asked, having misread another situation. He tried to keep his face blank.

"Don't give me that shit," Horton said.

"I heard what happened. Someone carved an eagle or something."

"Don't play dumb."

"He's not playing," Perkins said.

"What seems to be the point of contention now?" the Senator said. "I remember when a man could have a nice peaceful drink out here."

"This asshole stripped wood off the side of my garage and left a space that just happens to look like a carving of a hand giving the finger."

Perkins and Trouper laughed.

"Did I ring your doorbell and leave a flaming bag of dog crap, too?"

"I had to postpone a job on them," Horton explained. "Not cancelled, mind you, postponed. Brink understood that economic conditions brought this about, but apparently such complexities are beyond Cam's grasp."

"What's not beyond my grasp," Cam said, "is your bullshit."

"I'd have been pissed, too, Nate," Lenny said.

"Look, I don't want to get into it," Horton said. "I'm just

saying."

"Of course you don't want to talk about it. It makes you look like an idiot," Cam said. "You didn't even come through on the drinks you promised us."

"Nothing was definite with that," Horton said, his face reddening. "Crystal had made dinner plans that we couldn't break. Don't think that it's going to happen tonight, either, after what you've done."

"I told you it wasn't me," Cam said.

"I know Warren has too much sense to pull a stunt like that, so that leaves you."

Cam doubted that even if he had a picture of Brinkley in the act, Horton wouldn't have dared to accuse him.

"Maybe it was a ghost," Trouper said. "That place of yours is supposed to be haunted on account of that rum runner that sunk on the rocks out there in twenty-six."

"Now that's bullshit," Brinkley said.

"Well, someone took an axe to his place and it wasn't a fucking phantom," Byron said. "I can attest to that."

"Nate," Perkins said. "You must have pissed someone else off beside him, because if it were Cam you would have been lucky to get F, U, K in spray paint."

"Thanks a lot," Cam said.

"You can barely draw a straight line across a blueprint," Brinkley said.

"If he's no good," Horton asked. "Why do you have him working for you?"

"He can hammer a nail all right."

"Is this garage like the grilled cheese with the picture of Jesus in it?" Trouper asked.

"I should really go out and look at this," Cam said. "It must be something."

Horton looked at him, narrowing his eyes into a glare.

"So if *he* didn't do it," Byron asked, snorting, "and *you* didn't do it, who the hell did?"

"Any high school punk who took an art class could have managed it," Brinkley said. He leaned back in the chair. "How many of your neighbors' kids have you booted off your dock?"

"So some teenager could do this but I couldn't?" Cam said.

"What kind of dupes do you think we are?" Byron said, his voice rising.

"Why don't you just relax, friend, and enjoy your martini?" the Senator said.

"Admit that you did it," Byron said, standing. His stare began on Brinkley and landed on Cam. "Otherwise, you insult our intelligence."

"Take it easy, Byron," Horton said. "It's no big deal. Brinkley's probably right; it's more than likely one of the little pricks at the corner of the road."

"The hell with that." A blue vein stood out on Byron's neck.

"Have another drink, Byron," the Senator said.

"Yeah, if Nate isn't going to worry about it, why should you?" Lenny Perkins said.

"Let's get Sandy over here for another round," Trouper said.

"You're going to let these guys get away with this?" Byron asked.

"It's a joke and it's probably not even them," Horton said.

"I wouldn't stand for it."

"I forgot what a hard ass you are," Horton said. He looked around the table. "His admin winds up in tears on a weekly basis. Just ignore him."

Byron looked down at his friend. "You're a clown, Nate." Then he gazed at Cam and Brinkley. "And you two are liars."

"You can leave anytime if you don't like the company," Brinkley said. "It's still a free country up here."

"Don't try to run me out. I'm not him," Byron said, pointing to Horton.

"If I wanted you out, you'd be gone," Brinkley said. His

voice was calm, but he stood up. Brinkley's nostrils moved in and out with each breath. Cam heard the whistling.

"Easy, Brink," Cam said. Jeremy had come out to the bar and was talking to Sophia and Holly, oblivious.

"Big fish, small pond does not impress me," Byron said, glaring at Brinkley.

Brinkley's hands flew to Byron. One went to his collar, the other to his belt. Before the man could speak, he'd been dragged across the table, drinks scattering to the deck. Brinkley hoisted and carried him, feet dangling, three steps to the rail at the river's edge. Brinkley then grunted and lifted, positioning Byron out over the water. The high tide was slack beneath them.

"You want to see how big the fish are here?" Brinkley asked. "Be my guest."

He let go of Byron who landed flat on his stomach in the water. The deck became quiet except for the splat and then the splashing and swearing from below. They stood at the rail and watched Byron tread water, his face crimson.

"Brink," Jeremy called, shaking his head and jogging over. Lenny Perkins was directing Byron to swim downriver to the boat slips.

Brinkley leaned over: "Ain't no big fish in this river."

"I'll have that son of a bitch locked up," Byron yelled as he dog paddled. Lenny, Trouper, and the Senator sat back down, trying not to laugh.

Cam grabbed Horton and said, "You better get down there and help him up. Tell him, he's lucky." Nate nodded and ran to the gate that led to the slips. Byron swam toward the dock.

Jeremy pulled up next to Brinkley and Cam. He put his hand on Brinkley's shoulder.

"You know there'll be shit if that jackass calls the cops. I heard how he was with Sandy."

"Hell, I'd like him to come up and take a poke at me."

"Let's get you out of here before we put Turk in a tight

spot," Jeremy said.

Cam took a few steps and waited. Brinkley, a smile on his face, watched Byron climb onto one of the docks.

"Come on," Cam said to Brinkley. "Jeremy doesn't need the trouble and neither do you. He's the type."

"I'd appreciate it, Brink," Jeremy said.

Brinkley pulled a twenty from his pocket and handed it to Jeremy. "Buy the fucker a martini in a real glass," he said, and started walking to the parking lot. Cam followed. The Senator caught Cam's eye and shook his head. They'd seen it before.

Brinkley's Harley was parked in the triangular No Parking zone next to the dumpster. A couple in a Lexus circled, eyeing the spot until Cam waved them on.

"They'll have something to talk about in Boston tomorrow, won't they?" Brinkley said.

"By the time the story gets there, you'll be eight feet tall, snorting crank, and pissing nails."

"He deserved it."

"I know, but you didn't have to."

"That's what I get for sticking up for you. You don't care that Horton thinks you fucked up his garage?"

"Why would I? He's an ass."

"You can't only have principles when there's money involved." Brinkley started the Harley and strapped on his helmet.

"Hey," Cam said. "If you're looking for something to do, take a ride by my doghouse and see if you don't recognize the shade of the siding."

"Nothing to brag about," Brinkley said, dropping the bike into gear. "If I find you went back there and apologized for me, you'll be the next one in the drink."

"I know that much."

"Good."

Brinkley roared out of the drive and Cam returned to the deck. Jeremy was over at Senator's table, handing a stack of bar towels to Byron. Cam asked Zora to pull up his tab. Sophia and Holly looked at him and did half-synchronized eye rolls. He wasn't about to say anything.

"Thanks for the beer, Sophia," Cam said.

"You're welcome." He paid and left. He was halfway across the parking lot when he heard her calling after him.

"How does that guy end up in the river?" she said when she caught him. She again became the Ferret, biting down on her bottom lip. "It's not the garage, is it?"

"Of course it is."

Cam looked over her shoulder and then back over his, as if they were discussing state secrets. "It wasn't the sign, itself. Horton's pal didn't believe Brinkley when he told him that we—as in he and I—didn't do it. You know Brinkley."

"He's a bully."

"He's a guy who lives in black and white."

"There's an annoying part of me that feels responsible," she said.

"He deserved it."

Byron was still muttering as he and Horton came out onto the path from behind the restaurant. Both pairs stopped talking. Cam readied himself for a sucker punch. But Byron stormed past, as if headed to the principal's office to scream about stolen lunch money. Horton mouthed to them: "He's drunk."

Sophia looked up at Cam, her thin shoulders slumping and her eyes flitting away. Why her disappointment bothered him, he didn't know.

"Are you asking Holly about that property?" he asked.

"No way. She'd have it all over town by dark."

"Do you realize that our entire relationship is based on keeping each other's secrets?"

"I wasn't aware that we were calling it a relationship," she said, blinking.

"I didn't mean anything by it," he said. "There are all kinds, and some don't even include drama."

She nodded and took a few steps toward the bar.

"Thanks for coming to the pier," she said.

"I was only guessing."

"I trust you."

"About that building," Cam said. "With that back hitch, you might be able to put a loft up there, like an exclusive dining room. That would be kind of cool wouldn't it, overlooking the harbor?"

She nodded. "You were the right one to ask."

He wasn't so sure.

CHAPTER SEVEN

Jeremy could have been playing the lead in a neo-noir. With its rickety table and salvaged restaurant chairs, his kitchen had been perfect for the scene. Only the cheap whiskey and an ashtray full of cigarettes had been missing. He'd come home from snowboarding to find Sophia sitting there at dusk, the items from her drawer in her precious Adidas bag in front of her. Her hair was pulled back tight and her face was locked in concentration. He'd dropped his things at his feet when he saw her. "Stagnant" was the word that she used, or at least the only one he heard as she explained that this encompassed them individually, as well as together. He could have understood had she'd known of Turk's sister who managed a restaurant at Sugarloaf.

"Fine," he'd said. "If that's what you want." He was still standing there when she got up to leave. His feet might as well have been nailed down. The skinny bitch had to turn sideways to get out the door and that's just what she did.

When he now swung around the curve and saw her on the pier gazing into the morning tide, he lost the rhythm of the song he was tapping along to. This setting was equally appropriate for what was about to transpire, a reversal of fortune for which he'd waited three months. He had never doubted it would come.

"What do you think?" she asked, smiling, showing her teeth. She tugged down on the faded purple T-shirt—one of his castoffs—that nearly covered the miniskirt below it.

"I'm glad you called," he said, stomach fluttering.

"It's perfect," she said.

"Well?" he asked. He prepared to catch her when she leapt forward. The way she fit against him, her legs wrapped around his waist, flashed in his mind.

"This is our restaurant," she said, patting the rough siding of the bait shed as if it were a pet. "We can be open by the end of summer."

"This is a bait shed." He struggled to keep his face intact. His guts threatened to empty.

"No," she said, pointing to the new building. "That is the bait shed. This is vacant, and seeing how it's still owned by the town, it's just sitting here. All we have to do is talk to the Senator and get a lease, which will probably cost us next to nothing. Then, we turn it into a restaurant."

"What will we serve? Rotting pollock and mackerel heads? Have you ever been in there? It reeks. Nothing will get rid of the smell."

She took his hand. He could barely grip hers.

"Close your eyes," she said. "Let me help you see it. Of course, we strip everything down to the frame. We rebuild on the same footprint, with a loft, which will serve as a private dining room. The walls are done in teak; windows with antique hurricane shutters line the walls. The tables are cherry. The lighting is orange and red, sunset colors. The only lobster buoys, gunwales, and tillers seen will be on the boats outside. It is a place where a man will feel right in a sport coat with an open-collared shirt and a martini. She is in her little black dress drinking a cosmo. They'll stand at the bar looking out over the harbor."

She kept talking, but he had stopped listening. His eyes locked on the peeling gray clapboards in front of him. She was right. It was a restaurant. If people drove out here for scenery alone, they'd come in greater numbers to be in *his* restaurant. Everyone always asked him when it was going to happen. It wasn't why he'd come here today, but he'd waited long enough for this, too.

"You're wearing your de la Renta jacket," she was saying, "and maybe the violet mock turtle; you walk over to the couple at the bar and lead them to their table. They smile at you, ecstatic. 'How wonderful it is that the owner is taking a personal interest in us.'"

Picturing it was easy. There was nothing like it. No place in Laurel, or on the entire coast, would have its—his— personality. The Sea Squall, the best there was now, situated in the middle of town, was fine but pedestrian, serving the same swordfish with pineapple salsa dished out in every other restaurant from Cape Cod to Canada. Jake Huffington, the owner, was a nice enough guy and happy to visit with every table, but he and his customers were closer to seventy than thirty. A bomb threat couldn't create excitement there. The Port Tavern, a few doors down, was burgers, chicken fingers, and steamers. The two lobster-in-the-rough and box wine spots north of town didn't enter the discussion. The Dockside's menu was positioned in the no-man's-land between the Squall and the Tavern. If it weren't on the river and carried by its bar business, it would have sunk long ago. Jeremy, not the owner, Marv Daniels, supplied the sizzle at the 'Side. It couldn't have been clearer: If there were going to be a destination restaurant in this town, it was the oversized shack staring him in the face.

There was Sophia, too. How many times had he sat on this pier while she swirled fogs of color on her canvases? They would be thrown together day after day, and she would see him at his best. Their relationship would be reignite; evolution would surpass the stagnation she had imagined. This very restaurant was what he was born to do, and Sophia had just delivered it to him. That could only be fate.

The menu was written as he stood there. There'd be oysters stacked on a mound of shaved ice at the head of the mahogany bar they'd put at the south end. He'd begged Daniels to put a raw bar out on the deck of the Dockside, and he'd refused to do it. It would cost him now. They'd grab fish right off the boats: Yellow fin, haddock, flounder. They'd find a chef who would let flavors come through without drowning them in overdone sauces, someone young and hungry with something to prove, who wouldn't break the bank. The place was going to burn.

"It's going to work," he said.

"I know."

They hugged. Jeremy might have misread the emotion involved if he hadn't already returned to where Sophia had placed him—at the end of the bar in his de la Renta. He watched a group of three couples from Boston drinking martinis and cosmopolitans and red wine, sporting the same jackets and designer dresses they'd have worn in the city. They were talking and laughing, their smiles only widening as he walked over to say hello. The owner.

CHAPTER EIGHT

Typical. Only a week earlier they'd had a taste of summer. Now on a sun-drenched day Cam Preston looked at his family bundled in winter jackets and wool hats. He stood behind the console of Brinkley's Mako, its tuna gear stowed below. The east wind had kicked up and if he wasn't careful as he forty-five-degreed the swells, they would get drenched. In the bow seats, his parents held gloved hands, his father's glasses wet with mist. His uncle Dan sat next to them, having flown in from California. His tan faded as the boat crested and plunged. Clutched in Dan's lap was a white and blue piece of ceramics that resembled the base of an antique lamp. Behind him on the deck seats were Kiernan and her husband, Spencer. Thankfully, the throbbing of the engine prohibited conversation.

They headed north, out and around the Senator's estate on the point, then ran along the coast beneath the granite bluffs. They passed below Sophia's father's house and her garage. The town of Laurel seemed caught between winter and spring. The air had the sting of early March, and the gray oaks on shore had just started to sprout their leaves. Marsh grass and lawns were patched with more brown than green. Cam angled through the three-foot rollers at quarter-throttle. His sister got seasick on a Sunfish and she was already as white as the boat. He guessed her being pregnant didn't help, yet she had refused to wait back at the house. When they reached the tip of Gray Gull, he circled around the ledge at the seal rocks, coming out just past the shoals that protected the beach. That's where they would spread the ashes of his grandmother, Francine Bailey.

Cam brought the engine to an idle thirty yards ocean-side of the shoals. A half-mile out, the beach house was nothing more than a gray rectangle, nearly indistinguishable from the rest. By checking the rocks, he could see that the high water mark hadn't yet been reached. They had timed the ceremony so that the ashes would start in toward the shore just before the tide turned, then go out to sea.

Cam scrambled to the bow to throw the anchor. He wrapped the line around a cleat and waited until it grabbed. The wind pushed them in, but the anchor held. Back at the console he cut the engine.

"Did you have to get a permit from the town?" Sherri Preston asked. Of course, she had researched the legalities of dispersing someone on both national and state levels. She had emailed him document after document about the guidelines, but had left the procedural duties to Cam.

"You don't need anyone's permission," Cam said. "You just need to file an EPA report within thirty days."

"Are you sure about that?" she asked.

"If we had a body, then we'd need a permit, and we'd need to be in six hundred feet of water so this summer kids wouldn't see it being picked apart by crabs at low tide."

"Don't be disgusting," Kiernan said.

"Anyway, I don't anticipate a Coast Guard Cutter plowing through to stop us," he said, not having bothered to check with the town. His grandmother had lived on this beach for forty-plus years. If anyone had a problem with what they were doing, Cam didn't want to hear about it.

"What if someone complains?" Sherri asked.

"Spencer and Kiernan can handle it," Cam said.

"I don't know that that's our field," Kiernan said.

"Do you really think anything's going to happen?"

Water slapped against the hull as the boat rolled. Wind ruffled the nylon of their jackets. Cam could make out a few figures walking the beach. It might have been more comfortable had they come out in the afternoon when things had warmed up, but catching the tide had been their main concern.

"Well," Dan said. He hadn't moved from his position on the bench. His arms were wrapped around the urn as if ready for a goal line plunge.

"Let's let Gram finally rest," Kiernan said. Spencer helped her onto the seat next to Dan. Her belly was just starting to show under her LL Bean coat. "She's waited long enough."

Her remains had spent the last two months on a shelf in his parents' house in New Hampshire waiting for the end of winter. This was the first spring weekend that Dan had been able to return.

"Does anyone want to say anything?" Martin asked.

"She's going to be where she loved to live," Kiernan said, tears streaming from her eyes.

"That's one thing we can agree on," Cam said.

"All of us," Sherri added. The family stood together. Dan's wide chin quivered as they gathered around him. All except for Cam kept one hand on the rail. The boat rose and fell, rose and fell.

"I'll do it if you want, Uncle Dan," Cam said.

"I can manage," Dan said.

Sherri looked at her brother and he nodded. She took the top off of the urn for him.

"Well, this is it, Mom," Dan said.

"God be with you," Kiernan said. Spencer made the sign of the cross.

"Good bye." Sherri wiped her eyes with her gloves.

"Farewell, Francine," Martin said.

Dan braced his stomach against the rail and raised the urn out over the water. Cam stood just behind him, watching Dan's hands shake. His throat was dry. Tears rolled down his mother's cheeks. Cam felt the boat rise, but as he steadied himself for the fall, his father's eyebrows arched up over the frame of his glasses. His father, the math teacher, was making the calculation. Before Cam could get, "Wait" out of his mouth, the boat swung on its anchor line. Dan upended the urn. The white ashes cascaded toward the ocean. But instead of falling straight down or flying toward shore, they were caught in the wind and blown sideways. The tail end of the plume flew into the boat. A coating of ash spread across the foredeck.

"Nobody move," his mother said.

"How did that happen?" Dan asked, his jaw trembling.

"Shit for luck," Cam said.

"This is horrible," Kiernan sobbed, collapsing onto the seat cushion.

"The question is," Spencer asked, "what do we do now?"

Cam waited for a whirlwind to whisk the ashes into the air and deposit them in the ocean where they belonged. No miracle came forth, however. They seemed stuck to the deck. Wiping them up with towels or Kleenex wasn't an option. There was really nothing they could do, Cam decided, but to flush them to the sea through the drain hole in the transom. It was how they cleaned the boat when it ran red with fish blood. He pulled the plug on the reservoir. He took off his gray hooded sweatshirt and rolled up the sleeves of his base layer shirt.

"I'm going to need that," he said, pointing to the urn that Dan still held. He passed it carefully, as if further damage was a possibility.   They watched as he went to the opening at port and dug the urn into the water.   He brought it up and a chill ran down his back.   He scanned the distance between the boat and the rocks.

"Where did the rest of her go?" he asked.

"Did anyone see?" Martin asked.

"Oh my god," his mother yelled.   Their heads swiveled around the Mako.   There was no line of ash along the surface. Some of the foam bubbling against the rocks was darker than the rest.   That could have been her, although in other spots, it was lighter, and that could have been her, too.   Or, she could have just sunk or started for England.

"What have we done?" Sherri said.

"Nothing right," Cam said. "Again."

Once they'd docked at the marina, Cam sent them to the house ahead of him.   He had to stow Brinkley's boat properly and was already too distracted.   If Miranda wasn't driving up from Boston, he'd have been tempted to go to the Tavern and spend the afternoon getting plastered.   Their excursion had been a disaster, this after a funeral that had been bad enough.

Though his grandmother hadn't wanted any kind of service, the week she passed they held one in a room of the Parish Center of Holy Angels, the Catholic Church that Sherri and Martin attended in Londonderry.   With its rows of fluorescent lights, the room was fine for bingo but horrible in every other way.   Two dozen people were spread out in rows of folding chairs.   Some were friends of the Preston's and distant cousins. Others were teachers from his parents' school or neighbors.   If there were contemporaries of Francine Bailey still kicking in Laurel, a trip spanning two states was likely prohibitive.   A lectern stood at the front.   In one corner were poster boards with pictures of his grandmother, grandfather, and the rest of his family. His boyhood, mop-haired self looked fairly happy in her company in several of the photos. He had a hard time looking at them without tearing up, so he sat by himself at the back. If he had had his truck he might have gone for the sledge and demolished the mandatory coffee pot, donuts, and pastries. But the vessel that drew his eyes rested on a table next to the podium, his grandmother reduced to a handful of charcoal stuffed into that base of a lamp.

Father O'Neil, bearded and apparently peeved that he would be denied saying a mass, welcomed everyone, made a few remarks about Jesus and Francine Bailey, and then introduced Sherri. His mother spoke, but Cam couldn't listen to the words; it was enough to hear her voice as it cracked and splintered. With her navy blue jacket, her hair sprayed into a helmet, and make up layered on her face, she wasn't herself anyway. His uncle Dan talked of how hard it had been to move across the country away from her, but how her scoldings kept him grounded even as he drove to work in his Porsche or relaxed on his deck overlooking the Pacific. Without his Shelby there, there was no talk of Francine Bailey coming back in the form of a butterfly or the wind. Kiernan, her eyeliner running, told of Gram teaching her to swim in the frigid Atlantic, and how she'd never swim again without thinking of her. When Father O'Neil asked Cam if he would like to say a few words, he shook his head. It wasn't because he didn't have anything to say.

He'd last seen his grandmother after News Years when he'd looped through New Hampshire on his way home from Miranda's. He usually expected her to look awful, but she'd seemed thinner than she had at Christmas, a week earlier. The yellow lighting of the facility colored her skin a translucent gray. She was sitting up, watching *The Price is Right*. The loose flesh that hung at her throat tightened only slightly when she saw him and called out. That she recognized him was a relief. He went over and kissed her on the cheek.

"You must be bored to come down and see me again so soon, Cameron," she said.

"I'm on my way up to Laurel and you know how quiet it is up there this time of year. I thought I'd stop by for a little excitement."

"You're not even going to get that much," she said, raising her hand and then dropping it on the blankets.

"Do you want to get up and walk around?" he asked.

"No thank you. I'm whipped already." She shook her head. "How's my house?"

"Still standing. I really want to rebuild the deck this year."

"Who do you want to impress? The McCarthys?"

The McCarthys hadn't lived next door for ten years.

"It's embarrassing," he said. "Everyone looks lopsided."

She dismissed the idea with a wave.

"So what are you doing with yourself?" she asked.

"I'm working for Brinkley. Remember him? He's down in Florida but he'll be back in a few weeks. I might do some skiing."

"Did you fix that leak by the chimney?"

"Yes, Gram." That had been two winters ago. "I rebuilt the chimney, too, and put in some new flashing. It's fine."

"Good. You know water will wreck the place."

"I do."

"How much did it cost?"

"It's all set, Gram. I got a deal on the materials and did it myself."

"Okay, then. What about that waitress girl you've been going with? Wedding bells?"

"Don't know."

"I guess we could call that progress. You'd think one of you two could have given me a great-grandchild by now."

"Talk to my sister. She's the one who's married."

She sighed. "The house is good?"

"Yes, Gram."

"God, we're lucky to have that place, aren't we?"

"If things go well, maybe I'll buy out the neighbors and we'll make it a compound."

"I won't be around forever. You take my house. That's enough for anyone."

"You never know, Gram. You might wake up tomorrow and feel like a million bucks."

"If you people freeze me like they did to poor Ted Williams, I'll haunt you. Don't forget that."

"Got it."

"But the house is good?"

"You know I take care of it," he said.

"I know, I know." Her eyes closed. "Why don't you bring me home then?"

"I'd like to," he said, chuckling, "but I think they'd consider it a jailbreak."

"I want to go home," she said, her voice on the edge of a scream. Her eyes bore into him. "I hate this filthy place. It's disgusting. Get me out."

"Take it easy, Gram. Let me just ask if I can, okay." Although his mother had told him she often asked to go home, he hadn't imagined it like this. He needed to get a nurse. "Maybe for a quick visit."

Her eyes began to water. His welled up.

"Goddamn it, Martin. Take me home. I'm not staying another minute in this goddamn place." She pounded her palms against the metal side bars of the bed. Her voice quieted. "Why did you put me here? Why?"

He didn't know what to say. If he tried to move her they wouldn't make the length of the hall. He plucked a Kleenex from the box on her nightstand. When he reached out to wipe her cheek, she slapped at his hand.

"Don't touch me, you bastard," she screamed.

"Gram, take it easy." She started whimpering. He stepped back, unsure of what to do. One of the nurses whisked into the room; she smiled at him and shrugged as she began soothing his grandmother in a voice used to lullaby a baby. He retreated to the hall and paced outside the door.

"Does this happen all the time?" he asked, when the nurse appeared five minutes later.

"None of our residents have an easy day, every day."

"Can I go back in?" he asked.

"She's asleep. Please don't wake her."

He watched her hollow chest rise and fall under the thin, tan blanket. He wiped his eyes with his sleeve and left.

As he sat alone at the service, he wondered what she'd thought in her last moments. Did she imagine herself at the beach? He couldn't shake the image of her blue, twisted lips as she begged him to take her home. Even if the attempt would have been a debacle, he should have tried. He had owed her that, but hadn't possessed the guts. She had every right to be angry. Cam chose not to speak of that failure or his part in removing her from her home in Laurel. He saw no reason to share any of it with a group of casual acquaintances and wedding-and-funeral relatives. It was all he could do to shake their hands and make small talk. By the time the service was over, he had sweat through his sport coat.

Now at the beach, he found his family waiting in his grandmother's kitchen. His father looked at him and shifted his eyes to his mother, who held out her arms. She sniffled and heaved against him. Plates of tuna and egg sandwiches and Barbecued Humpty Dumpty potato chips were spread across the table. Kiernan sat with a bowed head, her hair falling like a veil. Spencer, so serious and straight-edged to begin with, rubbed her back and whispered in her ear. Dan was the only one eating. Cam had no appetite. He'd barely slept these last few days, presumably due to a squirrel that had infiltrated the attic. Instead, Cam grabbed a beer from the refrigerator and asked if anyone wanted one.

"Too early," his father said. Spencer and his mother shook their heads. Kiernan didn't even look up.

"I can't have a beer," Kiernan said, screeching. "I'm pregnant."

"Sorry, I forgot," Cam said.

"You're a dick," she said.

"Kiernan," Sherri Preston said. Spencer gave Cam a keep-quiet look and adjusted the wire rim glasses on his face. He usually stayed out of their crossfire.

Kiernan looked up across the table at Cam. Her eyes were ringed with red. "I could have told Gram about it the last time I saw her, but we had just found out then, and I didn't want to tell *anyone* before three months, with all that can happen. It's what people do. She'll never know how much it would have meant to me for her to know."

"You couldn't have seen the future," Dan said.

"Really, Kiernan, you can't blame yourself for that," Cam said.

"You don't know how it feels to have that guilt on your shoulders."

"I've got enough," he said. "We all do."

"Not like this. I should have told her. Every time I saw her since the wedding, she asked."

"She wasn't doing it to pressure you, honey," his father said. "I'm sure that wherever she is, she knows and she's happy."

"She could probably tell anyway, knowing her," Dan said.

"Don't take it all on yourself, Kiernan." Spencer stroked his wife's hair. "You're human like the rest of us."

Martin Preston pursed his lips and tilted his head. Sherri poured herself a cup of coffee.

"You know your grandmother wouldn't want you to feel bad," Sherri said. "She wouldn't want those feelings transferred to the baby."

"So," Cam asked, "How pregnant are you?"

"Just about four months," Spencer said.

"You're going to name him after me?" Cam asked.

"That's what we were thinking," Spencer said. "Jackass Remlinger."

"Now that has a real ring to it," Cam said.

"How can you joke at a time like this?" Kiernan looked up, her chin quivering.

"I think Gram might think that one hysterical grandchild is probably enough," Cam said.

"You're such a bastard."

"Just because I don't care to carry on like a punch-drunk Ophelia doesn't mean I don't feel bad. I just had to wash her ashes out of a fucking fishing boat." Cam pushed his empty bottle to the center of the table.

"That's not even the right play," Kiernan said.

"Both of you stop," his mother said, snapping a tea spoon against the table. "The least you can do today is be civil. You managed to get along at the funeral. I suppose it's too much to ask for it to happen again."

"Fine," Cam said. He grabbed another Budweiser out of the refrigerator and went out onto his lopsided deck.

"How are you doing?" his father asked, joining him.

"Well, I'm not out to win an Academy Award," Cam said. His father sat down on the chaise lounge.

"Have a seat," Martin said.

Cam sat and put his feet up on the cafe table. He looked over at his dad, who shook his head.

"You know you two could barely get along when you were little. I assumed you would grow out of it at some point. It makes your mother sick to think about it."

"I suppose it's my fault?"

"Don't look for me to take sides. It isn't you against her. It's us, or at least it's supposed to be. You need to see it like that and for the life of me, I don't understand why you can't."

"Because I inherited Gram's intolerance for that kind of nonsense. Someone needs to tell Kiernan that this isn't about her. It's about Gram. I've been hearing the same crap my whole life. You remember that stupid band concert when she was a freshman and the trumpets screwed up? She wailed for a week because it ruined the climax or whatever it's called, as if it were a tremendous blow to her, the first clarinet. Greenie, my dog, gets hit by a car. I cried for an hour. She cried for two days. What the hell?"

"Did it ever occur to you that she really feels those things? That she's not acting? You take things in stride, maybe a little too easily. Others are different, like your mother and sister, and they should be respected as such."

"That's a hell of a lecture, Dad, but no. In Kiernan's case, I don't buy it."

"You're wrong for that, Cameron."

"Would it have hurt her to tell Gram she was pregnant?"

"That very guilt is what's making her feel so bad. It's simple logic, and I know you can follow it."

"It's her own fault, then."

"You may come to realize that people make mistakes. You're familiar with that concept?"

"I am. But I don't care to flounce around like a beached mackerel to make sure everyone knows I'm suffering."

"No, you pout and sulk."

Cam raised his eyebrows and smiled. His father smiled back. Miranda turned the corner onto the deck.

"Well, you two look like you're doing okay," she said.

"We were just saying that," Cam said, grateful to have her there.

Inside, Miranda's eyes watered as she hugged his mother and made her way to Spencer and Kiernan. He caught Dan checking her out as Kiernan clutched her. Then Cam had the pleasure of introducing her to his uncle. Cam started the stopwatch function of his Timex Ironman.

"Miranda, this is my Uncle Dan, my mother's brother." Cam smiled and squeezed her hand. She'd heard him talk about Dan often enough. The weekend that Dan visited last summer, Cam spent at Miranda's complaining about him.

"Dan Bailey," he said. "You're the girlfriend, I take it."

"That would be me."

"You're a waitress or something? Cam's been rather closed-mouth."

"I was a waitress when we met. I live in Boston now. I'm in advertising."

Dan put his hand to his chin and nodded. "In what capacity?"

"She walks down Beacon Street in a sandwich board advertising Mr. Chicken franchises."

Dan shook his head as she cuffed Cam on the elbow.

"I'm in creative at Quigley and Walter. I've been focusing mainly on print and public spaces."

"Well, if you ever get into multi-media you make sure that Cam gives me a call. I don't know if he told you but I work in the Industry in LA. With all that's going on out there, we're always looking for good people. If you have any kind of a track record, there's a place for you."

"I imagine it's hard to get your foot in the door," she said.

"That's where I come in. For years, I've been telling Cam to get his ass out there, that I could place him in the Carpenters' Union and he could spend his days building sets amongst the best weather and most beautiful women on the planet, present company excluded. But he won't budge from his little backass town."

"So you know people in advertising out there?" she said.

"Rob Thomas is working on a new series. Just the other day he was telling me how hard it was to get good people in marketing. Charlie Sheen was saying the same thing about the team that promotes his new show."

"3:10," Cam said, checking his watch.

"What?" Dan asked.

"Nothing." Dan had surpassed his usual name-dropping three minute mark by an entire ten seconds. The emotional trials of the day were extreme, after all.

"I'm in entertainment law," Dan said. "There's quite a bit of business integration."

"Aren't there also enormous amounts of bullshit, Uncle Dan?" Cam asked.

"You can step in that anywhere. You've just got to know the right places to scrape off your soles."

"I don't know if I could deal," Cam said.

"When you're pulling up to the lot in a Porsche 911, you can put up with quite a bit, believe me." Cam stifled a giggle—4:12 for the car.

"Well, I'm sorry about your mother," Miranda said. "She was so nice to me."

"Thank you, Miranda. I'm sorry she never had the chance to come out west. I think she would have liked my beach, too."

"I'm sure she would have," Miranda said. Cam was dubious, and exhaled loudly when Dan resumed his assault on the sandwiches.

"He's not such a bad guy for someone in the *Industry* who talks with Charlie Sheen and Rob Thomas, whoever that is, and drives a Porsche."

"Maybe you should go out there. Wouldn't you like to be surrounded by starlets and sports cars?"

"I'd rather live with Ralph the dog at his place."

"I bet you would," she said, her smile falling flat.

They settled in around the table. The awful sandwiches were there to remind them of Francine's favorite lunch, one she subjected them to five days a week during countless Julys and Augusts. As they nibbled, reminisces came out. They recalled her fondness for Carlton Fisk, blackberry brandy, and hydrangeas, which she had been unable to grow and often left her cursing. Kiernan recounted falling down the stairs as a four year old, one of her earliest memories, and making Gram accompany her every trip for the rest of that summer. As a sophomore in high school, his mother had kissed his father for the first time below the sea wall, telling Francine the next day that she'd met the man she was going to marry. Dan engineered his first car accident by crashing into the old shed. After that, Gram told him he could ride his bike back and forth to town for his dishwashing job. Cam related that when Miranda first started coming by, it was to hang out at the beach with a group of friends. Gram had asked him when he was going to take the poor girl out, and he'd explained that it wasn't like that. Francine had laughed and asked how big of a fool did he imagine she was. The room became quiet as the laughter petered out.

"I'm going to buy this house," Cam said.

"How are you going to do that?" Kiernan asked. His mother, father, and Dan looked at him as if expecting a punch line. "We talked about it, we can't afford it, and we're both lawyers. Have you been robbing banks in your spare time?"

"I've got a two-year plan," he said.

"So, you're not writing us a check now?" Dan said, laughing.

"Holly doesn't think it's going to take that long," his mother said.

"I don't know about that," he said.

"How are you going to come up with that kind of money?" Kiernan asked.

"I'm going to build some houses next year, on my own."

"Really?" she said.

"It's what I do," he replied.

"You've got these jobs lined up already?" Martin asked.

"Not yet. Brinkley doesn't even schedule that far out. I've got time."

"I hope you're right and that you can manage it," Sherri said, lips tight. "Good luck."

Kiernan was looking at him, exasperated. Dan smirked, thinking him a joke or, more likely, imagining Miranda naked. Spencer and Miranda were nodding politely. His mother then asked if anyone remembered the McCarthy's terrier that dug up Francine's tulip bulbs. The subject of the house was dropped.

So that's how it is, he thought: His plan wasn't worth considering. Had they chosen to ask, he could have provided hours of details. Apparently, they didn't want to waste time by dismissing him in earnest. Their attitudes would change down the road, however, when he brought them back here and dropped a fat green bank check onto this very table. That might be something they would find worthy of discussion.

CHAPTER NINE

By six o'clock he was grinding out Route 295 on his way back from dropping Dan at the Portland Jetport. None of his family had stuck around, all high-tailing it to their real homes as if they'd done something wrong. True, his parents had school the next morning, Spencer and Kiernan had work, and Dan supposedly couldn't miss a meeting with Charlie Sheen's production company, whose receptionist had fantastically enhanced breasts, not to mention a liking for him, which was convenient now that he was separated and headed for divorce. Cam had begged Miranda to stay, but she refused, citing a breakfast function that she couldn't chance being late to, even if it meant driving two hours to Laurel, then two more back, after only a four hour visit.

Cam couldn't relax. He flipped the radio station after every other song and lasted less than a minute on sports talk. He adjusted his seat. As night fell, the air regained the winter snap it had possessed that morning. Instead of making the turn toward the beach, he cut towards town and the Port Tavern. He wasn't quite ready to sit by himself in the house and listen to it creak and moan. He didn't want to consider that the scratching in the attic wasn't being made by a portly squirrel.

Even on a Sunday the Tavern was busy. Wood paneling gave it a rustic feel, and the place retained just enough grit to be authentic. Janie, as usual, was working the bar. Her father owned the place. She dressed in all black, even down to the lipstick, mainly to irritate summer tourists. They barely noticed, however, as the look was probably common enough in the cities and suburbs they were trying to escape. She was a year older than him, but carried herself as if the difference was ten.

Brinkley had a beer waiting for him.

"Tough day?" he asked.

"Yup," Cam said. "Thanks for the boat."

"Don't mention it."

Cam gladly listened to Lenny Perkins tell them how Henry Schlissfut, a three hundred pound plumber, got stuck in a bathroom vanity he was installing at a house in Wellport on Friday. He was on his second Budweiser when Holly James came in. He waited until she got settled, said hello to eight or nine other people, and received her glass of pink wine. Her brown hair was cut short, similar to his own as a twelve year-old. He supposed she thought it made her more business-like.

"Holly, I've got a question for you," he said.

"Shoot," she said.

"How long do you really think it'll take to sell my grandmother's house? Off the record."

"Hard to say. We could hit this June. But with a house like that, you've got to get the right type of people to see it. To be honest, it'll take some luck to move it before fall. Being a fixer-upper, it will have its challenges. But it won't get past September. A lot of prospects will be looking then."

"What are the odds of it going into next year?"

"Your parents are paying me to see that it doesn't."

"But it could, right?" He was getting a continuation of the pitch she'd made his folks. "What about the places that have been sitting on the Shore road?"

"I'm not selling those, and I'm really good at what I do."

"Never mind, modest."

"You're funny." She smiled and then turned to talk to the person next to her, who happened to be Adam Francis, owner of the Monastery, the kind of person that he would expect Holly to suck up to.

He felt a hand on his arm. "Hello, there," Sophia said, coming up behind him. "Wow, you look like hell."

"Thanks," he said, choosing not to look at himself in the mirror behind the bar. "I appreciate that."

"I'm sorry," she said, a sincere expression on her face.

"It's been a rough week," he said.

"What's happened since Monday?" she said.

"It's a long story."

When Holly joined Sophia, Cam was able to drift down the bar. Lenny Perkins and Brinkley had started buying drinks for a few of the waitresses from the Seacoast Brewery. Cam half-listened to the banter, trying to convince himself that Holly didn't know the market any better than the limitations of her own ability.

According to Miranda, none of their orbits ran beyond the Dockside, the Tavern, and the Brewery. The Senator, for all that he possessed, preferred the walls of the Port Tavern and the deck of the Dockside to anywhere else. Although Miranda hadn't come out and said it, she feared that would be his future, as well. Since escaping to Boston, her voice often dropped when they conversed about his comings and goings, and the trajectories of those he considered his friends. At least she'd seemed somewhat excited about his trying to buy the house. He didn't need a city like Boston or some soul-gutting job to prove himself. He knew what he wanted, and it was right here.

"What are you guys talking about?" Sophia settled onto the stool next to him, having abandoned Holly. Cam sat up straight. He couldn't remember her ever joining them unless Jeremy had requested her to do so.

"We were wondering who was going to buy the next round," Perkins said. "Usually it's the last person to sit down."

"You're full of it," she said.

Cam had found the Ferret different than he had known her as Jeremy's girlfriend. Previously, he'd never considered her more than a small blond appendage. While she might have been lost when considering how her ex- currently felt about her, it was also clear that she had ideas, and they weren't any more ridiculous than his own. She wasn't mean or self-serving or judgmental. She liked him, that was clear, but she didn't expect anything. That was a relief.

Lenny and Hank Blanton, who owned the Commercial Street Gallery, were soon arguing about whether the Chamber of Commerce should install public restrooms in the parking lot behind the business district, the burning issue of local politics. The town had refused to do it. They left it up to the businesses, and Lenny was making the point that if it was the businesses that were going to profit from them, they should be the ones to foot the bill. Cam doubted it would get resolved before July or even the following summer.

"Are you going to tell me what happened?" Sophia said, quietly, while the debate continued.

"We spread my grandmother's ashes off of Gray Gull beach today. She died this winter. It was the first chance we had."

"That's her house that you live in, isn't it?"

"It was. We lived there together for two years, until she had to go to a nursing home. Alzheimer's."

"You're all alone there?"

"I have been for some time. But it's different now. A squirrel or something got in the attic this week. At first I thought she was haunting me."

"Maybe she was."

"Ghosts don't scratch and scritch when they hover, do they?"

"You never know," Sophia said.

"Yeah, you do." Cam said.

"You don't believe in the paranormal?"

"Not as much as in oversized rodents."

She shrugged.

"If you're scared," Sophia said, "I can come over and keep you company. I'm not afraid of either squirrels or ghosts."

"Maybe I'll leave the lights on." He needed to change the subject before he looked even more pitiful. "So how's your restaurant coming?"

"Don't say it out loud."

"Who's going to hear us, this stack of napkins?" Everyone around them was fully occupied in conversation.

"Please. Jeremy and I aren't taking any chances."

"So he's in?"

"He's in all right. But speaking of paranoid, Jeremy's having a bit of an issue. You haven't mentioned it to anyone, have you?"

"No." Cam couldn't imagine that Jeremy would be excited about spending time with her again. He could barely make it through fixing her a drink.

"He gets up everyday expecting to find our plans posted on the Coast Star's homepage."

"I haven't said a word."

"He's so pumped," she said. "I could do a rain dance naked around his apartment and he wouldn't notice. He's submerged in catalogs and business plan writing books, and he's already sent a rough sketch to this architect he knows. We're meeting with the Senator tomorrow, and if that goes well my father will fly in. Then we're before the Board of Selectman. I probably shouldn't have told you any of that. It's all highly classified. But I *was* going to call you."

"About what?"

"I don't understand much of the building issues. Jeremy's been spewing about this and that and the other thing, and I don't even get the language. I have a notebook at home with a list of things I don't understand. I've got to know this stuff by the time we sit down with my father."

"Jeremy won't explain it?"

"I suppose he would if I asked. But I'm not sure that he knows what he's talking about. I don't want to look like an idiot, and I have the feeling that you'll be able to put it in English for me, not to mention get it right."

"I guess I could help you with that."

"Do you want to come over later?" she said.

"Oh no, I'm on fumes as it is." With Lenny sitting next to them, Cam could see the report going straight to Jeremy if he and Sophia walked out together. Nor was he up for another debate on what a night cap meant. "Could we do it some other time? I could meet you here or at the Brewery?"

"A public discourse would violate the Prime Directive of Secrecy."

"You're going to need to put in a high ceiling to fit Jeremy's ego in there. I can tell you that much."

"That's what you need to pull off something like this. Absolute belief."

"I've never considered fat-headedness a positive attribute," Cam said.

"Why don't you come over on Wednesday night? I'll cook."

"Really?"

"You don't think I can?"

"I'm sure you're a better chef than me."

"It settled then. Thanks." She kissed him on the cheek. He felt himself turning red as he made his way back to Lenny and Brink.

CHAPTER TEN
"Senator Grimes"

They walked into my office, eyes up then down, as if coming to confess. They couldn't help but be intimidated. Over my shoulder was the picture of me and Ronald Reagan, and it is there for a reason. My father, the Senator, is just off to the side, invisible to the camera. Reagan is looking at me fondly, with a slight smile and his head cocked in my direction. Those who see it cannot help but assume he is endorsing an idea I have just shared. He looks appreciative, but he was an actor. We had conversed for less than half a minute, at the end of which he offered me these words of wisdom: "Work hard at Yale, Edward." My given name is, of course, Eugene.

I came out from behind the desk to shake their hands. They were here to discuss a subject of such importance that it couldn't be broached on the deck at the Dockside. The boy had even put on a tie, as if thirty-six inches of silk could color what I'd had come to surmise about him over the past ten years. Sophia Harding's eyes finally landed on the Winslow to her right before returning to me. Jeremy stared straight ahead and nodded when I suggested they sit. I returned to my chair.

The desk, mahogany and massive, is not the one used by

my father in Washington. That relic, along with his pictures and correspondence, was shipped to that supposed hotbed of collegiate political thought in Waterville, where his office is recreated in a prominent section of their library. This space is my own domain.

"What can I do for you?" I asked.

"We're interested in the old bait shed on Laurel Point pier," Jeremy said.

So it is not a plea to use these grounds for a wedding, which I had considered might be the case. It is a frequent request from friends and strangers alike, and one that I never grant. My own nuptials took place here in 1986, and it is not a scene I wish to see repeated. The use of a dilapidated building owned by the town, however, was another matter.

"I assume that you do not wish to operate a bait business," I said. "What is it then, a gallery?"

They looked at each other before he spoke.

"You know I've wanted to open a restaurant here for a while, and that old shed is just the place for it. Naturally, we'll renovate. But it's just sitting there now and no one wants it except us. We'd like to lease it and figured we'd better talk to you."

"I'll be delighted to help, both personally and on behalf of the town. The first thing to do is make certain that the zoning regulations allow a restaurant as a conditional use."

"I've checked. It does," Sophia said, as I reached into a drawer for my copy of the codebook. She blinked rapidly and shifted her bony ass in the leather chair while I paged through to the appropriate section of the ordinances.

"You are correct," I said. "It's a commercial zone whose possible uses include restaurants, hospitality, and food service." This business model was a possibility I had not regarded in my position as a steward of Laurel, perhaps because the building was currently such an eyesore that traditional, logic-driven thought could not imagine it otherwise. Our current official assessment was that we would soon have to invest in tearing it down. I had just been presented with a more intriguing option, however.

"So how do we go about getting a lease?" Jeremy asked.

"That will have to be negotiated through the Board of Selectmen. I might be of use to you there, provided there is benefit to the town."

"Of course there is," Jeremy said, practically shouting. "We'll create jobs, expand the tax base, and add a destination spot that will increase tourism. We're going to bring a certain quality in the area of hospitality that doesn't exist here."

"Exactly what kind of place do you foresee?"

I listened. Although I didn't care what color the walls would be or how the various menus would be presented, they outlined a clear vision and they did so with passion. As she described their restaurant, Sophia rose from her seat and leaned forward, her small, pert breasts edging to the scoop neck of her shirt. I became hard as I listened to her. With such maniacal enthusiasm on display, I could see why Jeremy might have been so inconsolable. But his heartbreak had apparently been overcome by the prospect of this restaurant. He spoke as if the possibility of failure did not exist, having yet to learn that wanting is not all it takes.

Money, it appeared, would not be an issue with the Harding's bankrolling the project. Their plan was logical and the personalities, so important in that business, were right— meaning that Jeremy did command a following. While I would not be able to help them with Code Enforcement and EPA standards, there was little doubt that I could gain the approval of my fellow selectmen and secure a lease. There were no residents on the pier to complain about traffic. The fishermen groused about everything, and they wouldn't like it at first, but certain insignificant steps could be taken to placate them. Because the town would benefit, the deal could be brokered quickly. Everyone would have a chance to prosper.

"From the town's perspective," I said in a measured voice, "there are several considerations. First, what impact will there be on the roadway and use of the pier? You never know with those fishermen. Will it interfere with their access? What is fair market value for a lease and what would its duration be? How much will the business expand the tax base? Will it truthfully fill a need in the community? Merely saying these things will be addressed isn't enough; there must be substantive evidence provided."

Like a puppy, Jeremy attempted to respond to each feint, and I raised my hand to stop him.

"I believe the failure rates for new restaurants run at roughly ninety percent," I said. "It could be a risk for the town should the business fail under an outstanding lease."

"Senator, come on," he said. "That building is just standing there, empty and decrepit. We're going to rebuild. Even if we flopped in a week, the added value of the real estate would still benefit the town. This isn't a lark. Restaurants that fail are ill-timed, ill-conceived, and ill-managed. You know me. Those won't be problems here."

"How are we to determine the value of the space? A rent too high or too low could potentially damage your enterprise and, in the process, Laurel."

"It's not unusual to have an agreement based on percentage of sales. We wouldn't be opposed to that. We'd all be invested in that case."

"You would use local builders, I assume."

"Of course," he said. "Friends of ours."

"The location is on the waterfront, on what is termed 'the critical edge.' You'll need to get EPA approval. That can be tricky. And expensive."

"We're prepared for that."

"Good to know," I said, leaning back. "I think this is doable, insofar as I can present it to the board at the next meeting. I'll put a discussion of leasing the original bait shed right on the agenda." I smiled at them as I set the hook, letting my face cloud. "Of course, you will need to attend the meeting. Who do you anticipate will compete with you for the space? Your current employer, Marv Daniels? Huffington from the Squall? A group from Portland?"

"That's something we wanted to discuss with you," Jeremy said, his eyebrows knitting into a 'V.' "Is there a way that we can avoid the kind of free-for-all that opening this up might create? Can't you just go ahead and lease it to us? We're ready to move as soon as possible. We can be open this summer."

"Wouldn't the nature of supply and demand dictate that it's in the town's best interest to allow competition?"

"Senator, if we can get in there quickly, that's an extra year of income for Laurel. If there's a protracted process, it's going to cost the town money in the long run because even if a higher rent is agreed on, you'd be losing that entire first year of payments. Not to mention that certain other parties might try to throw a wrench in the works, not because they want the space, but because they don't want the competition. You've got cash on the barrel right here."

"I understand your concerns," I said. "Although there are no legal restrictions limiting our ability to operate as we see fit, there is the concept of fair play. This is a very open community."

"But giving us our shot is fair play," Sophia said. "The building has been there for a year now, unused. Anyone could have come up with this idea, but they didn't. We did."

"True," I said.

"We've been friends for a long time, Senator," Jeremy said. "That's got to mean something. Can you do us a favor here?"

"A favor is carrying an empty glass to the bar so that a waitress doesn't have to bother. Giving preferential treatment in a serious financial matter is rather different."

"So are you going to insist on opening it up for bidding?"

"I didn't say that," I said. "But to presume that I can

facilitate this for you without some sort of quid pro quo would be a little much. You're asking me to compromise the best interests of the town with that of your own."

"So you want something from us?" Sophia said.

"Like money?" Jeremy asked.

"Don't be crude," I said, chuckling. "I will expect a certain level of treatment, and this would remain strictly between us: A table of my own, if you know what I mean. In addition, I think that my efforts might be recognized with some complimentary meals, perhaps an annual year-ending event for some of my closest associates. A drink or two on the house when I visit. I'm sure you'll recognize this as being fair consideration. Think of what a business would have to pay a lobbyist to influence legislation. I'll be promoting your agenda and to thank me all it will cost you is a bottle or two of Gosling's and an occasional filet or sirloin."

Their faces ran through a series of subtle contortions, though if they had a more realistic knowledge of how business and government intersected they wouldn't have been surprised.

"Do you find that unfair?" I asked.

"Not at all," Sophia said, "but as that theoretical lobbyist, you'd only be influencing yourself."

"Please remember that you are the ones who asked me to do something out of the ordinary. It wasn't I who suggested channeling what could be a very profitable lease to an interested party at the exclusion of others. Some might construe that as below board. Others might look at it as savvy. To be quite honest, I am happy to proceed either way."

"I don't see a problem, Senator," Jeremy said, practicality apparently having won out. "A drink or two and a few dinners isn't much in the grand scheme of things. We'll be glad to do it."

"I think you know you can trust me. I'll certainly be showing my trust in you."

"I've noticed that Marv has never bought you a drink,"

Jeremy said.

"The Dockside has never been able to get the permit to expand its deck, either."

"I thought that was because of the EPA."

"Perhaps it is."

"It's a deal, then," Sophia said.

"But you'll make this process easy for us, right?" Jeremy said. "No hoops to jump through, no roadblocks, no pressure, no surprises."

"That I can do for you," I said. "Have we come to an understanding?"

"I'd say so," Jeremy said.

"Agreed," said Sophia.

Although they did at times appear a bit disconcerted, they left smiling. It wasn't a reason to doubt their capabilities, this naiveté. In fact, I was sure that they would be successful. I would benefit from their accomplishments, as they would from mine. The business of politics has always run best when well greased, even if only a squirt or two of the all-purpose is needed. I learned that much growing up in this family and town.

CHAPTER ELEVEN

Cam sat at the breakfast bar of her kitchen as Sophia stood at the counter chopping romaine lettuce to make them a salad to go with the pasta she was boiling. Not that he minded, but he had expected she'd have grander plans than the kind of meal he cooked for himself. It was a Wednesday, however, and the Sox were off. He wasn't missing anything, and really, he didn't have anything better to do. He raised his eyes from the nearly indecipherable curlicues of her notes to explain what HVAC meant, only to be distracted by the way her golden hair flowed over the red tank top, drawing him to the toned legs in black running tights. She started slicing a cucumber into the salad bowl.

"Are vegetables sensual or sensuous, I forget," he said.

"I think they're healthy."

"Don't you know *Animal House*?" he asked. "With Otter and Mrs. Wormer in the grocery store?"

"Is that the one you read in eighth grade where each animal represents some government or something?"

"No, that's Orwell's *Animal Farm*. This is a four star movie, comedy."

"I'm sure." She shook her head and pointed to the papers

spread in front of them. "Are you making any sense of them?"

"I promise you'll be an expert by dessert."

"To be honest, I was worried you were only coming over to drink my wine."

"I hadn't planned on drinking at all," he said, looking at the piss colored liquid in his glass. It didn't taste any better to him tonight than it did the last time.

"Don't you want to have fun?"

"It's preferable."

"My grandfather always said, 'You don't need to drink to have fun, but why take the chance?'"

She sat to his right at the counter while they ate, so that she could make a fresh set of notes based on his lecture. He went through each of her bullet points, explaining the terms and having her describe them back to him. He detailed the building process from how an estimate was formed to the finishing punch list. He also pointed out areas where they wouldn't want to skimp on the construction. She scribbled as he talked, then had him pretend to be her father and question her. Her performance impressed him. She had actually listened. By the time they finished, the sun had set and they were in shadow, the empty wine bottle in front of them.

"Jeremy is horrified that Daniels will find us out and try to cut us off on it. Or the owner of the Squall. He's so nervous he's got a rash on his shoulders."

She had no idea how much she tortured her ex-boyfriend. Although Cam's critical thinking skills hadn't been the greatest of late, he had a hard time imagining their partnership would work as smoothly as she imagined.

"I probably shouldn't tell you this," she said. "But you might be doing the job."

"What do you mean?"

"Jeremy's going to talk to Brinkley. That's who he wants to build the restaurant."

"Really?" Cam sat up in his seat. That would turn the

summer around. Not exactly a doghouse, a restaurant on the pier would more than replace the funds that Horton had snatched from them and add another prime item to his portfolio.

"He thought your idea about the loft dining room was a good one," Sophia said.

"That would be cool, wouldn't it?" The hair on his arm prickled when they brushed against each other.

"All we need is to get the lease."

"Your ATM is ready to spit out the money? The one who doesn't like your partner?"

"The one who likes to make investments that pay off."

"This could be a great thing for all of us," he said.

"What did I tell you the other day?" She smiled widely. "The hell with it. I'll give you the whole plan."

She went on to describe the restaurant, from the layout to the menu holders. Darkness fell in around them, and Sophia didn't bother to adjust the lights. A project that could make a name for him had fallen into their lap. Of all people, he had the scattershot girl in front of him to thank for it. For the first time in weeks, he felt at ease.

When their glasses were empty, he helped her clean, handing her plates as she loaded them into the dishwasher. His mother and sister had conditioned him where that was concerned. Sophia kept talking, going on about some food that Jeremy wanted to serve at the restaurant. Cam had never heard of it. She put the salad bowl in the drying rack and opened the cabinet under the sink so that he could throw out the napkins he'd piled on the counter. When she closed the door, they were inches apart. A fast-car-on-black-ice hollowness rose in his stomach.

She leaned in almost imperceptibly and he matched her. Then he had her by the waist and she was pressing him into the refrigerator. Her hands found his Levis and she pushed them towards the floor. The two of them followed their clothes, Sophia pulling him on top of her. She wrapped her legs around him and moaned. His eyes were clenched as he traced the edges of her small breasts with his tongue. He stole a glance: Her head was flung back as if searching the ceiling for stars.

"Do you have anything?" Cam whispered.

"Like a condom?" she said.

"Yeah."

"Trust me, don't need it." She pulled him back down. Cam told himself to slow down and breathe: Baseball. Red Sox. Line-up. Ellsbury. Pedroia. Ortiz. Middlebrooks. Salty. And as Miranda—Christ, Miranda—had trained him, it worked. Sophia shuddered and twisted so that she was stuck to him, and he let go. She rocked hard again as he jerked and his muscles constricted at once.

Sophia wrapped her hands around his neck and tilted his head down so that their eyes met.

"Hello," she said. She kissed him again and then rolled them over so that she was straddling him, sitting up. He raised his hands to her flat, taut stomach. She reached onto the island where she'd placed a bottle of red wine and took a swallow. She dropped her head to his and emptied the wine she'd drunk into his mouth.

"It's not so bad that way," he said.

She reached down and wiped his lips. "It looked like you were bleeding," she said.

"I'm fine," he said. She lay down so that she covered him like a blanket.

"Why did you come to Horton's with me that night?" he asked.

"I'm not sure."

"I don't believe that."

"We don't have to stay here on the floor," she said. "I have a bed, too."

"I'll try anything once," he said.

CHAPTER TWELVE

At six-thirty in the morning, he crept along the back roads of Laurel, slouched behind the wheel, Sox cap low over his eyes. Presumably, Sophia the Ferret was still stretched out across her bed, breathing inaudibly as she slept. Christ. He hadn't been drunk. Nor had he spent the previous weeks longing to be with her. In fact, on several occasions he'd run away. Not to mention that he was—in theory—committed to Miranda. Yet, it had happened. He also had to admit that he'd enjoyed himself. What he couldn't do was allow that to complicate things. He'd go home, take a long, hot shower, and get his mind right. At least his grandmother wouldn't be in the kitchen having her coffee when he came through the door. One look and she would have known. Cam sunk lower in his seat.

He'd broken his collar bone at fourteen. He'd been at Hunter Masticola's A-frame on Sandy Point. It was his second or third time drinking beer. He'd leapt from the loft to the couch below imitating a Randy Savage off-the-top-rope-elbow-smash. Instead of landing flat on the cushions, his shoulder had scored a direct hit on the back of the couch. The snapping of his clavicle echoed like a gunshot. Cam howled, and Eddie, eyes bugging at the instantaneous lump growing on his friend's shoulder, called the cottage. Cam's parents were out to dinner at the Break Point, but Gram showed up minutes later. As he tried not to cry, she asked how he'd done it, and he told her the truth, pointing with his good arm. She shook her head.

"I'm dead when Mom and Dad find out," he said, when they got in the car.

"Look on the bright side, you could be dead now," she replied. When they passed a variety store, she stopped to get him some gum so he wouldn't "smell like a brewery" at the hospital.

By the time the doctor, stooped and pale, entered the canary yellow exam room, Cam had already been poked, prodded, and X-rayed by a nurse. His shoulder throbbed. The doctor puckered and sighed.

"How the hell did you do this?" he asked.

"He went over the handlebars of his bike," Gram said, before Cam could answer. "Trying to show off some jump or other for the young ladies, I believe."

"It's a good break," Dr. Donahue said. "I hope they were suitably impressed."

"I don't know about that," Cam said.

He was given a sling and a prescription for Tylenol with codeine. Gram was handed a stack of paperwork. They hadn't pulled out of the parking lot before he had thanked her for covering for him.

"Let me tell you a few things," Gram said. "The Masticolas are good people. If word got out that there was underage drinking going on, the hospital might find it necessary to notify the authorities. None of us deserves that headache because you and Hunter refuse to use the brains that God gave you."

"What are we going to tell my parents?" Cam asked.

"What do you think we should tell them?"

"The truth might put me in permanent lockdown," he said.

"If you think you're going to get away with nonsense like this your whole life, you're going to wind up being an *asshole*."

It was the only time he'd ever heard her use the word.

Sherri and Martin had been waiting on the front porch when they returned from the hospital. Before he could get to the stairs, they were asking him what happened. Gram was the one who told them he'd crashed his bike. His parents still didn't know the real story.

He'd have to do the right thing and let Sophia know that this didn't mean he was a prospective boyfriend or interested in a relationship. It was a crazy hook-up, one he shouldn't have allowed to happen. Hopefully, she could live with that. As for Miranda, he'd have to make it up to her, which did not mean he'd be throwing himself at her feet and begging forgiveness. A confession there wouldn't do either of them any good. His stomach settled as he accepted this course of action. "*Asshole*," however, did not stop echoing in his splitting head.

CHAPTER THIRTEEN

As advertised, the Victoria Secret bra made her breasts look spectacular. Not as great as Gisele Bundchen's—Mrs. Tom Brady—but not bad considering what the nylon and fabric had to work with. Of course, nothing was easy. A Friday follow-up meeting with Will Nichols of Mr. Chicken had somehow been continued into a lunch on Newbury Street on Saturday that lasted for three and a half hours. They sat outside in the sun and discussed everything but business. As a result, the shoulder straps were digging into skin the hue of a tequila sunrise, and she wanted to go into the bathroom and chuck the thing into her bag. However, that would require donning the white cardigan draped over her chair, which would generalize the pain across a body that barely breathed through the yellow cotton sleeveless she wore. As she tried to conjure a solution, Miranda dredged up demographic data on eighteen-to-thirty-five-year-old females who used roll-on deodorant. Her phone rang.

Eddie Deperna wanted her to meet with them in Quigley's office. Ugh. It was moments like these that made her wish she'd given in to Cam and spent one more year as a waitress.

She walked through the series of cubicles. Some of the screens were colored with graphics; others bore the mundane black and white of Word. In the glassed-in creative conference room, several of her co-workers were building a pyramid with Red Bull cans.

She smiled as she entered the room. Deperna was seated on the window ledge, which ran the twenty-foot length of the office. The green of the public garden was poised below him. The treetops, window height, were the same green as the grass. Not so long ago, the fields were as brown as the branches.

"Mr. Quigley," she said to the company president who sat behind his desk. "Eddie." Deperna was her team leader, and she used his first name although she knew he probably would have been thrilled with more formal language. Quigley stood, ran a hand through his thinning hair, and asked her to sit down, motioning to the chair in front of his desk. A current sizzled through her overcooked skin. Quigley's eyes rested on her cleavage for an instant. She did not check, but imagined Eddie's eyes also locked in at some point.

Deperna stood up and settled into the chair to her right, pulling it to the side to acknowledge that while he was not Quigley, he was not on her level, either. She considered that a bad omen.

"How are you coming on the Roll-on roll out, Miranda?" Quigley asked. If he were not wearing his usual bow tie, she would have expected a smirk.

"Making progress. I'm currently researching how the target demographics match up with the historical. Once I've established that, we'll brainstorm tomorrow. That's the correct timeline isn't it, Eddie?"

"That's the plan. How is it going?"

"To be honest, I'm still digging. I wouldn't want to conclude anything just yet."

"Do you always proceed so cautiously?" Quigley asked.

"I'd rather have correct information than quick answers."

"What if in this case, I need to know right now? What would your impression be?"

"Based on stable sales figures, I'd say that women using roll-ons have used them for years and stay with the product. To expand that base, aiming for a younger demo would make sense on several levels, as they could then carry the product with them. Of course, a different deadline may allow for other impressions. Which I don't have to tell you."

Quigley nodded and looked up at the miniature Boston Celtic championship banners he had strung along the side wall. Dork. Cam wouldn't even string Sox pennants in his bedroom. Quigley swiveled to look at Eddie. "It will be interesting to see how that works out when you're finished."

"That's a more than fair assessment," Deperna said. "She's a thinker, vertically and laterally."

A thinker with great tits, she thought, considering where his gaze kept falling.

"But you're not too comfortable on national campaigns, are you, Miranda?" Quigley asked.

She looked over at Eddie, whose eyes mysteriously focused on his shoes. She wondered what she'd done to deserve the hot seat. Would there be downsizing? Suddenly, returning to waitressing did not seem like fun.

"I don't think that's a very fair characterization, Mr. Quigley. Since I joined the firm ten months ago, I've been placed on projects with local targets: Mr. Chicken, Amtrak, Olympia Sports. That doesn't mean I couldn't be effective on projects with a larger scope."

"Weren't those campaigns less challenging?" Quigley said, straightening in his chair. "A freshman marketing class could have been successful in those areas, if you ask me."

"If that's what you think, you're wasting a lot of money paying the people on this floor." She smiled, not about to roll over for them.

Quigley looked over at Deperna and nodded.

"You have done exceptionally well with what you've been given, haven't you?" Quigley said.

"The numbers speak for themselves. Following our Mr. Chicken campaign, their sales were up thirty-one point seven percent. And—"

"We're aware of the numbers," Deperna said.

"Did you ever see that television show *The Shield*, Miranda?" Quigley asked.

"Yes. My boyfriend watched it. The main character was that bald guy, Mattie. No, Mackey. Rogue cops and drug dealers. Changing morality lines, that kind of thing. Large male audience, twenty-five to fifty-five, as a market. But I thought it was off the air. Are we going to try to sell the DVD's?"

"*The Shield* isn't a client, Miranda," Deperna said.

"Do you consider yourself a leader?" Quigley asked.

"If anyone on Eddie's team is willing to take a lead role, it's me. Even though I don't have the experience that some do, I don't hold back. I'm the first to stay late and offer to help. In college, I was the captain of our marketing competition team. Of course I'm a leader."

"The thing about *The Shield* is this: Mackey led what they called a strike team. They're given the tough jobs, the hard cases, ones that need immediate and decisive action." Quigley watched to make sure she was following him. "What we've encountered in the last six months are requests from smaller clients, usually local, who also want quick action and immediate results. They don't want to wait for a ramp up, nor do they want the long march. They want the shock and awe, and a quick return on their advertising dollar, much like Mr. Chicken."

"I see."

"Their budgets are lower, but their expectations are not," Deperna added.

"This is where out-of-the-box, divergent thinking is going

to be needed. We're not talking about traditional advertising models. Is this something that you think you could excel at, being a member of a campaign strike team?"

"To be honest, I think that I can excel at any aspect of this business. If you'd like me to work on the team with this quick strike capability, I'd be glad to do it." She reminded herself that she was still in her first year and she had to be patient and flexible. She should look at it as an opportunity.

"I think you've misunderstood, Miranda," Deperna said, nodding to Quigley, who was now leaning forward.

"I can see that by the look on her face, Eddie," Quigley said, smiling. "She thinks she's facing a demotion."

"I didn't take it as that, Mr. Quigley. Honestly, I'll do whatever it takes to help the firm."

"No, Miranda. We've been very impressed by your work. You're getting a promotion—and a raise. You're going to lead the QST, the Quigley Strike Team. You're going to be our Vic Mackey."

"Thank you," she said, standing to shake their hands.

From what she remembered, the television character had been nothing short of a mad dog. Admittedly, she was surprised by the impression she'd made at Q and W. She knew that she'd done some good work and they were right: this suited her. A few summers of carrying trays stacked with drinks in a wall-to-wall bar had made dealing with sober businessmen manageable, and she was more than willing to kick ass. Back at her cube, she dialed Cam's number to tell him of her promotion. Would her slacker boyfriend find it as amusing as she did that she'd just been compared to a maniacal careerist?

CHAPTER FOURTEEN

Sophia came in from a twelve mile run to find the Mercedes parked next to her Jeep. She sighed as she balanced on the bottom of her stairs and stretched her calves. They would have dinner, but she would be the one getting grilled. In the end, he would give her the money. She'd just have to sweat for it. If she wanted to be smart, she'd go say hello and welcome he and Tia back to town. She sighed once more and walked over to the house.

Her father, in his pinstriped shirt and jeans, was at the desk in his study swearing at his laptop. A printed rough draft of the business plan she had sent him peeked out from under some other papers. When she said hello he came over to hug her.

"You still look like a kid," he said. "Are you ever going to age?"

"I'll probably go straight to gray when we get this restaurant going," she said.

He nodded. "Running a business isn't easy, especially that kind."

"I know," she said. She didn't catch the scent of the Paris

that Tia, just five years older than she was, wore. "Where's my prospective step-mom?"

"She's down in Newport with your brother, helping him outfit his boat for the season."

"How's it going for him?"

"You could pick up the phone once in a while."

"So could he. Well?"

"He had a rough start, but his booked charters for this season are up significantly over last year. It looks like he might turn a profit. It's impressive. There's a lot of money down there, though, as you know."

"There's some up here, too." Her eyes shifted to the window. "People love looking at the ocean, and they'll pay to do it."

"I wouldn't debate that." Rawley Harding picked up an empty coffee cup and looked into it. Then he put it back down. "It's pretty strange if you think about it. I have two children who never showed any interest in business or investing, one a writer, the other a painter. Now they both want to be entrepreneurs. How do you explain that?"

"Poor genetics?" she said.

"I guess I could just enjoy it." They stared at each other until smiles appeared simultaneously. "Where do you want to have dinner tonight?"

"Wherever you like," she said.

"How about the Hermit Crab Inn down in Ogunquit? I'll call Hugo and get us that corner table so we can go over your package."

"Remember, there's going to be three of us."

"You think this partnership will work, you and him?"

"Now that we've all graduated from Junior High, I think we've got the maturity to handle it."

"I get the same sarcasm from your brother."

"More good luck for you," she said.

"It is over between you and Jeremy? Definitively?" She

thought she detected a grin that he tried to hide by stroking the salt and pepper hair of his goatee.

"As I've told you at least twenty-five hundred times already, this is all business."

"It better be, because it's easy to lose money, even without partners. I know that from experience. So when I expect you to be exhaustive in research and diligent in planning, it's because I never want anything bad to happen to you. To be forewarned is to be forearmed. I expect to free up this money for you, but I need to see that this restaurant is a smart move. If you can't prove that it will work, I've got two choices and they both stink: I don't give you the money and we both feel like shit, or I do give it to you, you lose it, and we both feel like shit. I hope you can appreciate that."

"I get it, Father."

"What I don't understand is why you want to do it," he said.

"It's something I'll be good at," she said, without having to think.

"Painting is something you're good at."

"It hasn't exactly made me self-sufficient, though, has it?"

"Maybe you will start to sprout some grays. I'm proud of you."

"Thanks, I guess," she said, although she did not feel so enamored that she wanted to spend the rest of the afternoon listening to him.

CHAPTER FIFTEEN

A sport coat was required at the Hermit Crab, but she was still surprised by how professional Jeremy looked in his gray flannel suit. He was waiting for them at the bar, sipping a Pellegrino with lemon. The folder containing their updated business plan sat next to the glass with the sparkling water. She didn't doubt that if her father didn't like what was on those pages, he wouldn't supply the capital they needed. Jeremy and Rawley shook hands without either breaking into a grimace. They discussed the weather and the American League East. The venture they were considering seemed to have squelched the animosity that hung over them like the humidity in August.

They talked as if there were nothing important to discuss. Rawley described her brother Wren's luxury yacht charter and Jeremy expounded on the intricacies of chilling martinis. This lasted through cocktails and until the appetizer plates were cleared from the table. That's when her father requested their updated packet.

"It's all there," she said. "But before you look at the final numbers, let me help you see the big picture." She started with the profile the building would strike when one crested the hill and drove down to the pier with the harbor and the soft lighting of sunset as its backdrop. She described the interior from a customer's point of view. The food: panko encrusted tuna with the wasabi aioli, the uniforms, black jeans with black shirts, Robert Cray playing in the background. His eyes focused on her as she spoke. He nodded in places. His eyebrows raised in others.

"I can see how you would be busy all summer," Rawley said. "Is that enough to make a profit?"

"No, of course not," Jeremy said. "But we'll adjust the menu as the seasons change. More comfort food in the off months to encourage locals. If we can break even in March, April, May, November, and December, we're in good shape. Because we will rake it in at peak."

"What if there's a lousy summer, a lot of rain, high gas prices. What if—through no fault of your own—you stall right out of the gate?"

"We'll still get local business. That will keep us afloat."

Rawley raised his eyebrows and swept his fingers back and forth over the tablecloth. "Why? Every other place is open."

"You've been out on the pier," Sophia said. "It's beautiful. Where would Tia want to go if you were in Laurel?"

"But it's five miles from town."

"Everyone coming to Laurel drives," Jeremy said. "There haven't been trains here since the Twenties."

Rawley nodded and opened the revised prospectus. Jeremy studied the Hermit Crab's wine list. Sophia looked around the room, noticing less than ten customers. At close to fifty dollars an entrée and this being spring, there wouldn't be too many people around ready to drop big money on a Tuesday night. She and Jeremy were the only guests under forty. Her father flipped pages, taking his time. She wondered what kind of impression Cam would make on him, not that she had reason to consider it. He'd called, as she had hoped he would, but what he'd said wasn't what she'd wanted to hear. He thought she was great, of course, and he enjoyed talking to her and hanging out, naturally, but he was committed, unfortunately, to his girlfriend. That's what she got for pursuing someone who seemed normal, a regular person.

Rawley finally looked up at them. "Jeremy, how do you arrive at your sales figures?"

Sophia relaxed when Jeremy answered calmly, not as if his judgment was being questioned. That Rawley didn't dispute his answers was also a relief. Maybe the torture she expected would not materialize. Rawley asked about cost of goods estimates and labor. More questions followed, and for each one, Jeremy answered as if he'd known what was coming. He had prepared well.

"As you know," Rawley said, "I've never done anything in a restaurant but eat, drink, and tip. So, I will be running these numbers by some folks I know in the industry to see what they think. But to me, they look good. Your place in the market and operational plan are well thought out. That's a critical first step, and it's not easy. You've got expenses listed for equipment, wares, liquor inventory, food inventory, you name it. You're not flying by the seat of your pants, which was one of my fears, to be honest."

"I know this business, Rawley. I haven't just been filling space."

"That being said, there are some elements in any venture that need to be in line. Some aspects of the plan make me uncomfortable, one in particular that I find considerably problematic."

"What would that be?" Sophia was the one who started taking offense, in spite of the ease in his voice.

"Let's talk about the building," he said. "I compliment you on coming up with a way to get this done. However, I want to make sure you realize what a gamble it will be paying for the rehabilitation of that building. Should the restaurant fail—and I'm not saying that it will—you'll have sunk some serious money into a structure that you don't own, and you have only one way of recouping those expenditures."

"This restaurant is going to be a success," Jeremy said.

"But let's say that it's not. The only way to get a return on your investment is to rent it to someone else. Normally, that limitation would be deal-breaker for me. But with that location, it would undoubtedly be attractive to other enterprises."

"So you look at the worst case scenario instead of the positives?" Sophia said.

"If you want to succeed, you explore every angle."

"So we have to make sure it's done right is what you're saying," Jeremy said.

"Exactly. Now let's add that you've got to completely renovate the structure and how much that's going to cost," Rawley said.

"We've lined up the best contractor in town," she said. "He's built half the houses on our street."

"How many restaurants has he done?"

"None," Jeremy said. "But he's as good as anyone who has. I'll be glad to have him talk to you."

"Is this one million dollar build-out his estimate?"

"Yes," Jeremy said, "but it's rough, based on what we want done, materials, aesthetics, things like that. I calculated the cost of appliances and infrastructure. Of course, when we get approval then we'll really sit down and hammer it out."

"I hate to say this, but you don't need a hammer, you need a cleaver."

At that point, three servers showed up with their entrees. Sophia felt the blood rushing to her head as plates were set in front of them at the same instant. The pepper mill was offered as if it were nectar of the gods. A hovering busboy replaced the molecule of Pellegrino that had escaped from her water glass. They were asked if everything was to their satisfaction, though they had yet to taste.

"What do you mean by that?" she asked her father, not bothering to pick up her fork. Rawley cut into his filet. Jeremy sat with utensils in hand and his mouth open.

"The building is the problem, and not in one way, but two: the construction cost and the lease."

"I know where you're going there," Jeremy said, "but there's nothing wrong with a rent or lease based on a percentage of sales."

"That's not my issue. Other than the fact that people who are not you and work for the town will know your business— or at least what you're making. But perhaps you can live with that. I wouldn't want it, however."

"And?" Sophia said. She couldn't even look at the flounder on her plate.

"Any business, even a restaurant, needs to have its debt paid off in no less than five years. That doesn't happen here. Simply, you can't afford to rehab the building, especially for what you're thinking of laying out, and then pay rent on top of that."

"I'm not following you. We'll be profitable from year one, as far as most things go. Our prime costs will be in line from the start. It's just the building costs that will need to be paid off over an extended time."

"Which is exactly my point. At the end of your lease, you're handing the town a million dollar building, the way you have it. You would have also paid another half-million dollars in rent. So you've paid Laurel a total of one-point-five million, when, to make your numbers work, that number can't be over half a million."

"But we've already come to an agreement with the Selectman, Senator Grimes."

"Wasn't that just a preliminary discussion?"

"Yes, but we've agreed," Jeremy said.

"Well, you can't do it. You'll never make a cent."

"So, we have to go back on what we said?"

"It's not in writing. And people do it every day, even when it is in writing."

"Senator Grimes is not going to go for that."

"You are talking about the son, right?"

"The father has been dead for five years," Sophia said.

"He's a goofball," Rawley said. "But the modicum of intelligence he possesses should tell him that this isn't going to work, otherwise."

"Then he'll open it up for bidding to everyone."

"So what if he does?"

"Then we won't get it," Jeremy said.

"Not getting the space is better than losing a million of my dollars and your futures."

Sophia recognized the sick look on Jeremy's face. Hers must have been a match. Rawley placed his fork and knife down on his cleaned-off plate.

"You go back to him and show him the numbers. Factor in the cost of the building against your sales projections, and spread it out over fifteen years and figure out your three percent or five percent or whatever you think is fair."

"So once we pay off the building, then we pay rent?" Sophia asked.

"Right. But you don't do both. That would be suicide. You might be able to get them to take the building at the end of the lease without having to pay rent along the way. Your lease is going to need to be longer than ten years, as well. At least fifteen, as I just mentioned. You've got to be able to take some chips off the table before the town takes the building back."

"Why would they pull the plug on us if we were making them money?" Jeremy asked.

"You can't expect people to act rationally in business. You can think that they would, but it doesn't work that way. Business is a playground for frustrated adults. If there's some kid who doesn't like you, you don't get to play kickball. You can, however, for the most part, trust the legal system. All those lawyers exist for a reason."

"That is not going to be a pleasant conversation with the Senator," Jeremy said. Sophia could see the worry lines around his eyes come out. She knew he was imagining the derision the Senator would spew after hearing their revised proposal.

"Of course not," Rawley said, finishing the last of the Bordeaux in his glass. "But a change in selectmen down the road might mean they want to put it up for bid, and if you don't protect yourself, you've got nothing to show for all those years of hard work. Make it a single, not a double cost. The town ultimately gets the building, so you need to get your money upfront."

"Fine," Jeremy said.

"That's only one of the worrisome components. You're also going to have to cut your build-out in half. Those estimates are always low, and you haven't even touched the structure yet. You've got a million dollar cost for a restaurant that's only going to generate two-point-four million in sales over your first three years. That's your best case scenario. That doesn't make sense. You're forgetting that you really need operating capital for that first year, too. You've got to hold funds in reserve. You can't plan on generating maximum revenues from the start. If you can drop that build out to half a million and renegotiate the lease, then you've got a shot at sustained success."

"Impossible," Sophia said. "The building needs to be gutted."

"Have you thought about a location that doesn't require a complete build-out?"

"The pier is the point, Father, as you stated earlier."

"Location, location, location," Jeremy said. "You've probably heard of that."

"It's up to you to figure out how to do it. The structure of the building, that's one thing you can't change. How you do the rest of it, that's another thing. Maybe you buy used equipment. Go to some auctions. I don't know. But if you don't change these things, it's a recipe for failure. You've got to regroup."

"You're telling us is that we can't build the restaurant that we want," Sophia said.

"What should we do, open a fucking fish and chips?" Jeremy said, scrunching his napkin in his fist.

"There's the professional attitude I've been expecting," Rawley said, smirking. "You are just going to have to figure out how to get the kind of place you want on the cheap, or at least cheaper. That's the reality."

"I think you are missing the point, Rawley," Jeremy said, jabbing a fork into his swordfish and leaving it there, "if you don't mind my saying so. You can't serve the kind of food that we want to serve, you can't create the kind of atmosphere that we want to create, in a shack. We need to have a certain level of décor."

"It's my money," Sophia said. "Couldn't I buy a boatload of bird shit if I wanted?"

"If you want to piss away your income, you've got two more years to wait. By then, this point will be moot."

"But," she said, "if we can get our lease squared away and cut the building costs in half, we'll go ahead."

"Yes." Rawley pulled out a pen from his vest pocket. He wrote a number, 500k, on the back of one of his business cards. "This is how much you'll get from me. It's the highest point, when combined with what Jeremy's putting in, that will make the numbers work. If you can find a way to get it done for that—all of it, retaining fifteen percent for operating capital—I'll gladly sign it over."

"Why don't you just put a gun to our heads?" Jeremy said.

"Jeremy, you're going to have to work harder. You might have worked hard to get this far, but business isn't easy, not when the buck stops at your desk. It's got to make sense financially. Not having a fallback, you should realize that more than anyone. You might not get another chance if this opens and fails."

Jeremy, frowning, nodded in agreement.

Rawley's face puckered as if he suspected a bad oyster had been slipped onto his plate. "Now explain to me how this partnership works."

"We'll be equal," Sophia said. "Fifty-fifty."

"Does Jeremy have an equal share of the money?"

"You know he doesn't, but this doesn't happen without his expertise."

"I'm putting in everything I own," Jeremy said.

"How much is that?" Rawley asked.

"Eighty-five thousand."

"That's no small amount."

"I'm going to take a salary that will mainly go to Sophia so that I can reimburse her until, ultimately, we will have contributed the same amount. Profit will head that way, as well. I'll bartend a night or two to generate some money to live off of. Eventually, I'll have earned an equal share."

"You might be surprised to learn that I think that's fair, as long as Sophia retains one percent more. That's the reward for taking the financial risk."

"I can accept that," Jeremy said.

"Good," Rawley said. "I'm also concerned with the decision making process. How is that going to work?"

"It's fifty-fifty," Sophia said. "If we can't agree, it doesn't get done."

Rawley studied her. "You are all right with that?"

"Yes."

"You shouldn't be, and not because of whom your partner is. There are times in any concern when parties on the same side with the same goals won't agree, and they wouldn't if their lives depended on it. You can't foresee this kind of thing happening, but it does, and it can paralyze a business.

Someone has to have the ability to make a call. Because she's putting in the money, that has to be Sophia. It's simple."

"So, money talks and I'm out on my ass if it comes down to it." Jeremy's hands fell heavily on the table. The amber liquid in their snifters jumped.

"Jeremy, you know I'm not like that," Sophia said.

"Money gives her the final say," Rawley said. "That's the way the world works."

"I understand," Jeremy said. "I just hope that this doesn't give you the final say as far as how we run the restaurant. You know the vagaries of these financial aspects and partnerships and what-have-you. I can deal with that, and I trust Sophia. But to be honest, what I don't want is you coming into that restaurant and telling me how to run my business. As you said, you don't have the experience. I don't want you, intentionally or not, challenging my—or our—authority concerning operations."

Rawley nodded. Sophia had known this was going to come up sooner or later. At least it was out in front of them. She and Jeremy had discussed the prospect of her father bellowing at a busboy or handing out advice to them in front of their staff. They needed to be independent.

"You two will run the show. Although I do expect monthly sales reports and P and L's, I won't be doing anything in the building other than running up to the bar for a drink."

"Fine," said Jeremy.

"Now, what about your personal issues?" Rawley asked.

"Father, you are out of bounds."

"No, I don't think so. What did I just tell you about business? It's always personal. You two have a history. If Jeremy starts dating one of the cocktail waitresses, you might have a problem with that. If you develop a relationship with the chef, he can perceive it as a power move. That can effect decision-making and disrupt the entire work environment."

"There will be no relationship issues," Jeremy said.

"That's easy to say," Rawley said.

"We've moved on," Jeremy said, grinning. "She's already dating."

"Sophia?" Rawley's head shot back like a chicken's. Sophia remained composed. She'd had no idea that Jeremy was aware of what had transpired between she and Cam.

"I have a friend," she said. "It's nothing serious."

"We're fine," Jeremy added, looking solemn.

"I thought this was a business meeting," she said.

"So tell me about the chef, if you even have one yet," Rawley said.

CHAPTER SIXTEEN

Back in her apartment, Sophia poured herself a glass of wine. She had to admit that although the meeting hadn't gone as well as they had hoped, it hadn't been a catastrophe. She'd kept her composure throughout the discussion, but could now admit that she'd been rattled. Rawley had opened the door for them, but not all the way, and now they had to figure out how to squeeze through. The light in her father's bedroom across the way hadn't come on yet. He was probably in the study having a Remy Martin. She wondered what he really thought. Cam would still be up at the beach. Maybe he'd know if it were possible to build something out of nothing, and do it cheaply.

"Hello," he said, answering on the second ring.

"It's Sophia. What are you doing?"

"Watching the end of the Sox game." His voice was neither excited nor disappointed. Friendly, she thought, as promised.

"We talked to my father tonight about the restaurant. I have some questions for you, on a confidential basis, of course, if you don't mind."

"Not as long as you don't make me drink any more wine.

Which I guess is okay, because I'm here and you're there."

"He wants us to cut the construction costs in half."

"You're kidding, right?"

"How impossible is that?" she asked.

"You're pretty much starting out with a shack that's about to keel over. I don't know how you'd do it."

"I was thinking cardboard," she said.

"Some things you just can't change, like the structure itself: the roof, the heating system, the plumbing. It's the other stuff that you'd really have to choke back on."

"Like?" she asked.

"Siding, which I guess you actually couldn't, because who is going to go to a nice restaurant that looks like a dump? So instead of using all that cool wood that you want inside, you'll have to use the fake stuff. In a lot of places, I guess."

"Really? Will it look like hell?"

"I guess there must be a way to swing it. I probably just don't know how."

"Jeremy was going to call Brinkley."

"If anyone can do it, it's him."

"Well, thanks for talking to me."

"It's not too hard."

"You might want to know that you came up in conversation tonight."

"Am I banned from the bar already?"

"Jeremy mentioned to my father that I've been dating."

"Me?" His voice had shot up as if he'd sucked in helium. "I'm sorry. I didn't mean it like that. But we're not really, well, dating."

"It's okay. I know that. I didn't think that dinner was the time to get into a dissection of my social life. It just kind-of passed through the conversation. Jeremy's the one who brought it up and it didn't even faze him."

"That's good, I guess," he said, his voice returning to normal.

"Well, thanks again for the advice," she said.

"No problem."

Sophia looked at the blank canvas on her easel. She started to rise and then sat back down. Swirls of black and purple, the nighttime colors of the woods beyond the window, called to her. They were the same hues that she felt inside, and she wasn't sure she needed them to converge in paint. She didn't want to see the embodiment of her disappointment. She probably shouldn't have called him. What had she expected to happen?

CHAPTER SEVENTEEN

Cam lay in bed listening to rain pound the roof. He and Brinkley wouldn't be fishing today. He didn't know what he would do. His parents were headed up again, which was strange because they hadn't expected to return until Memorial Day. And because they were visiting, Miranda wasn't. She was planning on coming for the holiday, too, and between being wasted from another sixty hours of work and the prospect of spending two weekends in close proximity to Sherri, she'd decided to chill in the city. He couldn't blame her. Being with his parents was like attending an over-chaperoned high school dance. Maybe if Miranda wasn't too overwhelmed with writing jingles, he could go down there. He'd call later. But as of seven o'clock, when his body had stirred to consciousness, he couldn't see any reason not to go back to sleep.

That lasted until nine, when he heard Sherri and Martin rustling in the kitchen. The aroma of coffee rose through the house. He put on some sweats and went downstairs. Suitcases were stacked next to the table.

"Moving in?" Cam asked.

"They're empty," Martin said, avoiding his eyes. "We've waited a long time. We're cleaning out Gram's closet."

His mother poured him a coffee.

"We need to talk to you," she said.

The three of them were triangulated around the kitchen. His mother, in her jeans and red cardigan, stood next to the sink. His father sat at the table. Cam leaned in the back doorway, watching rain fall in gray sheets over the ocean. He caught his mother looking at his father, who shook his head ever so slightly.

"We've got some news," Martin said.

"Something that's not easy to tell you," Sherri said.

He wondered if his sister had lost the baby.

"We've got an offer on the house."

"This house?"

"Yup," Martin said, looking at his feet.

"At the asking price?" Cam said, his voice rising.

"Not quite," Sherri said.

"So, you're not taking it, then," Cam said. Because they finally received an offer maybe they thought more would follow and they wanted to prepare the place—and him.

"We haven't come to a final decision," she said. "But it looks like we are."

"I thought you were waiting until you got what you wanted," Cam said.

"We really can't turn down the offer," Martin said, looking right at him.

"How much is it?" Maybe if it were low enough, he could counter with one of his own.

"We're sitting at an even one million."

"That's not even close," Cam said. "Why would you consider it? You've just put the place on the market."

"It's still a lot of money," Sherri said. "Especially to us."

"You'll admit, Cam," Martin said, "that real estate is speculative. Things can go wrong. Didn't some big fish just cancel on you? The market could drop like a rock. Who knows?"

"If you can wait two years, maybe less, I'll give you one-point-one, that's an extra fifty thousand a year."

"I wish we could give you a chance," Sherri said. "I really do. But this is a solid offer. The buyer is a Wall Street VP or something."

"So it doesn't matter that I'm family?"

"Cam, it's a half million dollars for us and Dan. It's too much to leave on the table."

"I told you I'd better the offer."

"Cam, think about it. This guy's annual bonuses are probably more than your mother and I have made in our entire lives."

"That's not really the point here, is it?" Cam said.

"A bird in the hand," Sherri said.

"When did this guy even see the house?" Cam struggled to keep his voice reasonable.

"Holly showed him around a few weeks ago. You must have been at work. Anyway, she said he's primarily interested in the location. He barely looked inside. She thinks he's going to tear it down and rebuild, like all the other places on the beach now."

"Gram wouldn't have liked this one bit."

"Don't hit the panic button," Martin said. "No one is kicking you out. It usually takes a couple months for these things to close, especially when there's that kind of money involved."

"Dan wants this, too?"

"He's actually pushing for it," Sherri said.

"Fine," Cam said, standing, spinning, and heading up to his room. He changed into his jeans and his black Under Armor shirt and threw some clean clothes and his travel kit into his Nike bag. He wasn't about to hang around and listen to this for the next two days. He'd explode.

"Where are you going?" Sherri asked as he blew through the kitchen.

"Out."

"Don't storm off, Cam. Let's discuss things."

"The hell with that," he replied, snapping the door shut behind him.

He made himself drive the speed limit for the thirty minutes it took to hit the turnpike. As soon as he got on the highway, he called Miranda to tell her he was coming. He got voice mail. She was probably in bed, or maybe at work. Anyway, she'd see him when he got there. He couldn't find a song on the radio that he liked so he plugged in his phone and listened to the Howlin' Wolf compilation that he'd burned from Brinkley's collection.

His grip on the steering wheel gradually tightened, and his foot lay heavy on the gas pedal. As he dipped into the toll area he was pushing ninety. Slow down, he told himself. A ticket would only make things worse. Of course, it made sense for his parents to do what they did. They were typical, scared-of-their-shadow Middle America. They weren't about to take a chance. He should have seen it coming. While they had agreed that if he could get his act—and the funds—together in a few years, they'd give him a shot, they never thought that he'd actually do it. His grandmother's house, the place that really anchored him and his family, would be bulldozed. His own fate wasn't so different. He'd been living on a foundation built on false assumptions, most of which were his own.

He called his sister. He wasn't surprised by the confusion in her voice when she found him on the line. He couldn't remember the last time he'd done it, but she did stop short of asking if their parents had been in a car accident.

"I just talked to Mom and Dad about something that you need to be aware of," he said.

"Don't tell me you've gotten Miranda pregnant."

"Not even close. I haven't seen her in weeks."

"You're finally applying to law school?"

"Are you going to keep guessing or let me tell you?" he said. "They're selling the house."

"The beach house?"

"Yes."

"To that guy from New York?" she said.

"You know about this?"

"I knew someone looked at it a few weeks ago."

"Thanks for telling me."

"I thought Mom and Dad had done it. I'm not any happier about this than you are. I wanted it to stay in the family."

"But you don't want to buy it?"

"We can't afford it. You know what we paid for our house, and we've got the baby coming."

"I could've swung it in a few years, but they won't wait."

"Put yourself in Mom and Dad's shoes. It's a sure thing, and it's going to fund their retirement. Do you think they want to keep teaching until they're sixty-five?"

"They would have still gotten their money, only it would've come from me."

"I don't know what to tell you, Cam. There will be other houses for sale. If you find one you like, I'll do your legal work for free."

"Great," he said.

By the time he hit the Massachusetts border, the rain had dissipated and the sky was a light gray. The air changed, not in its quality, but the energy it possessed. Cars weren't going any faster or veering at random angles, but they traveled with purpose. He enjoyed the tension that came with it. Maybe he should have moved down here himself.

He'd had opportunities. If you could swing a hammer, Brinkley said, you could work anywhere. His friends from UNH, Eddie Grayson and Craig Lawrence, both lived in Boston. Grayson went to Gillette right after graduation and lived in the Back Bay. Lawrence was in Charlestown, fresh out of law school. They'd both tried to get him to make the transition. He used to visit them often enough, mostly incorporating Sox, Celtics, or Bruins games. But before the end of the weekend, he'd look out the window and see some dirtball in a white T-shirt letting his Rottweiler shit on the sidewalk; when he weighed that against the view from his grandmother's living room, it hadn't been much of a contest.

Miranda had asked him to come with her, too. She'd started talking about it before her last summer in Laurel had even started. He often drove her down for her interviews so she didn't have to worry about parking and traffic. She was dying to get there, and he hoped that she would get the job she wanted, and that she wouldn't. He'd waited two summers for her to realize that her University of Maine classmate-boyfriend was a scumbag. Cam had imagined Miranda moving in with him at Gray Gull for that winter, when they'd have the beach and the snow and the storms to themselves. At the same time, he wasn't sure that her sanity would have survived. While he could veritably hibernate, Miranda was one who had to keep moving. When she landed her job, she'd gone without him in September. They remained a couple, however. He had to admit, with himself to blame, that the results were mixed.

He turned onto Route 16 and came into Somerville the back way. He drove past Tufts, a school that had rejected him. He probably would've had a tough time there. The students walking along the fringe of campus looked serious and determined, and he guessed that wasn't a product of the urban environment, but the academic one. In classes that he had enjoyed, he had done well. Those that bored him, he had only been able to muster enough interest to pass. That might not have worked at an institution that his geek-happy sister had found difficult.

Cam cut toward Davis Square and got stuck behind two cyclists riding down the middle of the street. In matching black shorts and neon yellow shirts, they were cutting through the same residential crossways that he was. Their legs pumped as if turning the same axle. Normally, he would have been irritated at being slowed to fifteen miles an hour, but another minute or two wouldn't kill him. Miranda would be glad to see him, and she'd likely have an idea or two on why he shouldn't be going ballistic. In two hours-plus of driving, he'd been unable to come up with one himself.

The cyclists turned onto Cane Street and he swung in behind them. They coasted to a stop just up from the yellow three-decker that held Miranda's apartment. He pulled over so that he could back into their spot, the only free space on the street. He put on his directional signal and waited. If they had any clue, they would see him and hop up onto the sidewalk. His eyes went to the rearview and he rested his arm on the top of the passenger seat.

One of the cyclists was a woman, and in good shape. This neighborhood was full of young people. There was everything from lawyers to baristas. Miranda's roommate was a waitress at a barbecue joint not far from there, and up until this latest raise, she brought home more money than Miranda—the same Miranda who had just taken off her helmet and was smiling at the other cyclist, a muscled rider whose spiked blond hair had been freed by his recently removed helmet. He touched her shoulder, pointed toward the city and smiled with unnaturally white teeth. They hadn't noticed the truck, never mind that it was his.

He stepped out of the double-parked Ranger and walked around to the tailgate.

"Mr. and Mrs. Armstrong, would you mind moving so a guy could park?" he said, leaning against the fender.

"Cam," she shouted. Miranda started toward him and stopped. "Shit. What are you doing here?"

"If you'd give up this space, I'll tell you," he said.

Miranda motioned to her friend and they yanked their bikes up onto the sidewalk. He tried not to watch them as he parallel parked. But he didn't miss the weak smile that the two of them shared. He was tempted to put the truck back into gear and just take off. That's what his gut was telling him to do. Apparently, it was less taxing for Miranda to pedal all over Boston than it was to drive to Laurel. He walked slowly around to the sidewalk where they held their bikes by the handlebars.

"Cam, this is Will Nichols," she said.

"Hi," Will said, as they shook hands. He was half-a-head taller than Cam, maybe five years older, and fit. He looked extremely comfortable in the spandex shorts and shirt.

"Ah, the boyfriend," Will said. "I've heard about you."

"Good listening?" Cam asked.

"We're out there a long time," Miranda said. "You talk sometimes just to stay awake."

"I didn't even know you were riding," Cam said.

"You knew I had a bike."

"I didn't know you actually used it."

"Mainly it's for stress relief," she said.

"Do you ride?" Will asked.

"Not since I got my driver's license."

"Great sport," he said.

"So, what are you doing here, anyway?" Miranda asked, shifting her weight from foot to foot.

"I guess you didn't get my message."

"As you can see, I don't have my phone." She held up her hands.

"I was informed this morning that my parents are selling Gram's house—and not to me. So I skipped town before I blew a gasket."

"I'm sorry," she said.

"It's going right out from under me. They got a lousy offer and took it anyway. They're getting less than they wanted, and I'm not getting a chance."

"It was going to be a long shot with you, anyway, wasn't

it?" Miranda said.

"No."

Conversation stopped. Cam could feel Will looking at him. Discomfort, or something like it, tightened the contours of Miranda's heart-shaped face. Was this all cosmic retribution for sleeping with the Ferret? He doubted that the universe cared what he did. A more logical argument would prove he'd brought it all on himself. He was just another in a line of buffoons.

"If there's one thing that I've learned in business," Will said. "It's that nothing's written in stone until it is written in stone. Hang in there. It might not happen."

"You must be a Harvard B-School guy," Cam said. "What is it that you do?"

"I own a string of restaurants."

"You wouldn't be Mr. Chicken, would you?"

"That's me. More cluck for your buck, right Miranda? We've got eight stores and five more on the way thanks to a smashing advertising campaign."

"Terrific," Cam said. "I'm glad to see you enjoyed your bicycle date, or whatever this is."

"What it isn't, is a date. It's a workout," Miranda said. "Will lives around the corner." Only her bike prevented her from placing her hands on her hips as she did when she was frustrated with him. "I do occasionally interact with others. There are six million people down here. When you walk out your door, you're bound to run into some of them."

"It's a matter of luck that you naturally cross paths with work buddies in tight shorts?"

"Dude, it's not like that, honestly," Will said. "Chill."

"More great advice from the pompous ass."

"You're out of line, Cam," Miranda said. The lack of amusement in her voice was matched only by the absence of humor on her face. He knew she had every right to her anger.

"Well," Cam said, "good luck with your ongoing evolution

into a yuppie douche bag. I hope you enjoy it."

Will shook his head. Cam spun around and started to the truck. He was probably just helping the guy get closer to peeling off Miranda's spandex, but he wasn't about to apologize. Being reasonable was beyond him.

"Where are you going?" Miranda asked, close to yelling.

"I'm going to Mr. Chicken," Cam said. "More cluck for your fuck. Sorry, I meant buck."

"You're being an infant," she said.

"Fuck that."

Cam got in the Ranger. Now that he'd fully sunk himself by acting like a complete imbecile, he needed to show some restraint. The only way he could prove a bigger loser was to squeal the tires down the street and clip the fender of the Accord parked on the corner. He crawled five miles an hour to the stop sign. A left, another left, and then a right, and he was headed back to Maine.

CHAPTER EIGHTEEN

After two hours of white-knuckled swearing and steady ten-miles-over-the-limit driving, Cam crossed the bridge from Wellport into Laurel. The rain was still pouring as he pulled into the Port Tavern's gravel lot. He hoped the bar would be empty. Three people sat watching the Red Sox game. Barely anyone passed the window on the street. Cam imagined himself in one of those songs that Brinkley listened to, where the character would be ready to get off his barstool only when he'd figured things out.

It was impossible for anyone to be at their best all the time, especially under adverse conditions. Regardless, he'd acted poorly: With his parents; with Miranda; with that Mr. Chicken jerk-off. He would have to take this defeat—engendered by him alone—like a man. Miranda was probably a lost cause. They were apart in distance and in direction, and now in attitude. Whether she had been fooling around with Nichols was moot. He'd fucked another girl. Maybe he'd known subconsciously that a reckoning was coming. How else to explain Sophia the Ferret? The emergency road trip had ended in disgraceful retreat. All he could do was get drunk, and that he could manage successfully.

"What are you doing here in the middle of the day?" Janie asked.

"I'm drinking to forget," Cam said.

"What?"

"You name it. Dashed dreams. Broken romance. Lack of prospects."

"Don't forget self pity."

"Thanks for reminding me. I've heard that beer enhances the taste of bitterness so I thought I'd give it a try."

"You're not going to go out and get a tattoo later are you? That would be too much of a cliché."

"Like your outfit?" She was dressed in her usual black.

"Aren't you perceptive in your sorry state?"

"Easy for you to say. Someday all this will all be yours." He swept his arms to encompass the entire woodened bar.

"Can you imagine how disgusted I'll be then?"

"Maybe a chicken-frying prince will swoop in and take you away."

"I stay away from the cooks. And I don't believe in dreams, just in low costs and high margins."

"I'll drink to capitalism," he said. "The bane of my existence."

"You're not going to turn into a problem, are you?" Janie said.

"Not for you, anyway. You have my word on it."

He drank by himself for close to an hour before two women came in and sat next to him. They were in their forties and weighed down by bags from various shops. They loved the town. It was beautiful, even under a gray sky, like a painting. One of them was going to drag her husband out to look at a cottage on the Shores. Cam wondered which one they were talking about, but didn't care enough to ask. They talked about their kids, apparently in high school and college. One was getting a 4.0. The daughter had a boyfriend in premed. A son started at goalie for a prep school lacrosse team. The children had no observable faults. How lucky, Cam thought, with such liars for parents.

In the midst of his fourth beer, Cam decided that he would have to move out of his grandmother's house as soon as he sobered up. Let his parents claim their sweepstakes. They'd done nothing wrong, and it wasn't like they'd have another chance. They deserved what they could get, even at his expense. He wouldn't hang around, though, glomming on and pretending he was happy about it. He'd been run over, but he was getting up before he was ground into the dirt. He needed to make his own way. He was just late to realize it.

A middle-aged man sat down. He ordered a house white wine, then started talking to Cam. He'd driven here from New Hampshire in his BMW M5, which Cam determined to be some sort of expensive sports car. The man normally didn't drive it in foul weather, and Cam wondered if by foul weather, he meant rain. The man rambled on, saying that you didn't want to abuse a car that cost that much money. Red veins lined his nose like a road map.

"BMW stands for Bavarian Motor Works, right?" Cam asked.

"Yes."

"Doesn't it snow in Bavaria?"

"I'm not sure," said the man.

"You think the Germans would put that much into a car that they could only drive half a fucking year?"

The man nodded, asked for his check, and left.

Hank Schlissfut the plumber came in. He bitched through three beers about how goddamn busy he was. He was the worst plumber in town. Brinkley wouldn't use him, not even if they couldn't get anyone else. Brink would wait until one of the guys he liked was available, even if it cost them days and especially if it was new construction. Back when they worked for Sarofian, Cam had caught Henry sniffing around the underwear-filled laundry basket of a woman whose kitchen they were remodeling. Cam again considered the concept of karma.

He closed his tab with Janie at six o'clock when she left for the day. Rico Rogers came on, stoking the sidebars of his goatee as Janie estimated how much longer she thought Cam might last. Rico was nearing fifty and as far as Cam could tell got the Saturday night shift because he didn't put up with any shit. Rico surveyed the length of the bar and then put his money in the drawer. Janie said goodbye to Cam and zipped out the back door. Cam watched her.

"Don't even think about it," Rico said. "High maintenance."

"I wasn't."

"You've been here awhile."

"Some."

"You want another beer?"

"Sure," Cam said. Rico leaned in as he placed the bottle in front of Cam.

"I get paid to put up with the assholes that come in here," Rico said in a low voice. "I don't know why you'd choose to do it."

"This is where the alcohol is."

"Good point," Rico said. "I don't care if you piss yourself later, as long as you don't do it here and you don't drive home. You're not planning on getting behind the wheel, are you?"

"Nope."

"Okay."

An old couple came in shortly after that. They were short and thin, and neither of them could have weighed a hundred pounds. His gray hair was swept back in a wave and oiled. He helped his wife onto her chair and took her sweater off for her. He nodded at Cam when he sat down himself. Even at his most sappy, Cam had never pictured he and Miranda at such an advanced state of togetherness. The man ordered them a pair of vodkas on the rocks. They sipped them and split a club sandwich.

The man got off his stool and held his hands out so the woman could get down. He smiled as she shuffled to the bathroom. Cam asked him how long they had been married.

"The hell with that," the man said, and then Cam noticed the absence of a wedding ring. "We're shacked up."

"The fuck you are," Cam said.

"Do I look like an idiot to you?" the man winked at him.

"No, sir. How long have you been together?"

"Twenty years."

"It still works?"

"Hell, yeah."

"What's your secret?"

"You just got to lay it out for them, say how it's going to be. Early on, I cuffed her around a little. It wasn't such a big deal then. Treat them like dogs and they'll treat you like gold."

"That's fucked up."

The woman returned and the man helped her on with jacket, and started walking her to the door. Just before he left he stopped and told Cam: "Remember what I told you."

Cam thought he might be drunk enough to have imagined that conversation, but feared he wasn't.

"Do you know what that guy just told me?" Cam asked Rico.

"I don't know, and I don't care."

"He hits her."

"What the fuck are you talking about?" Rico said.

"He said that he cuffed her."

"The guy was a mouse."

"That's not what he said."

"Bullshit." Rico glanced at his watch. "How are you doing?"

"I'm ready for another one."

"Probably your last," Rico said. "Don't you live out at Gray

Gull? How are we going to get you home?"

"I'm too drunk to drive," Cam said.

"We've established that. You have someone you can call?"

"My phone's in the truck. But one of those guys must be over at the 'Side. Brinkley or Perkins or Trouper."

"So I'll play your secretary."

"Sorry," Cam said, giggling.

"I'm going to charge you for babysitting, you know that, right?"

"I'll have a vodka on the rocks," Cam said.

"No," Rico said, sliding his tab and one more beer in front of him.

Cam sipped it and emptied a fistful of crumpled bills, which he picked through to settle his tab. By the time he'd done that and finished his beer, Sophia the Ferret was next to him.

She smiled and said, "I heard you need a ride."

Cam looked at Rico, who shrugged.

"Brinkley or one of those guys is coming," Cam said.

"No, they're not. I'm the driver."

He stood up and held onto the bar to steady himself. "Did I pay, Rico?"

"We're good," Rico said. "You're an angel, Sophia."

"Thanks." Sophia looked at Cam with a crooked grin. He smiled back and took a step forward. It was easy. The next thing he knew he was climbing up into her Jeep. She buckled him in.

"Your forehead is awesome," he said.

CHAPTER NINETEEN

He knew where he was when he woke up. That was a bonus. He was fully clothed. A puffy lavender comforter was strewn over him. His head pounded. He stood up and went to the bathroom to find some Advil. He took four with a handful of water. He zombie-walked to the couch and flopped back onto it. When he saw her standing in the doorway of her bedroom, he made it to a sitting position, wrapping the blanket around him.

"I take it you found the painkillers?" she asked.

"Was there something better than Advil?"

"No."

"How much of a problem was I?" he asked. "Should I apologize now or after you tell me?"

"You were a cupcake. Although when I was fixing you on the couch, you were stroking my forehead and trying to scratch behind my ears like I was a cat. You don't remember that?"

"Not really."

"You were feeling pathetic."

"I was mad at the world."

"No, mainly just at yourself, your folks, and your

girlfriend."

"Ex-girlfriend is probably more accurate."

"Really?" She acted like it was no big deal.

"I'm sorry you had to get hauled away last night. Wasn't Brinkley or one of those guys at the Dockside?"

"They were."

"How did you wind up driving the paddy wagon?"

"I volunteered."

"You're kidding."

"I'm not," she said.

"Anyone curious as to why?"

"I told them if you were drunk I might get you to go down on me."

"Great," he said.

"Why do you care what they think?"

"I don't."

"You don't act like it."

"I'm not having the best twenty-four hours," he said.

"Were you heartbroken that you weren't named homecoming queen?"

"So, your advice is to stop acting like a pussy."

"It would be a start," she said.

"My truck is still in town?"

"I guess."

"And you're going running now?"

"It's what I do."

"I guess I'm going for a long walk then," he said.

"You can stay here, you know." She stepped toward him and smiled. She swung her leg up on the arm of the couch and stretched her hamstring.

"You'll give me a ride when you get back?"

"I will, but that's not what I meant," she said, straightening up. "You were pretty adamant about moving out of your house last night, which you may or may not remember. I don't know if it was the liquor talking, or if you really want to do it.

Either way, it's okay. You can stay here."

"I still had my wits when I decided that. I just hadn't figured out a landing spot."

"You've got one if you want it." She gave him a shrug. "Let me know." Then she left on her run.

He decided he would stick to his principles, even if they were the result of a drinking binge. He'd take that hike into town to reclaim his truck, then grab some clothes. He'd crash here for a few days. It was either that or Brinkley's basement which was a cluster fuck of tools, boat parts, and unfinished furniture projects. And why not? The important thing was to get out of his grandmother's—now his parents', soon some rich fuck's—house. He wasn't going to over-think it. He was going to act. Another thing he wasn't going to do was spend any of his inheritance on the security deposit of some dump. That money was not being touched until he was buying his own place—which once again wouldn't be in sight of the Atlantic. He could find an apartment later that week. With summer approaching, rentals would be jacked for two-month profiteering. He'd probably have to move inland, maybe even south to Wellport with its condos and cheesy townhouses. That would mean mosquitoes and dead air and heat. Too bad for him.

"Yes, Mom, I'm well aware that I acted like an idiot," he said as his parents crowded into his room. He was scooping clothes from his bureau into the three sports bags spread out across his bed.

"How do you expect us to take you seriously when you run off for twenty-four hours and not tell anyone where you are?"

"I'm twenty-five, and I live on my own. Apparently, more so now. I apologize for the hideous transgression."

"So, where are you going?" Sherri asked.

"I'll be staying with a friend."

"To clarify," Martin said, "you don't have to go anywhere. No papers have been signed. We're still waiting. There's no telling how long this could drag out."

"This isn't my place anymore," Cam said. "Do what you want."

"Don't let sour grapes dictate your actions," Sherri said. "You're cutting off your nose to spite your face."

"Just what the hell does that mean, Mom?" He zipped up the bags and sighed. A glance at his mother revealed downcast eyes and a look of concern. His father seemed exasperated. He hoisted two of the bags and reached for the third. His father grabbed it.

"Who is this friend?" his mother asked. "Where can we reach you?"

"You don't know her. She lives over on the bluffs. You might try using my cell phone from here on out."

"What will Miranda think of you living with some girl?"

"I'm not living with her, and what Miranda thinks isn't an issue."

"What do you mean by that?"

"Just like it sounds."

"What's going on with you?" His mother's voice rose, as if it were her right to know.

"What do you think?" he said. "I'll talk to you later." He had to wait for them to step out into the hall so he could leave. Sherri's face was twisted, clearly angry. His father followed him out to the truck. They threw the duffels into the back.

"So, you're going to do this?"

"Yup."

"You know you're acting completely illogically."

"What am I supposed to do, wait around until I get kicked out?"

"Why not? You could plan, save money, give yourself some time."

"Because planning has got me where?"

"Your mother is very disappointed."

"She's not the only one."

Martin nodded. "Be careful," he said.

"You too," Cam said, unable to come up with anything else. Then he left.

"Where do you want my stuff?" Cam asked.

"We can't have it cluttering up this spacious living room," Sophia said. "So I've cleared out a drawer for you in the bedroom."

"Thanks. I'll go to the mall and pick up a sleeping bag this afternoon."

"Why would you do that?"

"It will be less of a hassle than making up the couch every night."

"You don't have to stay out here, is what I'm saying." She cocked her head and grinned.

"Oh," he said. He smiled back. It wasn't the scenario he had anticipated. Perhaps he should have.

"Come on, I'll show you your glorious bureau space." He followed her into the bedroom, unsure if these were the living conditions he wanted.

Sofia was still in her shorts and running bra. She pulled out two empty drawers in the smaller of the two chests. She helped him unpack and refold the clothes. They laid them in side by side. She held a salty scent that wasn't unpleasant.

"What about these?" he asked, holding up the empty shells of the nylon duffels.

"Who cares?" she said.

It started with a kiss. Afterward, they lay on the bed. She nuzzled into the crook of his shoulder. He stared at the ceiling.

"You've never told me why you came with me to Horton's."

"I thought I did."

"Not the truth," he said.

"What does it matter?" she said. "What's happened has happened."

"I'd like to understand why," he said.

"I went to the Squall because you said you'd be there."

"So you were stalking me?" He laughed.

"I wouldn't say that."

"What would you say?"

"You might take this the wrong way."

"Try me."

"I thought that you might be interesting because you seemed so normal, like a real person. And sad, too. You know how people are around here: Always trying to impress everyone, putting on a front. But not you. You had lost a job and you were upset, and you wanted to do something about it, but there wasn't anything you could do. So you were being funny, and I liked that. But you were alone in the middle of the whole thing. Really, so was I. Neither of us deserved it."

"You make us sound pitiful," he said, shifting uncomfortably.

"We're just people who are honest with themselves," she said. "Maybe that's why we've become friends. It's nothing bad. If you think about it, we knew each other for three or four years. We'd say hello. No big deal. But sometimes you can't see what's in front of you."

"It's crazy, isn't it?" This was the kind of talk from her that he used to dismiss. Now he found himself thinking that it might make sense.

"That's why I don't paint people," she said. "If you paint what you see, it's never the truth. It's just a picture, and a camera can do that."

What was he supposed to do now?

PART TWO

CHAPTER TWENTY

Although Jeremy hadn't actually been to a Selectmen's meeting, he'd watched enough of them on the town's cable access channel. Or at least, he'd seen parts of them. They were interminable. Discussions of parliamentary procedure seemed exciting when the business at hand most often centered on public rest rooms, tour bus parking, and tax bills. The selectmen, the Senator included, haggled endlessly over the wording of obscure ordinances. The mandated public forum that accompanied each issue seemingly existed to allow townspeople to oppose spending of any funds other than those that kept the streets plowed in winter. The meetings often made the discourse at his bar sound as if it were taking place in a Washington think tank.

Jeremy planned on being persuasive, concise, and erudite. He'd written his talking points down on a series of index cards and rehearsed in his living room. Everyone would be left with the understanding that their proposal should be accepted without question. Leasing the building to him and Sophia made sense and money for Laurel. Even the Senator hadn't protested when he'd gone back to him with Rawley's revised lease; he'd known that its original conception was too good to be true. In addition, the Senator would have his back, guaranteeing an easy go. Tonight, Jeremy would symbolize the restaurant itself: winning and sharp.

The meetings were held in the small auditorium at the Fire Station. Sophia met him out front. She wore a conservative but pretty navy blue dress and had tied her hair back in a pony tail. She carried a portfolio with the architect's rendering of the building and some sketches that she'd done of the interior. Only ten cars were parked in the lot. He took that as a good sign. Fewer people meant less chance for resistance, although he couldn't see why anyone outside of possible competitors would be opposed to the rescuing of an abandoned, dilapidated shack.

The Senator had placed them on the agenda under "Pier Prospect" and scheduled them last on the docket. Jeremy had checked the town web site and it hadn't gone on until the previous day, as planned. He half-expected Huffington from the Squall or Daniels to show up and demand that the shed be opened for bidding, but there was little reason to suspect that would happen. Hopefully, the few people who knew of the plan had kept their mouths shut.

His palms were sweating as he entered the room. Ten rows of folding metal chairs were set up on each side, with a lane through the middle. Eight bodies were scattered throughout, including Ed Nottle, the reporter from the Coast Star, who sat up front with his notebook. Jeremy led Sophia to the back. This way he could make an entrance to the podium opposite the Selectmen's desk. Behind them, a scraggly kid from the high school audio visual squad set up his camera for the public access broadcast.

The selectmen stood behind two pushed-together, skirted tables; Senator Grimes, Freddy Wilpon, and Sally Shannon talked quietly. Wilpon owned one of the jewelry stores in the town center. He was in his sixties, bald, and thin, with birdlike fingers that flitted while he talked. He drank white wine spritzers and never had more than two. Shannon's family had owned the motel on the way to Gray Gull for fifty years. They hadn't improved it in the last twenty-five. But business was good, it being convenient for families whose interest in Laurel was the beach. Both Shannon and Wilpon were pro-tourist, which played into Jeremy's hands, as well.

The Senator nodded and a red light came on the camera, then he instructed his associates to take their seats. He called the meeting to order. In unison, each selectman opened a manila folder and removed a stack of papers. The Senator welcomed everyone to the May Laurel Board of Selectmen's meeting and let everyone know there were five items on the docket. The selectmen then rubberstamped the funding of three summer lifeguards for the town beaches. Thanks to Turk, Jeremy knew they'd already been hired. The Board then discussed when to install the No Parking signs for the downtown areas (there was simply no need for parking regulations in the non-summer months). It was decided that they would be posted on June first, just as they had the past ten years.

The debate over funds for paving potholes on the Fox Farm road resulted in Jeremy grinding his teeth for fifteen minutes. Thanks to an abnormally large amount of spring snow, the highway department didn't have the money for the needed repairs, so they had requested an allocation from the general fund. The issue was opened to the public hearing. Immediately, a pot-bellied, red-faced gent in a fedora stepped to the podium. He believed fixing a road under attack by axle-grabbing craters was a waste of town money. His position was countered by a gray-haired, heavy set woman dressed in something that looked like a housecoat. She not only demanded that the road be fixed immediately, but that the town pay for a new set of tires for her Chevy, as apparently neglect of the pavement had cost her several Goodyears. The

Senator smiled and told her politely that that was not going to happen.

"Excuse me?" she said, as if she had not heard him.

"Madam, while we can possibly repair the road, we cannot reimburse you for tires. Surely, you cannot determine that the Fox Farm road is responsible. It is not the only road you have traveled on, is it? Nor can we determine the original quality or condition of the tires."

"Oh, stick it up your ass," she said, before turning and heading for the door.

The Senator sighed. Wilpon shook his head. Shannon looked dazed. They waited until she left the room before voting to improve the road.

It was finally their turn. The Senator spoke quietly to his associates, and then to the camera. He probably thought he was Reagan-like: "This last item added to the docket is one that could benefit the town; meanwhile, it is time sensitive to those involved. It involves the lease of the old bait shed on the town pier at Laurel Harbor."

"Weren't we projecting that it would eventually have to be torn down?" Wilpon said.

"Indeed," said Senator. "At our expense."

"What are these folks proposing to do with it?" Sally Shannon said.

"I believe the concept is a fine-dining restaurant."

"In that building?" Wilpon slapped his hand down on the table, laughing. "I find that hard to believe."

"I put it before the Board," the Senator said, "that we allow the principals to speak and detail their plan. Would someone from the restaurant group please approach the microphone and present?"

Jeremy rose and strode to the Selectmen's desk, giving each of them an outline of the proposal. He then assumed his place at the dais and leaned over the microphone.

"Hello, I'm Jeremy Riley and I am one of the partners,

along with Sophia Harding, of The FishHouse Restaurant Group Incorporated. What we are proposing is to take a lease on what is now an unused, dilapidated building on Laurel Pier, referred to around town as 'the old bait shed.' As anyone with eyes can see, it needs major reconstruction, which we will undertake at our own expense." He shifted from foot to foot. He found himself talking directly to the Senator and reminded himself to look at the others. "We envision—and we plan on using a local construction company—having one of the finest restaurants on the coast. A destination."

"What about the smell?" Wilpon asked. "That place reeks."

"As I said, we'll be doing a complete renovation. We don't anticipate that being a problem."

"You better be right or your only customers will be seagulls," Wilpon said.

"You don't expect the town to pay for rebuilding that shack, do you?" Shannon asked. Everything about her was wide: her face, her smile, her hair.

"No. We will undertake the construction costs."

"You're not going to drop a Burger King out there, are you?" Wilpon said.

"Hardly. We plan on keeping the same footprint, which is mandated by the zoning regulations. That's fine. We'll be seriously upgrading the shell, as well as the interior. Let me show you a rendering of what we expect the building to become."

He motioned to Sophia and she stepped forward with the mock-ups, as well as the interior drawings. He narrated the details, such as the number of seats, the hours of operation, the expected traffic, and parking. The selectmen nodded along, looking completely pleased with each aspect of the presentation. He had hit on all of his key points.

"That's a fine looking structure, if you can get that smell out," Wilpon said. "Will you pay rent based on the building being the way it is now or as you project it in the drawings?"

"As you can imagine, the construction costs will be substantial, and technically we will be upgrading a piece of town property. The building will have more value as a restaurant than it did as a bait shack, and certainly more than it would have if torn down."

"So, you're proposing to pay rent as if it were still a bait shed, in other words?" Wilpon said.

"Not exactly. We would like the town to consider the value it will assume at the end of the proposed fifteen year lease when the property reverts to Laurel."

"Please clarify, Mr. Riley," Shannon said.

"Our construction costs will be factored in as part of the lease. Laurel will receive the building at the end of the term. That has enormous value, and those construction costs make our paying rent prohibitive until we get the building paid off."

"So, you don't want to pay any rent. That's rich." Wilpon was shaking his head. The four people left in the audience giggled. Jeremy could only imagine how many more at home were confused.

"We will be paying rent," Jeremy said, "but in an innovative, non-traditional sense."

"Are you going to pay us in baked stuffed haddock?" Wilpon asked. "Is that what you mean?"

Jeremy knew that Wilpon ran a tight ship at his store, and that this was a concept he should have easily grasped. He was having fun at Jeremy's expense. All he could do was take it.

"No," Jeremy said. "I mean at the end of the lease, the town will own the building, a much better one than now stands, obviously."

"Come on, Mr. Riley," Shannon said. "A circus tent would be an improvement over the current structure."

"Isn't the value of a busy, functional restaurant fairly evident?" Jeremy asked.

"So, you expect the restaurant to be busy?"

"Yes, we do," Jeremy said. "As you know, I—"

"What if it's not?" she asked.

"It will be."

"Do I have to repeat that question?" Wilpon said.

"Only if you want me to repeat the answer, Fred," Jeremy said. He had his hands crossed across his chest, waiting to see what would happen when Wilpon realized that he wasn't going to take any more shit.

"Gentlemen," the Senator said.

Sophia nudged up to the microphone and lowered it so that she could speak.

"Of course, when the building is rebuilt, it will gain value. What we are concerned about is the initial viability of the project. If we can agree on what would be a fair rental agreement under normal circumstances, we'd be glad to begin paying once the build-out cost matches what we would've paid in rent. I'm sure you understand that if we paid a substantial rent and for the construction of the building, the business model would not be feasible. If we can reach a compromise here, then we will both benefit."

"Well, why didn't you say so?" Shannon said.

Jeremy wanted to point out that was exactly the point he would have made had they not repeatedly interrupted him. Instead, he watched the smile spread across Sophia's face as if she had saved the day.

"I would be happy to negotiate that lease on behalf of the Board," the Senator said, "and then submit it at the next meeting for approval."

"Before we get carried away, there are other issues to discuss," Wilpon said. "I know plenty of men who work on the pier and moor their boats there. All that traffic isn't going to make them happy. There's not a hell of a lot of parking."

"At this point, we're just opening in the afternoon for dinner. They'll be gone before we do our peak business in the evening. We'll be utilizing existing infrastructure."

"By that do you mean the fishermen's parking lot?" Wilpon

asked.

"Yes."

"Now that is convenient," Wilpon said.

"Won't you need people to gut the fish and slice cheese to get ready?" Shannon asked.

"Excuse me?"

"I don't know what they're called, the guys who come in early and wash the lettuce and things like that."

"The prep people?" Jeremy said. "Yes, a few will come in the morning, but they won't be taking up more than a spot or two."

"What about delivery trucks?"

"Hopefully, the lobstermen will be fishing out on the ocean and not in the parking lot." Jeremy saw annoyance flash onto Wilpon's face. Good. "Even so, deliveries don't take too long."

"You know," Wilpon said, tugging at his pink necktie, "I haven't been convinced benefit to the town has been established."

"We'll be creating twenty or more jobs, paying taxes, and bringing visitors to the town."

"How many people from Laurel do you think you'll employ?"

"I don't really know. But it's smart business to hire locals who know the area."

"What if they don't know the food service business?"

"Then they probably wouldn't want to work in a restaurant."

"Isn't that kind of elitist?" Wilpon said.

"No, it's kind of logical."

"Are you going to take this tone and attitude with your guests, Mr. Riley? If so, you might not be very successful."

"I don't plan on it."

"Well, that's good news," Shannon said.

"I'm glad to answer whatever questions you have," Jeremy

said, in his nicest tone.

"We thank you for that," Wilpon said. "Now, what about the construction? You said you are going to use a local outfit?"

"We've been working with a local builder. Yes."

"What if an outside construction company comes in and quotes you substantially less?"

"We're committed to using someone from the area."

"Even if it costs more?" Wilpon asked, eyebrows raised. "Is that good business?"

"There are other issues to consider, as well."

"Would you care to explain?"

"If there are repairs needed, or adjustments, and you use someone local, they're right there at your disposal."

"So, you expect them to do a lousy job?"

"No, I don't. But those things happen in restaurants, as well as houses, as I'm sure you know."

"If you say so."

Jeremy rolled his eyes.

"How many people did you say anticipate serving on a nightly basis?" Wilpon asked.

"We would expect a few over two-hundred on average in peak season."

"That is a lot."

"I'm fairly certain they'll be the kind of people who might stay over in local motels and buy goods from local merchants. That would be another benefit for the town, wouldn't you agree?"

"That's why we are here," Wilpon said. "To look out for the town's best interest."

"Well, Mr. Riley has certainly answered all of our questions," the Senator said. "I will now open the public forum. Would anyone like to speak on the proposed renovation and lease?"

None of the few people in the audience moved. Jeremy

looked to the glass door. No one was bursting through. He exhaled.

"I put it to the board: Should we grant this group a thirty day option to come to an agreement on a lease? All those in favor?"

The three of them raised their right hands. Jeremy forced a smile.

"Very good," said the Senator. "We have thirty days to come to an agreement on a lease, considering value and time, as well as respective responsibilities. I will act as the agent for the town. Please contact me, Mr. Riley and Miss Harding, as soon as you are prepared to sit down and present a draft of terms. Or perhaps you would like to hear my thoughts, first. Either way, I will be glad to begin at your convenience."

"Thank you," they said in unison.

Jeremy returned to his seat. His jaw was clenched and he could have slapped Sophia when she smiled and patted his knee. The more he thought about it, the angrier he became. The Senator's agreement to "facilitate" had been a joke. This meeting should have been nothing more than a formality, but the Senator let it turn into an inquisition, with his associates batting Jeremy around like a badminton birdie. Yet, he had triumphed. The town would be thanking him soon enough. The stupid bastards. He told Sophia, who was shaking she was so excited, to go on home, and he would make an appointment with the Senator.

He waited outside the entrance to the station after the meeting closed and leaned against the handicapped ramp. The Senator walked out by himself and Jeremy fell into step next to him.

"What the fuck was that?" Jeremy asked, keeping his voice low.

"We cannot just roll over for you, can we? How would that look?"

"I was made a fool of."

"If we don't make a fool of you, it doesn't seem like we're doing our job."

"But this is in the best interest of the town."

"Of course. That's what our questioning determined. That's the beauty of representative government."

Jeremy sighed. The man had a point. It couldn't appear to be a bag job. "You could have let me know it was going to be like that."

"We don't rehearse or script these meetings, Jeremy. They are an organic enterprise."

"But—"

"The results are what you hoped for?"

"Yes."

"Well then, I recommend that you move forward. You come over later this week and we'll bang out that lease. We've already agreed in principle, and now it's just a matter of putting the numbers down. Then the lawyers do their work. It's nearly a done deal, even if you didn't like your part in the show."

"I didn't like it one bit."

"Never forget that appearances are important. This may be a small town, but its people are not completely gullible." The Senator reached out and put his hand on Jeremy's shoulder. "You were smart to come to me first. There's no doubt about that."

"I get it," Jeremy said

"I assumed you would."

Jeremy watched the Senator stroll over to his Mercedes. His restaurant was one step closer to becoming a reality, and all it had cost him was a sliver of dignity.

CHAPTER TWENTY-ONE

Cam had been at Sophia's for a week. Miranda hadn't called him, and he hadn't called her. That didn't surprise him. What did catch him off guard was that the last seven days had proven surprisingly easy. He'd actually become acclimated enough to notice a difference in Sophia's footfalls on the stairs that night. Usually, it sounded as if her feet skimmed the boards. But now she seemed to be channeling all of her one hundred pounds into each step. Her eyes ignored him as she whipped open the door and shot into the kitchen. A wine bottle landed on the granite counter with a just-short-of-shattering clunk. Her hand feverishly worked the corkscrew.

"What happened?" he asked.

"As if you don't know."

"I don't." He wondered what he could have possibly done. Had he parked in the wrong spot? Was his truck leaking oil on the driveway? Had he turned the laundry pink? He felt like his brother-in-law Spencer, well-intentioned but never quite sure why his sister was barking.

Sophia walked out from behind the breakfast bar with a glass in one hand and the bottle in the other. She glared as she sat down on the couch, leaving a full cushion space between them. She shut off the pre-game show he'd been watching. After gulping her glass, she refilled it and sat the bottle on the coffee table, not bothering with a coaster.

"We just had a meeting with Brinkley," she said.

"If his quote came in high, it's not because he's trying to screw you. He's as honest as it gets in this business. It's a hard project, and your budget is tough from what I understand."

"Oh, it's not that. He—you—are not doing the job. He told us it wasn't something he felt he could do."

"He can build anything."

"So you say. He told us there's some other project that *'he's more comfortable with.'* This, despite the fact that he and Jeremy have been friends for years. But it's business, not personal, right? That's supposed to be an acceptable answer?"

"Honestly, it's news to me. I haven't heard anything about any other project."

"Blissful ignorance. How convenient."

"It's the truth," Cam said, getting annoyed. "That's how he operates. It's not a democracy. I wanted to do the restaurant. You know I was looking forward to it. But Brink doesn't ask my opinion on things, and if he did he wouldn't care what I thought anyway. I'm sorry, but what do you want me to tell you?"

"You can explain how we're going to get someone else to do it and open before summer has come and gone."

"I can talk to him if you want," Cam said, reaching for his phone. "But I don't know that it will do any good."

"Don't you care?"

"Of course I do. It's my life, too."

He picked up his cell phone and wandered into the kitchen. A quick glance found her looking at him, disgusted. Brinkley didn't answer; he knew what would be happening. Cam could hear Brinkley's eventual response: "It's not my problem where you sleep."

"He's not answering," was all Cam could say.

"He's probably too busy throwing some innocent guy into the river."

"That guy was an asshole. Brinkley gave him every chance to drop it."

"You guys are all assholes."

"What did I do?"

"What do you think?" With that she stood up, sighed, and stomped into the bedroom. She shut the door behind her. It was less than a slam, but more than a closing.

It had been a mirage, after all. The past few days he'd come home and she'd been sitting out back in one of the deck chairs with a glass of wine. A kid's plastic beach bucket would be filled with ice and beer for him. They had talked, a lot. She'd explained the progress they'd made on the restaurant, surprising him with the level of detail involved. She'd ask him what he'd done that day and listen as he described the mundane shit that they were forced to do while they waited— he had assumed—for the restaurant to get approved so they could start there. When the two of them got hungry, they'd get in the Jeep and drive out of town for dinner. With each passing day, moving on had seemed less urgent.

Sophia was fuming; just what that meant was to be determined. It wasn't his fault, but that didn't matter. He was guilty by association. As emotionally invested as she and Jeremy were in their vision of the restaurant, reason was too much to ask for. He should have known that things could not have stayed as they were those first days. It just meant that he would need to find his own place, as he had planned. He went to the refrigerator for another beer. He turned the ball game on, the queasiness in his stomach something he was getting too familiar with.

As he watched the Sox starter issue as series of walks, he contemplated the worst-case scenario. She would emerge and kick him out. He'd have no choice but to crawl back to the cottage for a night or two. If his parents were in New Hampshire, where they should be, they wouldn't have to know. He'd have to take a day off from work to check out apartments, and that wouldn't go over well even though when he came down to it, Brinkley was partially responsible. Cam wasn't about to blow his inheritance on rent, so he'd probably wind up in another garage somewhere, one without tropical hardwood and marble counters. He was grateful that the Red Sox could at least occupy him until the Ferret escaped from her hole with his fate in hand.

It happened in the third inning with the bases loaded. The Red Sox were down by two and he tried to keep his eyes on the game so it wouldn't appear that he was anxious. She stood in the bedroom doorway, hovering on the edge of his vision. Her face revealed a half smile.

"I'm sorry," she said.

"So am I," he said. "But I'm in the same boat that you are."

"I don't doubt that. I was upset and I shouldn't have taken it out on you."

"It's okay," he said, though she was absolutely right.

"Have you eaten?" she asked, hanging her head.

"No."

"Let me take you to dinner. We can go all the way to Portland."

She came over to the couch and leaned down and kissed him. In the truck, she held his hand and scooted over into the middle seat. He hadn't ridden like that since high school. It wasn't bad.

CHAPTER TWENTY-TWO

Brinkley scowled as he stopped hoisting a ladder up to the second floor window. He watched Cam park his truck behind the Harley. Cam had been considering how he was going to approach the subject of the restaurant since he'd woken up early at five-thirty. He could try and wait it out, as they both knew what they both knew. But then Brinkley wasn't likely to explain himself out of a sense of obligation. He decided that he'd wait until lunch, and then make a casual reference to it, as if it were not a big deal. Maybe then Brinkley wouldn't dig in. There had to be a good reason they weren't going to do it, and Cam needed to know what it was.

"Hey," Cam said.

"Get that other ladder and get up here."

"Sir, yes, sir."

Cam put on his tool belt, slid in his framing hammer, and grabbed the flat bar. They were replacing the aluminum windows from old Captain Stillman's house. They'd been installed, poorly, in the Seventies. The wood under the sills had rotted and they were switching that out, too, turning a simple job into something more. Thermal, energy-saving

Andersens were going in, as specified by the new owners. Back to the future Brinkley called it. Wood was hip again.

Once Cam had his ladder up, they started working on pulling out the first frame, unscrewing the aluminum that had sunk into the spongy wood. They started at the top and worked equally fast, moving down screw by screw. When they had gone halfway, Cam couldn't take it anymore.

"So, we're not doing the restaurant?" Cam asked, using a tone that he might ask about the weather.

"I imagine your friend isn't too happy about it."

"That's putting it mildly." He tried to keep his voice light.

"It's no big deal," Brinkley said.

"It is to them."

"I didn't think it was a good idea."

"That's it?" Cam asked.

"Yeah," Brinkley said, leaning back on his ladder to make sure he made eye contact.

"That's a relief, because I thought you were going to get into a deep explanation like, 'Because I said so.'"

Brinkley ignored him and started taking out the next screw. Cam had no choice but to follow him and do so as well. When they had removed all the screws, he sunk his flat bar into the soft wood. The effort he put into it ripped his side of the frame out of the house. When they pulled the window, they each kept one hand on it and worked down the ladder. On the ground, Cam took it himself and placed it on the scrap pile. It seemed ridiculous that a house could come apart so easily.

"Why aren't we doing it?" Cam asked.

"The project has issues."

"Such as?"

"Look, I told you when you started that I wasn't going to go over every decision I made. That hasn't changed."

"I don't have a problem with that, in general. But I'm tied up in what we do, and you told me I'd learn things working with you. This restaurant is a big deal around here. So if there's something that I could benefit by knowing, like technical reasons why you didn't want to do it, I'd like to hear about them. There must be something that led to your esteemed genius turning down what will be a huge job."

"You're a pain in my ass, do you know that?"

"We all have our roles in this outfit, as you pointed out."

"So if you weren't fucking one of the partners and crashing at her place, you would still care as much? It's all about the building?"

"I'm just asking why, is all."

"Fine. Anything I say, it stays between us. Do you hear me?"

"Of course."

"First off, it doesn't matter if clients are our friends or not. We still do the same job we would for anyone. We make the same decisions, based on business."

"They were counting on us."

"I can't help that. If they're going to be business owners, they're going to face disappointment. That's the way it is."

"Thank you, Donald Trump. So, zero percent of the decision making process in based on people and relationships."

"What the fuck are you talking about? You wouldn't give the Ferret the time of day two months ago. Now, because you happened to get in the sack with her, I'm supposed to change how I operate?"

"I didn't say that. It just surprises me that you wouldn't want to help them out. You and he are pretty tight."

"Listen, your girlfriend's Dad has those two on a budget, one that's pretty fucking close to impossible. They also want it done yesterday. The difficulty in construction isn't a problem in itself. You know I'll take on a challenge. But this has failure written all over it."

"She's not exactly my girlfriend."

"That doesn't change the numbers, one way or another. That budget is a problem. Besides, we can make more money doing our regular work. That's why we're in this business. We're not the Red Cross."

Cam shrugged and started back up the ladder. If Brinkley thought building the goddamn restaurant was a bad idea, he was probably right. Cam felt something like anguish for Sophia. Brinkley was sharp when choosing projects, Horton's aside. In all likelihood, the construction would be problematic with that restricted budget. Cam didn't want to explain it to Sophia like that, however. That aspect of the project was already stressing her out. He'd have to tell her it wasn't financially advantageous for them. He knew it would sound like bullshit, but he just couldn't think of anything else.

CHAPTER TWENTY-THREE

Brinkley had them spend the last week of May roofing a mammoth house on Laurel Shores. It was another of the last-resort jobs that they avoided except in times of crisis. Cam supposed that was the state they were in thanks to one missed opportunity after another. When Brinkley called him over to his van before they left on Friday, Cam wondered what the bastard wanted. He'd already promised to spring for drinks at the Dockside; Cam wasn't sure whether that was compensation for keeping him two stories above the ground for forty-plus hours or loosening him up for their next and possibly even worse job.

Brinkley hopped off, having finished stowing his tools. He adjusted his Sox cap and grinned.

"I was going to wait until you had a few beers in you before I told you about the call I got on Tuesday. But then I figured it might be a better idea to get it out there before you got all liquored up."

"What's the next big money-maker, digging up septic tanks?" Cam asked.

"I know you've wanted a project to replace Horton's. Well,

I've got a line on one. It's a client with a lot of money who wants to do something interesting. We're coming highly recommended to him, from Horton as a matter of fact. You know how it is, though. It might not happen, but I want you to be aware."

"Stop dancing, Brinkley, and spill it." Cam found himself holding his breath.

"It's your grandmother's place. The guy that's buying is going to tear it down, but you knew that. He's another financial guy, from New York, and somehow he's buddies with Horton. I talked to him the other night and then he Fedex-ed some plans on Wednesday. For what it's worth, he seems like a good shit."

"I don't think they've even signed the P and S yet," Cam said.

"I know, I know," Brinkley said. "But it's going to happen fast. Apparently, there's no financing involved. I just didn't want you to get blind-sided in case someone like Holly mentioned it."

"So you're taking it if it's offered?"

"I am, and so are you."

"Fuck that," Cam said.

"Listen: I know you're not happy about it, but someone's going to make a lot of money of off this, and it might as well be us. I'll give you the same bonus plan as for Horton's, plus another percent or two. You deserve it."

"It's blood money," Cam said.

"You'll get over it when the time comes. Trust me."

"Don't be so sure."

"We bend to the world. It doesn't bend to us," Brinkley said. "Now let's go have a beer. I need one after watching you twitching up there all week." He nodded to the roof.

"Save your money for the bonus," Cam said. "I don't feel like drinking anymore."

CHAPTER TWENTY-FOUR

When Sophia finally got home at seven-thirty, her eyes rested on the empty bottles that populated the coffee table like a chess board.

"What happened?" she asked.

"Brinkley got a line on a new project. Tearing down and rebuilding my grandmother's house for some rich fuck from New York. The guy happens to be a friend of Horton's, too."

"Ouch," Sophia said. She sat down next to him on the couch and patted his knee. "I'm sorry."

"How did your day go?" he asked. "Did you get that estimate from CAF?"

She groaned.

"There's a bottle of Deloach in the fridge," he said. Anytime he bought beer for himself, he picked up some Chardonnay for her, and not the cheap stuff. "I'll get it for you."

"One might not be enough," she said.

Since Brinkley had turned them down, she and Jeremy had found it impossible to secure a builder who could give them what they wanted at her father's price. A commercial contractor from Portland had come in at sixty percent over budget. Another out of Freeport had been close, but they couldn't start until the following spring, a year out. Lenny Perkins wouldn't touch it—too much work in too short a time for not enough money—not that they would have wanted him anyway. To make matters worse, she and Jeremy had been granted final approval from the town, but that had come with a sixty day window to put the deal together.

Cam sat back down and handed her the wine. "Well?" he said.

"Two-hundred thousand over the budget that my father gave us and one-fifty over Freeport's." She jabbed the corkscrew through the foil, something she had taught him not to do. She grinned when he noticed.

"This is driving me fucking crazy," she said. "I'm like the ping pong ball between Jeremy and my father. One says we're spending too much money. The other claims it's not enough. My father won't move a cent. There's no compromise."

"Your father knows business."

"He's never owned a restaurant."

"Isn't it just about the numbers?" Cam said. "If we're building a house, there's a number that will make it work and there's a number that won't."

"But you can cut corners, right? Use cheap materials or leave something unfinished and then get to it later when they actually have the funds?"

"Sure. Why can't you do that with a restaurant?"

"Because people aren't going to drop fifteen bucks on a martini and thirty-five on a piece of tuna in a place that looks like a Denny's, and my father has us on that Denny's construction budget: five hundred thousand and not a penny more."

"Scale back. Isn't rustic hip now?"

"Not that rustic and not that hip," she said, draining her glass.

"If you're like this now, what's going to happen when the place opens?"

"Maybe I'll be borrowing the flask you're going to be packing when you start tearing down your own house."

"We'll need a double room at Betty Ford," he said.

She sighed. "I can't believe we're so close, but there's no way to lop off another hundred thousand. Will you look at the proposals again?"

"I will, but I still say that you can't do better than what Brinkley gave you and have what you want."

"Then what the hell am I paying you for?" she said, laughing and kissing his cheek.

"That's it," he said, as it hit him. "*Jesus Christ!*"

"What?" she asked.

"You're about a hundred thousand away, right, on the best estimate?"

"Sure, but that company can't go until next year."

He nearly lost his breath trying to speak. "I can get you to that one-hundred."

"What are you talking about?" she said.

"You can save fifty, sixty, maybe seventy-five grand by not paying the builder," he said, hyperventilating. He took a gulp of beer, hoping to calm down enough to get his idea into words.

"That will go over," she said. "When did you start drinking today?"

"When a contractor gives an estimate, whether it's Brink or CAF, anywhere from ten to fifteen percent of the total is profit worked in for the builder. You take that out of a prospective $625, 000 and you're within striking distance."

"How does that happen?" she said, shaking her head. "And we'd still be short."

"All you'd need is a little more cash and then you make some sacrifices in the construction."

"You know a builder who will work for free?"

"No, but I know one who will do it for a small stake in the business as a silent partner. Someone who also has access to thirty thousand in cash, and someone who could definitely cut out another twenty grand from the construction. There's your hundred-thousand."

"You?" she said, pushing her bangs off her face. Her eyes were wide. "You'd be able to do it, the actual construction?"

"There's no reason I can't."

"Are you fucking with me?"

"Not at all," he said. "I don't know why I didn't think of it earlier."

"Oh my god," she said, sounding more ecstatic than he'd ever heard her in bed.

"I've got to warn you. I wanted to buy my grandmother's house. I had a two-year plan, and it involved me doing my own projects, not even close to this extensive. None of my family thought I could manage it."

Her face twisted and she laughed. "They don't have any idea who you are, do they?"

"You think I could do this?"

"I have no doubt."

"But will Jeremy go for it?"

"He really doesn't have a choice."

CHAPTER TWENTY-FIVE

Cam picked up the phone and called his sister.

"I need your help," he said. It had been years since he'd asked Kiernan for a favor.

"Cam, I understand why you're upset. But Mom and Dad are doing what they have to do. I thought I'd explained this."

"I'm not calling about the freaking house."

"You're not in any kind of trouble, are you?"

"Why do you always assume the worst?"

"You know," Kiernan said, sighing. "I've been thinking a lot since this baby has come into our lives, about family. I'm wondering why we don't have any kind of relationship, you and me. Why aren't we friends?"

"We don't have to be friends. We're relatives. We're stuck with each other regardless. If I don't like the way you carry on like a drama queen, you're still my sister. If you think I'm acting like an obnoxious jerk, you can't trade me for a more civilized model."

"That's no excuse. Plenty of brothers and sisters have good relationships."

"They're not me and you."

"So what's wrong with us?" He was surprised by the concern in her voice.

"It's real simple. We're two different people."

"You just blurt these things out. What makes you think you know?"

"For example," he said, wondering if she would allow him to get to the reason he called. Perhaps he should have just found a lawyer in the yellow pages, his first inclination. "Do you remember when I asked you to buy beer for me one night in the summer before my freshman year in college?"

"No, to be honest."

"Well, not only did you not buy it, but you told Mom that I'd asked you, and that resulted in me getting grounded, and then not only did I not get the beer, but I missed the biggest party of that summer."

"If I had bought the beer for you and you got in an accident or got arrested or something, I would have been not only morally responsible, but legally, as well."

"Which may be true, but then why tell Mom?"

"I already said that I don't remember this. I guess to keep you out of trouble."

"But that wasn't your job."

"I couldn't just ignore what you were about to do."

"Enough of this," Cam said. "Can't we just accept the fact that we're different, from our values to the way we look at the world, and that we're never, ever going to think alike?"

"Coming to an understanding would be a start," she said. "At least it would keep Mom and Dad from worrying on us. Do you realize how much anxiety we cause them? That's another thing I've been considering now that I'm going to be a parent."

"Kids are supposed to drive their parents crazy." He wanted to scream.

"Not at our age," she said.

"Well, what I need stays between me and you. Mom and

Dad cannot be involved. I don't want a word of what I'm doing reported to them. I'm going to have my hands full, as it is."

"What have you gotten yourself into?"

"I was a little upset when they decided to sell the house."

"I know. We all know. You're not even talking to them. I don't blame you for being upset, but you need to understand their position."

"I do."

"They don't even know where you're living."

"I'm living with a girl."

"Like a girlfriend or a roommate?"

"Girlfriend."

"What happened to Miranda?"

"We were headed in different directions."

"So, is this serious?"

"Marriage-serious, no. This is also something I don't want Mom and Dad to know about. I don't need the questions from her or her advice. But there is something about this girl that might interest you. She and a friend are going to be partners in a restaurant, one that needs to be built. Only they don't have quite enough money to do it exactly the way it needs to be done. I'm going to build the restaurant, and I'm going to invest my inheritance money in it. Between that and sweat equity, I'm going to become a partner, too."

"What kind of place is this? Who are these people?"

"It's not a hot dog cart, if that's what you're thinking," Cam said. He took a breath and told his story, starting when he and Sophia had dinner together, and leaving out Horton's and Miranda, and Sophia and Jeremy's relationship, things that Kiernan might not have found reassuring. Of course, she had questions, and he answered them gladly. They came from the perspective of an attorney, as opposed to that of a sister: Who was doing the finance? How much money was involved? What type of cuisine? Who was going to make the decisions?

"So, what do you need me to do?" she asked, satisfied, a half hour later.

"You can do a contract, can't you?"

"Yes, yes I can."

"I don't want to get screwed," he said.

"That's a first," she said.

CHAPTER TWENTY-SIX

Cam was sitting back, watching the game, yellow legal pad in hand. An untouched, sweating beer sat on the coffee table. He was reviewing his critical path, what Brinkley would call a schedule, now at ten pages, and every time he looked at it, he added or rearranged something. Yes, he had doubts about his ability to pull this off. Brinkley had been hesitant to jump on the project—even before he had *his* fucking house lined up. Cam needed to be organized and prepared if he had any hope to succeed. He knew that much.

A knock on the door startled him. They'd had no visitors since he'd been there. Before he could turn, the screen swung open. Rawley Harding looked larger in person than he did in the pictures in the main house. He had a mid-summer tan and his blonde-gray hair swept across his forehead in a wave. His jeans were creased and his white button-down shirt, open at the collar, was pressed. He was fifty-two, the same age as his father, but looked ten years younger. Cam stood.

"So, who are you?" Rawley Harding said, strolling into the room. "The guy banging my daughter, the guy trying to leverage his way into being a restaurateur, or the builder about to blow the budget trying to build her a restaurant?"

"I don't like to pigeon-hole myself," Cam replied.

"You are Cam, I take it?" Harding held out his hand.

"Preston."

"You've lived here for a while, according to my daughter."

"Here, as in this apartment, or in town?"

"Laurel."

Harding settled into the leather easy chair across from the couch, glanced at the television, and placed his hands on his knees. He motioned for Cam to sit.

"My grandmother had a place at Gray Gull for years," Cam said.

"She recently passed away?"

"This winter."

"Your family is selling the house?"

"True."

"You wanted to buy it but didn't have the means."

"You seem to know the story."

"I haven't been here in a few weeks, but I do talk to Sophia. She thinks you're pretty sharp."

"I guess time will tell." Cam shifted and sat up straight. He glanced at his watch, figuring that Sophia wouldn't be home for at least another half hour and that it was not going to be a pleasant thirty minutes.

"I think you're pretty sharp, too." Harding had a habit of tilting his head when he wanted to emphasize a point.

"But not in a good way," Cam said.

"To take a small amount of money and a couple months' sweat equity and turn that into part ownership of what many suspect will be a successful business, that's no easy feat. I give you a lot of credit."

"Actually, Mr. Harding, I'm no carpetbagger. If you hadn't handcuffed them financially—and you have your reasons for that—I would have never come into the picture. The idea came to me when I was trying to figure out a way that Sophia *could* get the restaurant. There was no scheming master plan."

"How fortune smiled upon you."

"I'm willing to put everything I have, money-wise, into the project. It may not be much to you, but to me, it's a lot. I won't be getting paid while I do it. When the restaurant's done, I'll be back out looking for a job. If it fails, I lose big time. The way I see it, my neck's on the line right from the start."

"That much is true, I'll admit. What makes you think you can do this?"

Cam presented a verbal resume, naming any notable house that he had worked on in town that he thought Harding might have seen. Rawley listened attentively, but made no indication that he was impressed.

"You've worked for some good people," Rawley said. "But I've heard that when you first starting seeing my daughter you were building a doghouse. Is that the grand accomplishment of your own projects?"

"It was income. If someone wants to pay me well to build one of those magazine racks from junior high woodworking class, I'll do it."

"And your restaurant-building experience amounts to?"

"Nothing."

"Then you can see why I might be dubious about this."

"I'm confident that I can get it done, and done well."

"So is my daughter. Of course, Custer was confident at Little Big Horn."

Cam wanted to reach for his beer. If he did, Harding would think he was just lying around drinking beer, watching sports. Which was what he had been doing, but he was also going over his checklist. The permit was due to be issued in two weeks and he would be ready. Of course, if he mentioned that he was doing work and drinking, that wouldn't look great, either. But the way he was getting grilled, he didn't have anything to lose. He raised his eyebrows and stood up. "Do you want a beer, Mr. Harding?"

"Sure."

"I hope Budweiser is okay."

"I'm not a dilettante, if that's what you're thinking," Harding said.

"I was past that," Cam replied, as he handed him a cold one. "I thought it might have been taken as a compliment."

"So, you like it here."

"It's been great. Sophia's been great."

"In what ways?" Harding tapped the top of his bottle.

"She's smart, understanding, driven. She's really got a good grip on how to get things done. She's been amazing."

"Do you think it's smart for a girl to let some guy she's been dating for a few weeks move into her apartment?"

"It wasn't a few weeks. It was probably less."

"I can appreciate black humor," Harding said, standing. "You seem like a nice guy. You probably want to do well. But there's a lot on the line here, with my daughter and her money. I've been in business for a long time, and just because I'm not here every day of the year doesn't mean that I'm not connected to Sophia."

"I know where you're headed. You don't need to threaten me not to break your daughter's heart or send her spiraling into bankruptcy." He was going to have to stand up to Mr. Harding at some point, so he might as well get it over with as long as he could do it in a respectful manner. "I've been kicked around enough myself this year. I've fallen into this opportunity more than anything, and there's no way that this restaurant—or at least the building of it—fails because of me."

"I'm going to be honest with you, Cam. In the long run, I really don't give a fuck about this restaurant. I mean, I don't like to lose money. Not one bit. But my daughter hasn't done much other than splash some paint and run. Neither of those has gotten her anywhere since she graduated from Skidmore. So this is a gamble I'm willing to take. It's the first time Sophia's been passionate about anything tangible. She's finally moving forward with her life. If this restaurant becomes viable, she'll have turned the corner. Anything that can facilitate that, I'm in favor off it, even if it involves a kid carpenter who has never done anything on this scale, or in fact, on his own."

"I won't be the problem," Cam said.

"I've read the contract that your sister amended. You're happy being a silent partner?"

"I don't know anything about that business, other than how to act in a bar. It's probably wise."

Rawley shrugged. "Sometimes common sense can go a long way."

"Sophia and Jeremy want this pretty bad. His whole life is tied up into it. When someone's completely invested, the results are usually good."

"Your vast experience tells you that?"

"Am I wrong?"

"If desire were enough, I would've been the starting centerfielder for the Yankees. People have limitations. She's got about as much experience as you. The bigger issue is that he's got an abnormally high opinion of himself. That can be good in business or it can mean death. If you're going to partner to with them, you better be aware of that. If there are issues, you better be prepared to mediate. Legally, being the majority owner, Sophia can do what she wants. But she's insisting they'll be equals when it comes to decision making. His elephant-sized ego is going to get in the way sooner or later. You're going to have to jump in, and you need to come in on Sophia's side. Is that clear?"

"Of course, I'd support her over him. But if you read the contract, you know I don't have a vote. Sophia can handle Jeremy. I've seen it."

"You don't need a vote to have influence. When your money's on the line, you'll find that the 'silent' in partner is a myth."

"I wouldn't worry about that."

"Why should you, you don't know enough yet," Rawley said. His eyes went to the screen. "So, you're a Sox fan?"

"Yes."

"Maybe I've overestimated your intelligence."

"From this discussion, that would be hard to believe."

Rawley laughed. He shook Cam's hand and told him that he needed to get back to Tia, who was waiting over in the main house. He also informed Cam that he and Sophia would be dining with them the following evening. Cam was to bring the blueprints, his schedule, his lumber order, and any other relevant construction documents he might have in his possession. Cam said that he would look forward to it, all the time feeling like he'd been tenderized like a cheap cut of beef.

That next night Rawley gave him the official go-ahead. He hadn't had much to say when Cam showed him the plans, and explained his strategy and budgets. He just congratulated him and told Cam to get to work. Whether this meant that Rawley had faith in his ability to complete the project, Cam wasn't sure, but it didn't stop him from getting shitfaced on red wine during dinner. On his way out to cross the yard, holding Sophia's hand, he remembered that Rawley promised the first check would come as soon as the building permit was issued. They would sign the contract at the end of the week, before Rawley and Tia left for Newport. In two weeks, he would be building. He didn't have much time to find and put together crews for demolition and framing. He'd have to start lining up his subs. The list went on. He wasn't going to have enough hours in the day. To get started for real, though, he had to quit Brinkley.

CHAPTER TWENTY-SEVEN

Cam's hands were trembling. He hadn't wanted to say anything until he knew he was absolutely going to do the restaurant. Brinkley was uncoiling the power cord from the back of the house. They were going to start framing the addition of a master bedroom to a non-descript Cape on the Fox Farm road. Cam was on his toes as he walked over to the equipment. His arms tingled down to his fingertips. His head wouldn't stop turning over details, none of which had to do with this job, and he couldn't help but think that he had missed some obvious step in the critical path he'd gone over a hundred times. He remembered a salvage yard just outside of Boston, not far from Miranda's, where he might be able to get the claw-footed tub that Jeremy wanted to use for his raw bar. Cam took a deep breath.

"Brinkley," he said. "I need to talk to you."

Brinkley looked up, a crooked smile on his face. The white hair sticking out from his hat expanded as he took it off, brushed the cap across the leg of his jeans, and repositioned it.

"I'm not sure I can listen to another rant on the unjustness of the goddamn world," Brinkley said. "We're going to be doing your grandmother's house. Take the money and run."

"It's not that. I'm sorry, Brink, but I've got to give you my notice."

"Your what?" Brinkley put down the compressor he'd been connecting.

"I'm going to have to quit at the end of this week."

"Look, I understand why you don't want to work on your old place," Brinkley said. Cam could hear the whistling in his nose as Brinkley spoke. "But don't be a pansy about it. It's business. Don't do something stupid just because you're pissed off."

"It isn't that."

"Then what the hell is it?"

"I'm going to build the restaurant."

"Jeremy and Sophia's restaurant? Come on." Brinkley laughed.

"I'm going to be the GC."

"You've got to be fucking shitting me." Brinkley sat down on the lid of the tool box. "So, they couldn't get anyone else?"

"As a matter of fact, no." Cam hoped that Brinkley wouldn't notice his shaking knees.

"At least you're not completely delusional." Brinkley looked down and then back up. His gaze drifted into the trees. Cam waited for the inevitable tirade.

"I wish you luck," Brinkley said. "Now let's get going. We need to get this frame up today."

"It's an opportunity I couldn't pass up," Cam said. "Sorry I'm leaving you short."

"That's okay. It's going to be worse for you than me."

"What do you mean?"

"It's not a house. Maybe if you were putting up a simple ranch, I'd say good luck to you, go for it. A restaurant, though? Do you know how much extra shit that involves? It wouldn't have been easy for me. But I already told you what I thought. You don't have to listen." Brinkley started grinning;

small chuckles moved his muscular stomach in one motion.

"You're the one who told me that the principles of building are always the same."

"True. But when you go for your driver's license, they don't just give you the written test, you drive. They make you parallel park, stop at red lights, all that crap. Most folks do it in their father's Focus or Corolla. You, on the other hand, have elected to take your test in a tractor trailer filled with TNT in a blizzard."

"Whatever." Even if he could, Cam wasn't about to tell Brinkley about his stake and investment. That secret was part of the deal, at Jeremy's insistence. Cam could live with it. He hadn't even let his sister tell his parents. Let him get the job done first. That was the key to everything. He wouldn't need Brinkley after that. He'd have a resume, and it would include one of the finest restaurants on the coast of Maine.

By the time they sat down in the backyard for lunch, he'd stopped working five or six times to jot down ideas in the small notebook he'd brought in case he thought of something he could not chance forgetting. Every time he had pulled it out, Brinkley had grinned. Cam got up and walked off to the edge of the lawn to call a builder he knew in Dayton, hoping to get his crew.

Brinkley was smirking when Cam came back.

"I'm not going to have to put up with this all week, am I?" Cam said.

"What?"

"The snickers that come out while you contemplate my building that fucking restaurant. Why don't you just let me have it and get it over with?"

"There's no way I'm not going to enjoy watching you wig out."

"What are you talking about?"

"I can picture you at the end of the first week. You'll be rolling into the Dockside at sundown, dirty and pissed off.

Your hair will be as white as mine. You'll stagger to the bar and ask for your beer. You'll have a look on your face like you just got punched by Tyson. In fact, I'll even buy you the beer that you'll be sucking on like a baby's bottle. Then you'll really have something to complain about."

"So, you don't think I can pull this off?"

"You can probably build it. You don't know shit, but you know enough. You'll make some mistakes, but nothing you can't fix. It's working with the two budding restaurateurs that will be impossible."

"They've got a good plan. It's going to work."

"I tell you this: With different owners, I might have taken the job."

"Except for the budget, I know," Cam said.

"Wrong. You need to take your head out of your ass, Cam. Or out of The Ferret's ass, as you used to call her."

"So, because you don't like her, I shouldn't do it?"

"I'm trying to give you the benefit of the doubt. Go build it. It will be a good experience. But it won't be easy. Not with those two."

"Say it, Brinkley, so I don't have to listen to your little girl giggles."

"Your first problem, not necessarily your biggest problem, is that you're fucking one of your bosses. You don't think that will come into play at some point? Emotion and business don't mix, and you can be an excitable boy."

"But—"

"Let me finish. Your second problem, she used to screw your other boss, and he takes it a little more seriously than you do. You saw how he was all spring. It wasn't until the idea of this restaurant emerged that he came out of it. There's a potential land mine."

"They're through, and he knows it."

"Didn't you take any classes at that college? When you've got three people, two of whom have fucked the third, what kind of group dynamic is that? Do you think you're going to get any objectivity from either of them? You're a wedge. If you do something right, Jeremy's not going to be happy. If you do something wrong, the Ferret's not going to see it, or if she does, all three of you are going to be pissed. If everything doesn't come out just right, who do you think is going to get blamed?"

"I can answer that one. Me."

"Correct. It doesn't mean that it won't be a good learning experience. You've got that going for you."

"I ought to stick it to you right now and walk," Cam said. "You passed on the restaurant, so now you're going to run it down, no matter who does it."

Brinkley sighed. "What do you think of your bosses as decision makers?"

"Jeremy knows the business and Sophia has brains. You just don't realize it."

"Their first and biggest decision was to hire a builder who's never done anything on his own but a doghouse. That smart?"

"It is if that guy is me. You've already said I could get it done."

"Let me guess: You think the biggest problem will be figuring out how to get the exterior off that frame, and then putting another one on it without it collapsing like waterlogged pretzels. You think it will be hard getting the subs to show up on time. Or maybe you're worried about carving out the detailing Jeremy wants on his back bar—a fucking museum piece. The work, you'll figure out. You might not be fast, but you'll get it. That takes patience and perseverance, and you've got those."

"And the hard part?"

"It's the people, dumb ass. It's always the people. All the time you've spent in this business, have you ever seen me or Sarofian have a problem with the actual mechanics of a job?"

"I'm sure I have."

"For example?"

"I can't think of one at this particular instant."

"Exactly. Those problems have solutions. The gray hairs come from the people. 'Do this, do that, I wanted this, I wanted that'—all when they don't know what they want or when they change their mind in midstream. There's the stress factory. With those two, they never know what they want."

"You're wrong. That restaurant is extremely detailed already, down to napkins and silverware and salt shakers. All they've been doing for the past month and a half is planning."

"Be ready for the changes. The money won't go as far as it should. They'll make mistakes, too, and you'll suffer for those as if they were your own. At least your gaffs will be honest ones. It'll feel like they've stacked ten kegs on your chest. He'll be pissed; she'll be pissed; you'll be pissed, and you'll all be pissed at each other. Then factor in that you're fucking her, and he'd like to be fucking her. Hell, there might not be enough beer in St. Louis for you."

"You've got to get personal. What a prick."

"It's going to get personal. That's my point. Expect it."

"Can't we just get back to work?" Cam said, standing up from the picnic table. He couldn't tell the bastard that he was getting a piece of the restaurant, something that would pay off in the long run no matter what turmoil he encountered. He wasn't being impetuous or short-sighted. A few months ago, before he knew Sophia like he did now, he wouldn't have been in position to jump on this kind of opportunity, but things had changed. He wasn't about to flinch. Not now.

"What about your girlfriend?" Brinkley asked, not moving. "What has she done but live off her family money? What if you start fucking something up? You think she's going to be okay with that because you two have a relationship? That's only going to make it worse. You two will kill each other before the place is done."

"You don't know her."

"You sound like a kid trying to tell his mother that just because his date has tattoos and pierced nipples, it doesn't mean that she's not a nice girl. I know you don't think much of Jeremy. If you had an ounce of respect for the guy, you wouldn't be fucking his ex-."

"He'd sell his mother into slavery to get that restaurant. He won't let personal issues get in the way."

Brinkley smiled and spit to the ground. Cam wondered if this was Brinkley just trying to cover his ass. If he passed on a job that Cam succeeded in completing, how would that look to everyone?

"I've been his friend for years," Brinkley said. "But he's all about him, isn't he? You've noticed it. We've talked about it."

"That doesn't matter. What about all those people who flock to his bar? He remembers everyone who steps foot on that deck and he can name every decent chef from here to Florida. This is his life."

"I can tell you the batting average of every starter on the '86 Sox. It doesn't mean I can hit a curve ball. There's a difference between being a Chief and an Indian. Two different universes. Some people that can breathe in one choke in the other."

"You think Jeremy is one of those people?"

"Talk is cheap. Have you ever heard him say he's ever done anything wrong? It's always, 'The Chef has his head up his ass tonight.' If he's in the weeds at seven o'clock, it's 'The hostess overbooked the goddamn restaurant.' According to Jeremy, Daniels fucks up the Dockside left and right. Yet, Daniels has been there turning a profit for twenty years. Jeremy's biggest worry this spring was ordering shirts that matched his eyes. He draws up a plan and Rawley Harding tells them it's fucked and cuts it in half. You want that kind of captain piloting your ship?"

"If it's the only ship that will get me across the ocean, I'm okay with it."

"You've got a point there," Brinkley said. "I do have one piece of advice to you. Listen to her old man. He's got a clue."

"Well, it's my balls that are on the block."

"I'll give you credit for putting them there," Brinkley said, adjusting the brim of his hat. "I'm just floored that you're so willing to hop and skip through a field loaded with land mines. All you're seeing is the pretty flowers."

Cam rolled his eyes. He told himself not to take the bait. Let it go. He could add Brinkley to the list of those who didn't think he could handle it. He didn't care if he and Sophia and maybe Rawley were the only ones who thought he could succeed. It would be up to him, after all.

CHAPTER TWENTY-EIGHT

As soon as she left the pavement of the driveway for the gravel of the shoulder, her calves and quads would start to loosen. But Sophia Harding never felt right until she was a half mile out and hitting the hill in front of the fire station. Then she was running. As her stride opened up, so did her mind.

The morning air was cool, enough so that she had slipped a dri-fit shirt over her jog bra. There was so much weird about this summer. A man was in her shower right now, someone who'd been living with her for only a few weeks. She loved it, him being there. He was—she couldn't find the words as she cruised toward town. Innocent wasn't right; neither was low-key, naïve, steady, or driven. Comfortable and unassuming were closer, but he had enough confidence to make himself interesting. No, that wasn't exactly it, either. Considering her last relationship, any and all of those traits seemed endearing enough.

By the time she'd make it back home, he'd be on his way to Boston to meet with his sister about the contract. He was going to build them a restaurant. Of course, Jeremy hated the idea, and her father wasn't overly thrilled with it. But Rawley had probably doubted that she and Jeremy would have gotten this far. There was a hunger driving all three of them; hers she hadn't known she'd possessed. If she wanted to think truthfully, she couldn't figure out how she'd visualized that old shed as a restaurant in the first place.

The design on Horton's garage had been child's play on an adult canvas. She didn't really care about looking at it that morning. Her hope was that Cam wanted to see it with her. She'd had her doubts. He'd mentioned his girlfriend twenty-five times that night. Worse, he'd seemed embarrassed to have kissed her, and then didn't take her up on her offer of a nightcap, whether he thought there was more involved or not. Under normal circumstances, she might have written him off as uninterested. But out there on Horton's lawn, he had trusted her. That said something.

She had sat there on the boards of the pier waiting for him, loosening her hamstrings in the hurdler's stretch, and the restaurant that she and Jeremy had talked about so often had come to her: This setting, that building. It was perfect. That the inspiration had to fight its way to her consciousness as she contemplated the odds and significance of Cam's possible arrival made it even more of an enigma.

At the two mile mark she turned onto Archer Road which ran along the marsh. She was going good, and when she was in tune she enjoyed the quick scuff of her Nikes on the asphalt. Mornings like these made her think she should try racing again. She was fast in high school. In college, however, she'd lasted all of one cross country season. It was too much. Day after day the coach would follow them on his bike and read off their mile splits, as if any run that wasn't performed at red line was a waste. The freedom she'd found on the roads was taken away. By mid-October of her freshman year both her times and frustration had risen. Eventually, she saw little point in competing for the team, then not at all.

The marsh grass was green and high, and it swayed as one

in the breeze. The channels cut through it in straight lines were glassy and full. The sun colored the water a deep blue. One morning, when she could no longer run, she would paint it as it was, not as she saw it. That day, however, was still a ways off.

The elementary school stood at the three-point-four mile mark. It was a two-floor, square, brick building with large, four-panel windows. In the fall, posters of jack-o-lanterns and pilgrims would appear in them, to be replaced in December by elves, candy canes, and Santa Clauses. In the spring, there'd be flowers and bunnies and Easter eggs. Now the windows were clean and lonely. She couldn't help but feel jealous of those who had gone there. Events from its history were always popping up in conversations around town: Remember the time when Mr. Henry and Ms. Miggot came out of the supply closet after lunch and her hair was messed up and his fly was down. There was the Halloween when Mr. Vanders dressed up like Darth Vader, and Teddy Winslow, a first grader, got scared and peed his pants. Were you there when the raccoon family paraded into the cafeteria during the middle of lunch? They would all laugh so heartily, wherever they were. She couldn't even name four girls that she had been friends with in the school she'd gone to in Darien.

She passed the road that led to Jeremy's apartment at just over five miles. When they'd first been dating, she'd add on a three mile loop just to go by. She'd look to see if his car was there or if there were lights on. Maybe she'd be lucky and catch him out in the yard working on his jet ski. It was crazy, the passive-aggressive longing and hope. But was it any more nuts than her pursuit of Cam? She had sought him out at the Squall and then convinced him to bring her along to Horton's. After that, she chased him down while he was building the doghouse. His girlfriend was there, but the restaurant gave her an excuse to call him a few days later—a restaurant that never occurs to her if not for him. Maybe it was impossible to logically follow these things.

For as long as she'd lived in Laurel, she'd never given Cam much thought. He was someone she'd see in places that she frequented (not that there were many options), and they'd say hello and chat for a minute or two. But Cam opened a door for her that day at the Dockside when he was making fun of himself. Maybe it was simply because self deprecation was something that Jeremy could never do, like passing a mirror without checking his hair.

When she flew by the police station at six-point-eight miles, she thought of Alicia Turkington, a restaurant manager at some dive in ski country. Sophia had seen her once, the previous summer, when she was visiting her brother the police chief. He'd taken her to the Dockside. She was tall and stacked and her hair was long and blacker than black. None of those boys could help but stare. Sophia would have, too, if she were one of them. It was six months later when Sophia had gone alone to the Tavern for last call and stood behind Trouper and Lenny Perkins trying to order a drink. They were watching Turk hold court at the far end of the bar. She heard Trouper ask Lenny: "Do you think the Chief knows Jeremy porked his sister last week?" Sophia couldn't breathe. She also couldn't deny what she'd heard. She leaned against the bar to steady herself, and that's when they noticed her. Their conversation stopped. She would have liked to known the answer to their question.

At first, she tried to avoid Jeremy. Then she decided that he would never come clean to her if he wasn't presented the opportunity. She played along as if she knew nothing. Meanwhile she progressed through stages of hurt, denial, and anger. She settled on believing that perhaps it meant so little to him that he didn't think it worth mentioning. That changed when he told her he was going snowboarding at Sugarloaf a few weekends later. She wouldn't have been able to live with herself after that.

She and Jeremy had remained friends, as she knew they would. Jeremy was who he was. He had to be the sun in his sky. That didn't make him a bad person. She truly believed that he enjoyed making people feel good about themselves, and he was fulfilled by their liking him in return. It's what made him great behind the bar, and it's what would make him an even better restaurateur. He hadn't done what he'd done maliciously. It had probably just happened. But that didn't make going back to fuck an Amazon bitch okay, not when he was supposed to be with her. Jeremy had appeared confused and shocked when she walked out. She felt bad for him. Vanity and introspection were mutually exclusive when it came to her former boyfriend.

She scooted into town, and in the center where Route 9 intersected Main Street, she moved at a faster pace than the traffic. She enjoyed that. The Wellington Gallery sat on the corner. Two large seascapes were displayed in its picture windows. They were clichés of white caps and blackened waves. She wondered if she would ever desire to show her own work. Even, Tia, her father's trophy-girlfriend said her painting was original, and she didn't even like Sophia. So what was holding her back? It was simple, she supposed. If it were her canvases in the window, and they never sold, wouldn't that mean her last twelve years had been wasted? That was something she didn't want to contemplate, never mind face the evidence every time she went down the street.

Three-quarters of a mile later, thinking of people with money who didn't hold a job, she shot past the Senator's estate. A glorious structure, it commanded the point and the Atlantic with majesty. It was baffling, or more accurately, disgusting, how someone with so much could be so petty. To demand drinks and dinners to help out what presumably was a friend was dispiriting to say the least. As if Jeremy wouldn't have taken care of him anyway. The four or five dollars he paid for his rum-and-whatever or the thirty dollars he dropped on an entrée couldn't mean anything to him. Did the Senator have so low an opinion of himself—unlikely—that he had to boost his ego through petty extortion? He had to be compensating for something; what it was she didn't want to know. Let them get the FishHouse open and let him have his drinks. Any way she looked at it, it was small.

A half mile later, she veered left and passed the road that led to Horton's. That's where it really started with Cam. He had kissed her that night like he meant it. Maybe that was the difference. Something in Jeremy made it seem like you were kissing him instead of kissing each other. It couldn't have been that way at the start, she told herself. Then again, maybe it could have and she just didn't want to remember. Jeremy was such a vision to her in those days; she simply might not have realized it.

She wondered whether Horton had even bothered to fix the shingles she'd left pointing at him. People were phonies. He was a friend of Jeremy's, but that hadn't stopped him from hitting on her more than once, and at Jeremy's bar while he was working.

"My wife's at home in Wellesley," he'd said late one afternoon. "Jeremy's here all night. We could take a run out to my place. Got a bottle of Dom in the Sub-Zero."

"You're kidding," she'd said.

"Of course," he replied, his face turning red, sweat appearing on his temples. "You didn't think I was serious, did you?"

Yes, she did.

The road went over a bridge, and for a hundred yard stretch one could glimpse what would be the FishHouse. So much of their lives were tied up into making it something real and successful. It had all started with a flash of sympathy for a hawk-nosed, brown-haired boy who couldn't quite understand why things were happening—and not happening—to him. She wasn't so great with that, either.

By the time she landed back on her street, having gone ten miles, she had sweat wicking off her shirt. Her head was clear. Cam would be home with her later that night. She couldn't explain why he'd be there. But she didn't have to. His walking in the door would warm her, as if she'd been given a cognac on a blistering winter day in the middle of the summer.

CHAPTER TWENTY-NINE

Cam feared that he'd still be tossing and turning when the sun came up, and that he wouldn't be able to get out of bed. Sophia slept like a corpse beside him. How she couldn't be worried was incomprehensible. He was picking up the building permit from the town hall as soon as it opened at eight o'clock. Ordway's crew from Dayton would be waiting for him on the pier. It was going to happen. He had less than sixty days to complete the renovation for an August first opening. His mind jumped from a picture of the shed now to what it would be when finished. Although his mantra had been "one-step-at-a-time," the two images partnered to expose the monumental extent of his hubris.

At two, he climbed out of bed and moved to the living room. He turned on the television and found a sitcom he'd watched as a kid. The star of the show was a talking terrier. It was simplistic comedy, with stale jokes that were practically heralded by trumpets. At least he had made some progress in life. What he couldn't trace was the path that had taken him from a twelve-year old who liked the unbelievably vapid show to being twenty-five, shacked up with a girl he'd really known

only a month, and having a three-quarter-million dollar project
at his feet, all while being somewhat estranged from his family.
He was lost in the second episode when Sophia came out of
the bedroom. She had put on one of his t-shirts. Her hair
hung over her face.

"What are you watching?" she asked.

"One of my childhood favorites," he replied and turned it
off.

"Too excited to sleep?" she asked, sitting down next to
him.

"Petrified, to be honest," he said. "I can't figure out how I
got here."

"From the Squall?" They had had dinner at the bar where
they'd first collided. "You're too young to have a stroke." She
laughed.

"I might be too young for a lot of things."

She put her hand on his knee and looked at him, her eyes
barley luminous with the light in the room having vanished.

"Why do you doubt yourself?" she asked.

"Are you kidding me?" he asked, standing up. He began
pacing in the space between the sofa and the television. "This
chain of events is ridiculous, and I haven't had a hand in any of
it."

"What are you talking about?" She leaned forward, her
hands on her knees.

"Think about this," he said, stopping. "If Horton isn't an
idiot, I'm not pissed off at the Dockside that afternoon. I
don't get the idea to steal his shingles. I don't go to the Squall
and spend twelve bucks on a fucking hamburger because I'm
feeling sorry for myself. I don't run into you. I don't build
that doghouse. Miranda doesn't get pissed at me because I
have to work that weekend, which starts another ball rolling.
Of course, I'm still pissed because I don't get my
grandmother's house. I'm still Brinkley's guy. I never
entertain the idea that I could take on a big project. But that

doesn't matter because you never go to the pier to look at Horton's garage. The restaurant doesn't exist in your mind or anywhere else. I'm not living here. We probably never even hook up. How do you make any sense of that?"

"You don't," she said, her voice steady. "You just live. It's okay to give yourself credit for the decisions that you did make, too."

"Such as?"

"You decided that you weren't going to take shit from Horton. You decided to bring me along to rip off his shingles. You decided that you could buy the family house. It didn't happen, but that type of thinking led you to figuring how to get this restaurant done while no one else could do it. You decided to move in here, and that's worked out, hasn't it?"

"It's been great," he said, nodding. "But that's another thing I don't understand. You barely knew me when you let me move in. Who does that?"

"I liked you." She patted the couch next to her and he sat down.

"Why? I'm not tall and handsome and successful. I don't know everyone in town, nor do I want to. I did grunt work for a hard ass builder. By the end of most days I'm either filthy or drunk or both."

"You're normal. I know that doesn't sound like much, but it's something really good. There were other things, too: I knew I wouldn't catch you combing your hair for twenty minutes each morning. You laugh at yourself. And to top it off, you're the kind of guy who would put himself at risk building a house for a ferocious dog."

"So being a jackass is a good quality in your book?"

"I didn't run into you at the Squall by coincidence, and I didn't drive to Gray Gull just to scope out your work and ask you for a favor."

"Where you met Miranda, my girlfriend."

Sophia leaned back and shrugged. "You seemed lonely,

with her or without her."

"That's funny, because I thought you seemed desperate, if not slightly out of your mind."

"I was lonely," she said, with a matter-of-fact voice.

He looked down.

"There's nothing wrong with that," she said. "It's human."

"So you waited for me?"

"You weren't exactly running away."

He put his arm around her. "I guess I wasn't. But I may have led you to the edge of the cliff. If this restaurant turns out to be a disaster—I mean, my end of it—then what?"

"I'm pretty sure the world will keep spinning."

"That's a very philosophical attitude," he said. They spoke in what were nearly whispers.

"You're the one up in the middle of the night contemplating the meaning of life."

"I'd rather be asleep," he said.

"Then come to bed," she said, standing up in front of him. "You won't screw up."

"How can you be sure?" He pulled her close to him and pressed his head against her stomach. He breathed in the cleanliness of her skin.

"Now isn't the time to question," she said. "You know what needs to happen. Like the ad says, 'Just do it.'"

She took his hand and led him into the bedroom. She curled up next to him and ran her fingers through his hair. He lay on his back and closed his eyes. He tried to relax. Sophia soon fell into her soft, silent breathing. Cam knew he wasn't going to sleep. He'd get up in the morning anyway, whether he was ready for what faced him or not.

PART THREE

CHAPTER THIRTY

It was an odd conflagration of lifestyle. The Dockside hadn't seen him. He hadn't stepped on a beach, and his fishing gear remained stowed below in the garage. He went at it seven days a week, differentiating between weekday and weekend only by the vehicles he found in the pier's parking lot, the lobstermen's pickups and flat beds or the tourists' minivans and SUVs. From the moment he climbed out of bed at six-thirty, he was on the move and happy about it. He and Sophia rose together; he headed for the shower, she for her running gear. He left before she returned. Bradley's was the only stop, for a large coffee and a bagel, and he was on the job by seven. Things had gone as well as he thought they would, which was not to say they'd gone well. Just past the midpoint of June, the planned August First opening seemed pure fantasy. He saw no alternative but to keep his head down and plow through as best he could. Hopefully, something would give. It wasn't going to be him; he knew that much.

Obstacles had cropped up like dandelions right from the start, especially during those moments when he thought—finally—he had everything in order. He'd been able to hire the framers he wanted, Guy Ordway's crew from Dayton, forty-five minutes west. But he hadn't been able to get them for what Ordway called inland money. Given that, they still worked for less than what Cam would have had to pay a coastal outfit, even a half-assed one like Lenny Perkins'. They would frame, side, and roof, and Cam would put together his own crew to finish the place, hands-on. That meant for the two weeks he had Ordway, Cam needed to organize and coordinate, so that when Ordway left the critical path would fall into place. But it wasn't long before Cam came to realize that even his most assured decisions seemed only to stave off disaster, while others were destined to lead straight to it.

Ordway and his men started the day they'd gotten the permit signed by Benson, Laurel's three-hundred pound building inspector, someone never seen without his codebook. In less than two days, Ordway had nearly stripped the shed down to its existing frame, the south end all that remained intact in its decrepitude. Cam stood in the parking lot explaining to Jeremy and Sophia that they could have the place buttoned up within a week. Just as Jeremy started to reiterate for the fifty-seventh time that the sooner they could open, the sooner they would have money coming in, Ordway's troll-like right-hand man came over to grab Cam. "Big problem," Snodley said. Seconds later, Cam looked in disbelief as he stood at the south wall, his eyes narrowing at the blackened timbers revealed along a corner up to the loft. Ordway's crew, a tough group of Francos, looked at Cam as if he'd fired a gun over their heads. Charcoaled two-by-fours had crumbled as their hammers ripped at the exterior boards. The place could have easily toppled on them, and it was miraculous that it had not collapsed some winter, when feet of snow would sit on the roof for weeks at a time.

Ordway guessed that the fire had happened thirty or so years earlier. It must have been contained somewhat quickly, as it never made it outside. Those were the days before inspections and code enforcement, and whoever was responsible must have said, "The hell with it," and covered it with plywood. A bunch of lobsterman drinking beer around a barrel fire were probably the culprits, but now it was Cam's mess to clean up. They'd have to reframe that entire end of the building. He put in a call to Benson and thought of what Brinkley told him: People would be the problem, not the construction. He hadn't realized that they could be historical figures.

Any cost savings he'd gained with Ordway were lost in extra materials. Putting that side of the shed back together wasn't a complicated or mysterious job. To save time, Cam helped Ordway and his men. For two days, he was covered in soot, coughing like he had a three pack-a-day habit. The first week hadn't closed and they were already behind. He tried to tell himself that at least it left him time to make up the days.

When Benson came to check the new framing, he wasn't interested in hearing about the extra work they'd had to do. He heaved his considerable stomach and sighed, instead pointing to the intersection of the rafters and wall. He flattened his bushy mustache and said that they weren't up to code. Before Cam could protest, Benson pointed out that the building was on the critical edge, a term used for structures within five hundred feet of the water. Cam mentioned that he'd worked on plenty of houses on the coast and that they'd all been framed this way, reminding Benson that he himself had approved them. The enforcement officer sighed and pointed out that this was a commercial structure and needed to conform to the newly installed 2008 code, particularly hurricane requirements. Apparently, this would have been news to Jeremy's architect, too, because the blueprints had indicated nothing but standard framing.

"That's too bad," Benson said, tapping his pencil against his clipboard.

"Should I get the architect to redraw the plan or should I

just go ahead and do it the way that makes the most sense?" Cam asked.

"I'm here to inspect, not to advise," Benson said, and then shared the remainder of the list of commercial weather-related specifications that Cam needed to be aware of. At least he wouldn't need to waste any time kissing Benson's ass. If something didn't meet code, Benson wouldn't have looked the other way for free lunch for the rest of his life. Cam figured he could play by the rules, as long as he knew what the hell they were.

Cam had met the architect once. He should have known better. After agreeing to let Cam build the restaurant, Jeremy and Sophia had brought F. Donovan Lennard out of his Boston suburb for a meeting. In the cramped kitchen of Jeremy's apartment, Lennard had pointed out various parts of the building that he deemed would be difficult to construct. Cam nodded along, keeping quiet, realizing that it was likely that F. Donovan had never swung a hammer or used a Skil saw in his life. This would have been fine with Cam, even with the code blunder, except that when the windows arrived the following week, he lost another two days because the rough openings dictated in the plans did not match the size specified in the sheets that came with the Andersens. He was lucky that Ordway was still there, otherwise the reframing would have been a considerable project.

With the summer season well underway, Cam hadn't been able to dig up an all star team of talent for his own crew. Brad Whitworth had worked for everyone in town at one time or another. He was a good carpenter, but a bad drunk. If he showed up and wasn't hungover or still buzzing, he was capable, and Cam didn't need to look over his shoulder. But depending on him was like counting on the weather. Alex Paine also knew what he was doing, but he had three kids— one of which always seemed to be needing to be picked up for getting sick at daycare. His wife called nine times a day, which would have been grounds for ridicule had it not been so aggravating to the rest of them. Cam was lucky to get fifteen minutes out of him at a stretch. Dave Scapa had worked as a landscaper, a waiter, a stern man, and a trolley driver. He couldn't measure, cut on a straight line, or pop a nail in the right place. That he showed up stoned was another issue, compounded by his thinking that none of them noticed. At best, he was a live body and strong. That anything got done at all seemed incredible to Cam.

If Whitworth arrived in condition to work, Cam considered it a victory. He would give him his own project and leave him alone. He could give Paine a job that a normal carpenter could get done in two hours, and then figure him for three or four. There was only so much running for coffee, hauling, and picking up that Scapa could do. When errands were exhausted, Cam set him upon minimal building tasks, Cam thinking that if his mother could do it, then he'd let Scapa have a shot. This still required Cam to cut his wood for him and then check back every ten minutes, thereby preventing Scapa from getting so far down the road that his project would have to be scrapped and redone. Once he had everyone underway, he could then team up with Whitworth or Paine and push things ahead.

Naturally, Cam's phone rang even more than Paine's. He learned to leave it in his tool box, checking voice mails at lunch and again at four, in case he actually had to talk to someone before the end of the day. When everyone left at five-thirty, he could finally relax. He would tackle some detail work or cut for Scapa so he could have him ready to go the next morning. Sometimes he'd frame a door or put up trim. Cam never went home before ten. The work, he could live with. Jeremy was another matter.

Cam was ready to crucify him with a nail gun. Although he and Sophia were using his apartment as their office, it seemed like Jeremy rarely left the pier, a tall, dandy overlord. He thought nothing of calling Cam over and telling him things he didn't need to know: they'd gotten a great price on a used stove top; the dish machine could be delivered any day they wanted it; Sophia had come up with a great logo they could use on their signage. And questions: Why were they doing that instead of this? Was he still counting on using Blinn to install the kitchen gas, because Henry Schlissfut just called him and told him that he'd beat Blinn's price. All this did was keep Cam from what he needed to do: carpentry.

At the start of their fourth week, Eastern Seaboard Lumber showed up with the interior siding, a MDF paneling, which was going over sheetrock that was not yet hung. When painted with a glossy white enamel, the paneling would give the restaurant the atmosphere of a yacht without any of the kitsch. The problem was that they wouldn't need it for another two weeks. But by the time Cam had climbed down from the loft, the bullethead from Eastern had already unloaded it. Cam looked at the black clouds that hung low in the sky. He could send it back, but there were equal chances that they'd screw up the delivery again when he actually wanted it or that it would get soaked on its return to the lumberyard and then redelivered later, which would require sending it back again. He called the guys down and they started hauling the bundles into the restaurant, where it would at least be dry and close.

"Cam, can I talk to you," Jeremy said. Whitworth looked at Cam and grinned.

"No, Jeremy, you can't. Not unless you want to grab the other end of one of these bundles."

"Excuse me?" Jeremy's arms folded in front of his chest.

"I'm working, as you can see."

"Oh, I thought you were here for your looks."

Cam ignored him. Paine scowled.

"I guess there's no reason you'd want to know that the kitchen equipment has reached United's warehouse, and we can get it anytime we want. But you're only building a restaurant. No reason to worry about something like a kitchen."

"Does it look like we're ready to install the goddamn kitchen?" He dropped the end of the box he'd just lifted. Scapa scrambled to keep it from crashing.

"I'm just supplying you with critical information," Jeremy said. "You don't have to throw a tantrum."

"Leave us alone," Cam said.

"That's not going to happen. I've got a job to do, too."

"You need to get off of this pier," Cam said.

"Like it or not, I'm the cock in charge—of every aspect of this place."

Cam took two steps and faced Jeremy. His knees shook. Jeremy looked down at him, smug, as if Cam wouldn't dare take a swing, which is exactly what Cam was considering. He had confidence he could land the first shot and make it a good one, but wondered if his crew, on the edge of his vision and on the verge of cracking up, would jump in before he got his ass kicked. A rain drop landed on his nose. He didn't have time for it.

"Go fuck yourself," he said to Jeremy and then spun around, signaling Scapa to pick up the other end of a stack of paneling.

Fifteen minutes later Sophia's Jeep came screeching onto the wharf where Jeremy remained, glaring.

"All I want to do is build them a fucking restaurant," Cam said. "How hard could that be?"

"Harder than you think," Whitworth said, grinning. "You need to unionize. Then the Man can't tell you what to do."

"Cam is the Man," Scapa said. "They just don't know it yet."

"You're going to get it now that your girlfriend's here," Whitworth said. Jeremy's arms were flailing as Sophia stood across from him. Cam started over, expecting him to be stamping his feet by the time he reached them.

"Look," Cam said, preempting the tirade, "I can't get

anything done if every two minutes I'm being interrupted."

"You need to be aware of anything that's going on," Jeremy said. "Bottom line."

"No, I don't. I've got enough to worry about with what's in front of me. If your *fake yacht paneling* got wet," Cam said, knowing the term would piss Jeremy off, "it would be ruined. And, as you know, there's not a lot of room in this budget where we can afford something like that. So the fact that a bunch of fucking ovens can be delivered this week instead of in a month when we actually need them doesn't carry a lot of urgency."

"You need to learn how to multi-task," Jeremy said, shaking his head. "What about Schlissfut?" He turned to Sophia. "Henry called me this morning. He said he'd beat Blinn's price, whatever it was, by thirty percent. That isn't relevant either, according to Cam."

"Schlissfut sucks," Cam said. "He's the worst plumber in the fucking state. I wouldn't use him if he worked for free."

"That's what you say."

"Go call your friend Brinkley, you stupid fuck, if you don't believe me." Cam shook his head at Sophia. "I can't get anything done with him up my ass every ten minutes."

Sophia looked at the clouds and then from Jeremy to Cam. In a frown, her forehead seemed to elongate even more. He heard his guys laughing in the loft.

"You two need to communicate better," Sophia said.

"No," Cam replied. "Too much communication is the problem."

"How the hell is he supposed to be able to plan if he doesn't know anything?" Jeremy raised his hands and let them fall.

"Jesus, guys," she said. "Come on."

Sophia sucked in her bottom lip.

"How about this?" she said. "Every day at five o'clock, the three of us will sit down and go over things, Monday through

Friday, without fail. Sometimes it might not take ten minutes. Other days it might be two hours. But no complaints either way. Unless there's a matter of life and death, we'll leave you alone until then. However, even if you're in the middle of something at five, you need to stop and sit down. Anyone have a problem with that?"

"If you haven't noticed," Cam said. "I don't call it a day at five."

"Oh, I've noticed," she said, smiling and touching his arm. "We appreciate that. But taking a few minutes won't kill you."

"Okay," he said.

"Agreed." Jeremy nodded.

"Do you two shake hands now like little boys?" she said, laughing.

"We're good," Cam said, heading back to work, impressed with what he'd have to call his girlfriend.

"How did you make out, boss?" Whitworth asked.

"They're going to leave me alone until five o'clock."

"In other words," Paine said. "She threatened to put him on the couch."

Cam grinned. But even with that issue straightened out, progress was slow.

Things seemingly never could be done in the order he wanted to do them. At seven-thirty in the morning, as he waited for Whitworth's car to show in the parking lot, stress made an appearance. It ebbed when the Bondo-ed Cutlass showed and then resurfaced when Scapa's van crested the hill. Days that he wanted interior doors framed, Whitworth would go missing. When he gave Paine some detail work with Scapa to help him, one of his kids would bite someone, and he'd have to leave. Cam would weigh whether it was worth doing it himself and thereby leaving what he was engaged in for that night or the next day—or find something else for Scapa to do. He was thinking for everyone.

Despite the difficulties, and mainly because of Ordway's

initial efforts, the exterior was finished by the end of June. The restaurant, shingled with cedar, looked like it belonged on the pier. Forest green trimmed the windows and doors. The entryway was at the north end of the building. A black sign with varnished, carved gold lettering that Cam had done himself, proclaimed "The FishHouse." A smaller font added "Fine Food and Drink." The windows on that side of the restaurant were placed high to provide light and air, but no guest needed a view of rusted pick-ups and stacked lobster traps. Halfway down the building, a row of tall, potted evergreens hid the propane tanks that would power the kitchen. The kitchen itself started there and turned in an L around the southern front corner. Even Cam had to admit the layout was well designed. Views were saved for the customers: The wall that looked out over the water was all windows. That the building had once been a reeking bait shed would have been hard for anyone to believe, had they not seen its earlier manifestation.

Still, complications persisted. Jeremy had originally wanted mahogany for the bar and bar top. But this was based on having cherry on the walls, which had been scrapped due to cost. When the walls were downgraded to the MDF, Jeremy neglected to mention that this would affect the bar, too. Wood was shipped. Wood was sent back. Jeremy couldn't decide what he wanted. Cam told him to go the lumber yard and not come back until he found something he liked. He returned empty-handed. Cam suggested to Sophia that she take him to look at some of the weathered yellow pine planking they sold at a salvage yard in South Portland, which he could submerge under a few layers of polyurethane. He had Sophia float the idea, because if it came straight from him, Jeremy would have immediately dismissed it. Cam at least had figured out that angle. The bar would be done in recycled yellow pine, Jeremy decided.

Eastern Seaboard Lumber was a never-ending headache.

They had the best prices. Unfortunately, they were combined with the worst service. The wrong bathroom and bar tiles were brought. Twice. It ended up being a master stroke of luck, as the sub hired to lay them showed up four days late, arriving within five minutes of the correct tiles. Cam took it as a sign of grace, bad luck turning good. Of course, it only lasted so long.

CHAPTER THIRTY-ONE

He'd been expecting and dreading the call. It came on July first. He was glancing at his missed calls when the phone rang and he saw his father's number flash on the screen. Even if his sister had told them that he was the one running the job, not to mention an investor, they still would have expected him to drop everything and help. They had no clue.

"We're having a barbecue on Saturday the Fourth, around five o'clock, and we'd like to see you there," his father had said, after asking how he'd been. "Then on Sunday, everything goes from the house. It gets turned over the week after that."

"Great," Cam said. He'd pulled his things shortly after he'd moved into Sophia's. Most of it was in boxes in her garage.

"We could use some help, even with your sister and Spencer coming. We're donating most of it to Goodwill. They're dropping the truck off at ten on Sunday." His father spoke matter-of-factly, as if removing the contents of the house were simply a logistical problem. Had his mother made the call, her voice would have been coated in emotion. The reasonableness in his father's tone left him without offense.

"I'm going to have to work on the Fourth," Cam said.

"But I can spare some time to help clear the place out, I guess."

"You're working on holidays now? Can you possibly be that busy?"

"It's a time sensitive job."

"Really?" Doubt flooded his father's tone.

"I'll come Sunday morning and help with the furniture," Cam said.

"You can't spare an hour or two on Saturday to come eat with us?"

"Sorry, no."

"If you say so," Martin said. "It's unlike you to pass up burgers and beer for hard work."

"I don't know what to tell you," Cam said, and made an excuse to get off the phone.

It got worse when he told Sophia. Instead of being mad at him for abandoning the restaurant, she told him he should go to the family dinner. When he wouldn't concede that point, she insisted on accompanying him. Her presence, he agreed, might help him keep things in perspective. She'd been the one to get him focused on what lay ahead of him, not what was behind.

He spent the Fourth, eighty degrees and sunny, inside the restaurant, framing the kitchen. All day he watched people motor and sail through the harbor. They were tan and happy, and they waved if they spotted him. Brinkley cruised past on the Mako. Cam noticed his eyes on the restaurant until he was well past it. Sophia brought him lunch, and then dinner, and tried to get him to go to the Dockside. Cam worked through, until she finally brought him a quart of Budweiser and forced him to stop. They sat out on the pier behind the restaurant and watched the moonlight reflect off the water. He could have slept there.

They arrived at Gray Gull at eight the following morning. It was the first time he'd been out there in weeks. His twin bed was already sitting in the driveway, along with an assortment of dressers and night tables. They were old pieces, not the antiques sold in shops all over town. As soon as he stepped into the kitchen, he was greeted by the lemon-ammonia of Lysol instead of the cottage's usual scent. Leave it to his mother to clean something that had a razing in its future. She was folding linen with Kiernan in the living room, and she shrieked and bounded into the kitchen when she spotted him. Sherri held his face in her hands as if she hadn't seen him in years. Kiernan, showing a bowling ball for her stomach, smiled behind her. His father and Spencer came thumping down the stairs with dresser drawers under their arms.

He introduced Sophia to everyone, with his mother and sister sizing her up for different reasons. Kiernan hadn't told them of his actual involvement in the restaurant; Sherri wouldn't have been able to refrain from questioning him. Instead, she directed her investigation on Sophia: Where was she from? What did she do? Oh yes, a restaurant. They kept coming.

"So how is this restaurant progressing?" Sherri asked.

"Great," Sophia said. "We'll be open in a month."

"And Cam is working on it, too? Is that where you met?"

"He's been killing himself over there," Sophia said, smiling.

"Well, it's nice of Warren to give you the day off."

"Oh, Brinkley isn't doing the job," Sophia said. Cam exchanged a look with his sister. He'd asked Sophia not to say anything, something she had either forgotten or chose to ignore.

"Who are you working for now?" Martin asked.

"Her," Cam said, hoping Sophia would catch the tone and not reveal anything more than that.

"He's running the construction," Sophia said.

"For the entire restaurant?" Martin asked.

"That's right," Sophia said.

"Why didn't you tell us?" Martin said.

"It doesn't really matter," Cam said. "It's work."

"That's a funny way to look at it," Sherri said. "It must be an enormous undertaking."

"He's doing a fantastic job," Sophia said.

"When I leave here," Cam said. "I'm going right back there, so let's get moving."

"What about dinner?" Sherri asked. "I thought we could have one last supper. Your father was going to go to Alley's in Milltowne for pizza. My mother loved that greasy place, with its monkey meat or whatever she used to tell you two it was. I don't know why you aren't dying to explain what is that you're doing. You could at least share it over dinner."

"There really is a lot to be done," Sophia said. Cam wondered if she were backtracking now that his mother had started in on them.

"So you're working there, too?"

"Didn't we just tell you that, Mom?" Cam said. "It's her restaurant."

"She said she was opening the place. I don't presume to know what that entails. I'm sure she's not hammering nails or whatever it is you're involved in."

"I leave that to your son, Mrs. Preston."

"Please, call me Sherri. Well, that's settled then, you can tell us all about it at dinner."

"Can we just forget about the goddamn restaurant, Mom, and get this house cleared out?" Cam said. His sister and Spencer couldn't help but laugh.

"Are you going to invite us to this restaurant someday?" Sherri asked. "I'd love to see your work."

"When it's done, I might, if you don't bug me about it."

"For crying out loud," Sherri said. She turned to Kiernan. "What about your brother? Did you ever think?"

"No, Mom, I didn't," she said. "But why don't we get

going here before he pops his top?"

"You know if we do come up to go to the restaurant, we'll have to stay in a hotel," Martin said. He sighed. "If there's anything you want from here, Cam, you take it, okay? Otherwise, it's going to Goodwill."

Cam shrugged. "I don't need anything."

"You know," Sherri said, "you can put something in storage if you think you might need it later."

Cam looked at Sophia and grinned. Yes, this is what she had gotten herself into. She couldn't say he hadn't warned her.

"There's all those kitchen utensils and pots and pans," Sherri said. "The couch is in good shape."

"Believe it or not, there are some pretty nice amenities where I'm staying."

"It's just a garage apartment," Sophia said.

"Well it must be some garage if you can't use anything from a beach house," Sherri said.

"What do you need me to move?" Cam said, changing the subject before the interrogation broke them down and revealed that it was actually Sophia's garage apartment.

He hadn't given thought to getting his own place in weeks. The decision to jump into the restaurant had launched that far into the future. Even so, he wouldn't want anything from here. All it would do was remind him of his failure. He realized it was a bitter and selfish way to think, and that bothered him as he and Sophia maneuvered a mattress down the stairs. He would have his memories of his grandmother and living here with her, and that would be enough.

The small muscles in Sophia's arms tensed as they cornered the landing of the stairwell and went out through the kitchen. He hadn't expected anything when he'd moved in with her. If he'd had a few days to think beforehand, he probably wouldn't have accepted her offer. But their energies and desires had been synchronized from the get-go, even before they'd had the common goal of the FishHouse. He hadn't considered until now, as they heaved the mattress into the Goodwill truck, that things might change when the restaurant was finished. She would still have a purpose and he would be adrift. Ultimately, he would find another project, and they'd be the same people they were when they started living together. It was their connection that led them to where they were now, not the reverse. They were just living, and it was good. It didn't need to be intellectualized—if that's what one would call it. Moving in with the small blonde girl marching back into his grandmother's house had been an accident, one for which he was thankful.

The house began to look empty by the middle of the afternoon. Cam gazed at the walls, and saw the spots where the paint had changed hues from being hidden by furniture or a frame. From outside, it now looked stilted and weak. He couldn't imagine it surviving another winter, not that it would have the chance. It would be bulldozed before fall. Like its true owner, it was to be taken away.

When he left for the day, he refused to take a last glance at the ocean through the living room windows. He wouldn't step on the deck, still crooked, that had been his. He kept his eyes on the street and held Sophia's hand as he went out the door. The neighbor's house had its windows open and shadows crept across the screens. Ted Pearson waved from his porch, Miller Lite in his hand. The trees were full with leaves. Two small boys rode BMX bikes down the middle of the road.

"I can't believe you're going to go to the pier," Sophia said. "You didn't even take yesterday off."

"I wouldn't have lasted through dinner with them."

"We could get stinking drunk," she said. "We haven't done it all summer."

He pulled out of the driveway in the Ranger. He didn't have to look; it was all in his head. The faded cedar and glossy white trim. The brick chimney with the thin strips of silver flashing. The rectangular storm windows. The deep green of the lawn. The jagged boulders of the breakwater. The gray two-by-fours of the staircase. He was only headed across town, but he might as well have been leaving for California. He stopped the truck and put it into reverse.

"Are you okay?' Sophia asked.

"I'll be right back," he said. He reached under the seat and pulled out a hammer. He hustled back to the deck. When he'd built it, there was one rail that he'd cut short, his last one, naturally. He'd had to fill it in with a piece of scrap. He walked over to it and swung the hammer.

"What are you doing?" Kiernan asked, stepping out the kitchen door. "Did you forget something?"

"I won't be coming back here, ever." He yanked off the filler section and kneeled down to pry the post from the deck. "And there is something I want."

"A piece of wood?" she said, watching him.

"My wood," he said, and with a last effort, he ripped the one-by-one post from its base. It was soft from the years of rain, wind, sun, and sand.

"I'm happy for you," Kiernan said. "That girl must really like you if she stuck it out here all day."

"Thanks," he said.

"Don't be too hard on Mom and Dad. Put yourself in their shoes."

"Just don't say anything about what's really going on with the restaurant."

"I won't."

He walked over and hugged his sister, angling her sideways so he wouldn't squish the baby. She laughed. Then he was off down his steps.

"What was that about?" he heard his mother say, confusion in her voice.

CHAPTER THIRTY-TWO

It was a relief to get back to work the following day, even with his crew beside him. They were close to catching up to Cam's original timeline. Unseasonably cool weather, devoid of the humidity that usually drained them, had made working almost easy. When Scapa nearly cut the end of his finger off, Sophia was there to drive him to the Emergency Room. It was not a great loss, Cam reasoned. There were only so many times you could send a guy for coffee, and for a few days they got them exactly the way they liked them. Production increased.

The interior began to take shape. The original wide-plank oak floor had been sanded and refinished in the dining room, thanks to the unprecedented health and good behavior of Paine's kids and Scapa taking a miraculous proficiency to the work. The two of them also then put up the MDF paneling with startling speed and detail. Maybe it helped that the materials were designed so that your average homeowner could do it. Scapa's painting skills were also acceptable. Outside forces contributed, as well. Whitworth's girlfriend told him that if he didn't quit drinking, she was leaving. The resulting nervous energy poured into construction of booths and banquettes around the edge of the room. With everyone else occupied and productive, Cam had been freed to build the bar along the south end of the building. He crafted the back bar out of pieces of the same weathered pine, a subtle but noticeable contrast with the paneling.

To Cam, one day remained the same as the next. It didn't bother him that he hadn't watched much baseball. Instead, nights when he worked by himself, the games on the radio provided a rhythm. He'd run the saw between innings and build during the at-bats. He never yelled at the boom box the way he would at the television, not even when the Sox announcer was driving him crazy, dropping his voice with every Boston out. Cam's old routine had vanished, replaced by this one where he worked longer and harder. Yet, he was happy.

Sophia, usually preceding him by less than an hour, would be waiting for him at home. They would settle onto the couch to have a drink together, hardly ever more than one, and if he were lucky, they watched the last inning of a Sox game. If they'd missed it, she turned the television to TMZ and they listened to thirty minutes of celebrity buzz. Whatever game, gossip, or sitcom they found wiped their minds clean. They tried not to talk of the restaurant and often failed.

"We might actually make it by the first," Cam said, breaking tradition as a bottle-blond reviewed Miley Cyrus's dating habits. His watch told him it was the fifteenth of July.

"You're believing it now?" she replied.

"If conditions are perfect," he said.

"What would that entail?"

"Whitworth stays sober. The rest of Paine's family goes on vacation. Scapa's paintbrush becomes glued to his hand and his pot dealer moves. Jeremy gets laryngitis. No humidity."

"I could get the coffee again instead of Scapa if that would help," she said, running a hand through the mop on his head. He wasn't taking time off to get it cut.

"You've got enough to do," he said. She'd been working as hard as anyone, serving as the interior designer, business manager, and most importantly, voice of reason. She was the one who had floated the compromises that bridged dreams and reality. Sophia swung her legs over him so she was sitting in his lap, facing him. Her hair hung down, brushing his cheek.

"We're going to be great," she said. The glowing colors of the television turned her eyes red, then vacant.

"Really?" he asked. She smiled.

"The restaurant, too," she said.

Each night, they walked hand-in-hand into the bedroom and fell into an hour of sweat-dripping coupling, as if they had to exorcise the last vestiges of energy from their bodies before they could sleep. Sex had never come as often for him, or been as good.

CHAPTER THIRTY-THREE

The weather turned on them later in July, bringing ninety degree temperatures and even higher humidity. They had no choice but to push through the heat, downing Gatorade by the gallon. A sense of optimism cut through the heavy air. The end was in sight. Then the Chef showed up ten days before they were scheduled to open.

Chris Lamere had made his name at some restaurant on Cape Cod. Cam hadn't heard of the place, not that that meant anything. But he also couldn't recall Jeremy ever talking it up before he'd told them he hired Lamere. On principle, Sophia was peeved that she hadn't been given the chance to talk to the guy, too. Cam saw her point, but stayed out of it. Even though he hated to admit it, Jeremy had the kitchen design organized and under control. He had also hired an army of a kitchen staff. Cam assumed that Lamere's commitment to his former employer which prevented him from coming sooner was an indication of integrity. The good news was that they hadn't had to carry the dead weight of his salary. Jeremy and Sophia finally brought Lamere around on a Friday. Cam and his crew were working on finishing the dining room. Delivery and installation of appliances were scheduled for the following Monday. The kitchen was walled off, fireproofed, and sheet-rocked—ready to go.

Lamere was a six-footer with brown moussed-and-spiked hair that grayed at the temples. He couldn't have weighed more than a hundred and fifty pounds. Jeremy and Sophia whisked him into the kitchen through the opening where the swinging service doors would be hung. Lamere didn't even glance at the carpenters as he marched to his domain.

"You'd better come in here, Cam," Sophia said a few minutes later, peeking her head out of the opening.

"Is there a problem?" Cam said entering the kitchen, trying not to sound annoyed at the interruption.

"I wish you'd found me before you did this layout," Lamere said, looking from Jeremy to Cam. He had the schematic spread in front of him on the expediting bench.

"What's wrong with it?" Cam asked. He glanced at Jeremy, who raised his eyebrows.

"The stove top is too small. I don't know how you came up with a six-burner. Eight should have been the absolute minimum, and any real chef would demand ten. Those four extra burners make a huge difference. Otherwise, sauté is working with one hand tied behind his back, if not both."

"Isn't that stove the size United recommended based on the number of seats?" Cam asked.

"Those guys sell, but they don't cook," Lamere said.

"They put kitchens together every day of the week," Cam said.

"Well, believe me, someone who cooks for a living, they screwed this one up."

"Why would they have sold us a smaller, less expensive unit than what we actually needed?" Cam asked.

"Didn't you hear what I just said?" Lamere said. "They don't know what they're doing. With ninety seats and a bar, we need ten goddamn burners."

Cam sighed. "How many kitchens have you designed?" he asked.

"I'm the Executive Chef for a reason," he said.

"Impressive title."

"Save the attitude, dude," Lamere said. "You've got work to do here if we're going to turn this into a productive space."

Cam laughed.

"I gave United a budget," Jeremy said. "Maybe they were trying to fit it in what they could."

"If you're going to try to run this kitchen with a six-burner," Lamere said, looking to Jeremy, "you might as well not bother to open."

"You've got to be kidding me," Cam said.

"Lamere, this is Cam Preston, our, uh, builder," Jeremy said. "I should have introduced you."

"Hey, man," Lamere said, shaking his hand. "I don't mean to be a prick, but this is serious shit."

"Wonderful," Cam said.

"It doesn't stop there, either," Lamere said. Whitworth, who had come to watch and stood in the doorway, snorted and retreated to the dining room. "But it will be worth it. A little pain now will make for a smooth flow later, and we're going to need that, especially if we're going to do the numbers Jeremy projects. You've got to take a long term view."

Cam retrieved his notebook and followed Lamere around the kitchen while he critiqued every inch of it. At least with his clean shaven face and polo shirt, he looked responsible. He seemed to know what he was talking about, too, listing reasons for every proclamation. Cam could understand how a chef would have his own vision of a kitchen, but at times Lamere seemed like a dog who had to piss on every tree.

"I've got an idea," Cam said after they had completed the circuit, having filled four pages. "Let's tear it down and start over."

"Or we could get someone with a more positive attitude to

work with us," Lamere said.

"Are you two related?" Cam asked Jeremy. "Because you share the same tenuous grasp on reality." He held up his notebook. "This adds two weeks minimum to the job. Not to mention how much money it's going to cost in materials and labor."

"What the hell are you complaining about?" Lamere said. "You'll get paid."

"Are you signing the checks now?" Cam asked.

"He can tell you like I did, if that will make you feel better," Lamere said, pointing to Jeremy.

"He's the one who said six-fucking-burners would be enough," Cam said.

"Okay, guys, chill," Sophia said.

"Do you want to do all this?" Cam asked, looking from Jeremy to Sophia. Although it was in their agreement that his stake in the place not be disclosed, Cam wondered if they had told Lamere that there was a silent partner. "Each column of two burners adds a foot to the stove's length. We'll have to move the convection oven, rewire, take down a wall, and then reframe this entire end of the kitchen."

"We've got to," Jeremy said, obviously convinced by Lamere's soliloquy on kitchen design. "We're going to do some volume."

"I agree," Sophia said. "Let's suck it up."

"I'll get Osgood from United on the phone," Jeremy said.

"Great," Cam said. The decision came easy for them. It would be on him to make it work. How many times had he seen Brinkley and Sarofian go through this? He wanted to put his fist through one of the freshly painted walls. Sophia kept patting his arm, hoping to defuse what was building inside him. Lamere had better know what he was talking about.

Installing a sixty-inch stove would produce two extra feet of cooking area, and in addition to shifting a wall, they'd need to realign and expand their hood system, too. Benson had said that they were at their limit for venting. They'd have to order larger hoods and shoot up through the roof instead of over and out the south end of the building the way it had been originally cut. HVAC, electric, and plumbing layouts would all need to be adjusted, which meant calling and rescheduling a host of subs. It would have been easier had they ordered him to juggle chainsaws.

To complete these adjustments, Cam knew that they'd have to pull cash from their operating funds. Sophia and Jeremy had to realize it, too. Rawley Harding would go ballistic. But if Lamere was right, they had little choice. When they finished their brainstorming—if he could call it that—at seven, Cam went back to his bar construction. Sophia and Jeremy were taking Lamere on a tour of the town's restaurants, Lamere never having seen the competition. Cam was relieved to be alone, where he could work without thinking. That he had missed the first inning of the baseball game aggravated him more than it should have.

"Why don't you knock off and go with us?" Sophia said, having come back into the restaurant after leaving thirty seconds earlier.

"I can't," he said. "I've got to poly this. It's better to do it now when no one's here. I'm going to get the gas mask on and the whole bit. It will still stink in the morning, but it's got to get done."

"It's just one night," she said, "We've already blown your timeline."

"Sophia, to be honest, if I had to listen to those two talk about kitchens all night, I'd murder them. And tomorrow I've got a lot to do so some drunk chef won't have to work with *a hand tied behind his back*."

"Why don't you meet me at the Dockside when you're done? I'll buy."

"I'm just going home. I'll be loopy enough from the poly."

"Are you sure?"

"Positive."

She kissed him on his cheek and he was by himself. One coat tonight and another tomorrow; that's all he wanted. He put on his mask and opened the can. Sure, he would've liked to have hired someone or left it for Scapa. But doing it himself meant it would come out right. He stirred the poly and even through the mask, Cam could feel it oozing into his brain. He listened to the Red Sox start a rally and swept the brush across the bar. It was quiet between pitches. Eventually, he will have accomplished something. He wondered if he wasn't getting high from the fumes. He recalled that after he finished everything here, he'd have to go out and find a job. Again.

CHAPTER THIRTY-FOUR

At one-fifteen, the back roads between the pier and the garage were deserted even by the police. He could have sped and no one would have been the wiser, but he was tired and with one week to go, he wasn't taking chances. Cam had found no choice but to work longer and sleep less. It was the only way they'd finish on time, and he could handle it. He'd sent Sophia home three hours earlier, and when his phone buzzed, he wondered how she'd managed to stay awake. She'd been going at it as hard as anyone. In the darkness of the cab he glanced at his screen as he picked up. He almost dropped the phone when he saw it was Miranda. He'd never deleted her number. He couldn't imagine what she wanted at this hour after all this time.

"Are you drunk dialing me?" he said, smiling. Any anger had long since dissipated.

"That's presumptuous," she said.

"We haven't talked in a long time, and it is pretty late."

"Yet, there you were, ready to answer."

"I've owed you an apology for a while," he said. "I could have acted much less like an asshole that day, but I had a lot of shit going on, and you and Mr. Chicken in identical shorts weren't exactly what I was looking for."

"Understood and accepted," she said, with a bounce in her voice. "I ran into Grayson this week on Newbury. He told me that your parents sold the house and that you'd moved out. And that you're building a restaurant."

"I'm just coming home from work. We open in a week."

"You're working this late? Are they paying you to drink?"

"Actually, I was putting up faux bamboo molding until fifteen minutes ago."

"What's got into you?" she asked.

"It just kind of happened."

"Right," she said. He heard her sigh and breath in and out. "I've been drinking, myself."

"I guessed," he said.

"I owe you an apology, too."

"So you *were* going out with Mr. Chicken." He was proud of the lack of accusatory tone. They could have been discussing the price of beer.

"We'd been getting together. But we never did anything. At least not before you blew up at us."

"You're not with him anymore?"

"We broke up a few weeks ago."

"Too much cluck for your buck?"

"Something like that. So what about this restaurant?"

"Remember that old bait shed out on the pier? We've turned it—almost—into a beautiful space."

"Who? You and Brinkley?"

"No, me and my own crew."

"That's what Grayson said, but I figured he had it wrong."

"Why would you think that?"

"You weren't exactly a world-beater four months ago."

"I haven't changed."

"Don't bullshit me. You're hammering nails until one in the morning. So who's cracking the whip?"

"Me. Jeremy Riley from the Dockside and Sophia Harding are the ones opening the place."

"I know the hunk, but who the hell is she?"

"You know her, too. The little blonde."

"Who?"

"The Ferret." He pulled over to the side of the road. If Sophia was awake, he didn't need to worry her by finding him parked in the driveway talking to his ex-girlfriend.

"I apologize a thousand times," she said, snickering. "Are you going to invite me up when it's done?"

"That might be complicated."

"Why?"

"I happen to be living with Sophia now, too."

"As in roommates or are you two making wild, ferret love?"

"I'm not dignifying that comment with a response."

"So you're fucking the Ferret and you're building her a restaurant?"

"If that's how you want to say it."

"Those are connected in some way?" Miranda asked.

"Yes and no."

"I can't believe it." She was laughing, and he still wasn't annoyed. That probably said more about how things were between he and Sophia.

"You didn't even like her," Miranda said. "Aren't you the one that gave her the nickname?"

"It was the Senator."

"Now there's a fucking creep. So when did you start smooshing with her?"

"Nothing happened until after you. Just like you and Mr. Chicken."

"Oh Christ," she said, laughing again. "I'm supposed to believe that?"

"How drunk are you?" he asked. There was no point in telling the truth when they'd managed to let the hurt fade away.

"Warped enough to call when you're two hours away, and

we haven't spoken in months. I was actually wondering why we never talked afterward."

"We were probably ready to be done," he said. "I don't know."

"Maybe you're right. But now that I'm single and have spent the night sitting around with Marcie and a bottle of Goose, I decided that maybe you weren't so bad. Although after hearing about you and the Ferret, and picturing it, I don't know if I could do it with you again and keep a straight face."

"I wouldn't worry about your chances of finding out."

"I'm sorry," she said. "I shouldn't be so mean."

"Sometimes you can't help it."

"I guess you don't want to come down and see me, then."

"I'll have to pass."

"Well, if you finish the restaurant and she kicks you out, give me a buzz."

"I'll wait until I'm good and drunk," he said.

"I wouldn't hold it against you."

"Thanks for calling," he said. When she said goodbye, her voice seemed a mash up of laughter and melancholy. In another two minutes, he'd be home. He'd sleep for four hours. He and Sophia would get up together. He'd go to work. He wouldn't think about the call once all day.

CHAPTER THIRTY-FIVE

"Don't you have people to do that?"

"Fuck off," Cam said, recognizing Brinkley's voice. He was screwing in a faux brass plate on the men's room door. It was, in fact, something that he didn't trust Scapa to do and have come out level. He turned around and his former boss was standing there grinning.

"I don't know about who you got working here, but the jokers running the kitchen felt the need to tell me the place was closed. They must've thought I was coming in for dinner, and I'm not even in my suit and tie."

"Everyone's on edge. Soft opening tomorrow, then for good on Friday night. If I don't sleep, we might actually make it." He hadn't seen Brinkley in over a month. Of course, he looked the same. The wide stance. White hair curling out of the Sox cap. He must have come from the Dockside. He was in his jeans and a Harley t-shirt.

"Where's your help?"

"Whitworth fell off the wagon this week. He barely made it through the day. One guy's home with his kids. I've got Scapa painting trim up in the private dining room." Cam pointed his drill to the loft above them.

"I saw Whitworth at the 'Side yesterday and figured that might be trouble," Brinkley said. "But I've got to give you credit, man." Brinkley looked around the interior. "I had my doubts."

"Yes, and you didn't have any qualms about voicing them. So what's up?"

"Don't be so sensitive."

"I'm not. I'm just busy. You can give me all the shit you want next week."

"I didn't come to drive a stick up your ass."

"Which begs the question, why the hell are you here?"

"Well, we started tearing down your grandmother's out at Gray Gull and I found something."

"What?"

"An M-1. We came across this panel behind the pantry off the kitchen. I put a bar to it and this whole section came off."

"What the hell is an M-1?"

"A rifle from World War II. It's junk now, rusted up. Maybe you could salvage it, but I don't know. I figured you might want it. I've got it in the truck."

"It must have been my grandfather's. Gram must have forgotten about it, if she even knew it existed. He's been gone a long time." Cam drove the last screw and led Brinkley out the front door.

"How has it been?" Brinkley asked.

"Okay. I've got a punch list a mile long. Some of these details, if I'd known about them—god, forbid—beforehand, they might have been taken care of by now. But you know how that goes."

"You really got that much?"

"Seriously, I might not sleep until tomorrow night."

Brinkley opened the door of the truck and pulled out the rifle. The barrel was rusted and the canvas shoulder strap was musty and covered with mold. The dark wood had mottled.

Cam couldn't budge the action. He opened his truck and slid it behind the seat.

"Thanks, Brinkley, I appreciate it."

"The place looks good in there."

"I've done nothing but work. Lost fifteen pounds in the process. Sophia says I look more like a distance runner now than she does."

"Haven't seen you at the Dockside."

"Let me guess. Nothing's changed, even with the pretty boy over here."

"Thora's running the place. She hired a couple college girls to take his place. They're not too quick with the drinks, but they're pleasant to look at while you're waiting."

"Senator still holding court?"

"Always."

They stood there for a minute looking at each other. The lobster boats strained quietly against the tide. Yellow light poured into the parking lot from the high dining room windows. The evergreens were backlit by the kitchen. Cam noticed the spot illuminating the black sign created a glare. They'd have to change to a lower watt bulb.

"When does the house come down?" Cam asked.

"Next week."

"Good luck with that."

"It's a job," Brinkley said.

"Well, I've got to get back to my list."

"You got any work a dummy could do?"

"If I could get Jeremy to stop polishing his liquor bottles, I'd even use him."

"I can skip the Tavern tonight if you can use me."

"I could use you. I just can't afford you."

"Call it professional courtesy."

"Really?"

"Don't make me beg. You can buy me a beer with the fat check you're going to get in a few days."

"Come on then," Cam said, stunned, but realizing how much even a few hours of Brinkley could accomplish.

Brinkley walked into the restaurant behind Cam. What a relief to be able to point in a direction, explain what needed to happen, and rest easy that it would get done quickly and correctly. He let him work in the dining room, so he could talk to Jeremy, who was stocking liquor behind the bar. Cam went into the kitchen and humped for Lamere and his two flunkies, who were piecing together dunnage racks. Cam put up shelves. One thing the restaurant wouldn't be short on was storage space. At midnight, Lamere cooked burgers and herbed home fries for everyone. Although Jeremy and Lamere left after eating, Cam stayed until three and Brinkley hung with him. Sophia stayed, too. Cam's eyes hurt by the time he left. Sophia clung to him as if he were holding her up.

When they got home and the door shut behind them, clothes were shed. He thought back to that first night when everything seemed to come at a hundred miles an hour. They reached the bed naked and fell in next to each other. Her hair smelled of the Lemon Pledge with which she had been polishing the woodwork. He slid his hand over the sinewy muscles of her hips. She slid next to him so her ass cushioned his groin. Then they were asleep.

CHAPTER THIRTY-SIX
"Senator" Grimes

Few vehicles were left in the parking lot. The breeze lay nearly still; only occasionally could one hear water lapping against the hulls of the lobster boats. At the far end of the pier, a lone spotlight shaded the green water blue, and shadows floated on its placid surface. The metal bait shed, designed solely for functionality, commanded one end of the pier. In front of me was the FishHouse, with its illuminated black sign and carved golden lettering. Without my influence, neither edifice would exist. Yet, I was grossly overlooked this evening.

Some might take offense. It could have been construed a simple oversight had not my request for a reservation for Friday night, the grand opening, been denied, as well. But then, when one has wronged another, embarrassment over the initial action can compound the difficulty. I could have allowed the affront to dissipate over time, as these things are wont to do. But I could not overlook the failure of my so-called friend to fulfill what should have been an obligation. It was with a calm righteousness that I entered the building.

I was immediately confronted by a podium with the FishHouse logo, a silhouette of the building's visage that I had just witnessed from outside. Remarkable that they had been able to construct the place while spending so much time on unneeded decoration, as if one would forget the name of the establishment having just entered it. To the right was the main dining room with its wall of windows. A bar ran the width of the far end. The kitchen staff, in soiled chef coats, was gathered at a table with Jeremy. In front of the divider that separated the lounge from the diners, Cam Preston, Brinkley, and a few others sat at a round table littered with beer bottles. Sophia Harding was to Preston's left, practically in his lap. What surprised me was Jeremy's obliviousness to their heat. Perhaps his broken heart, the subject of much theater, had been overcome by the self-actualization of fulfilling his dream, even if it was nothing more pedestrian than the opening of a restaurant. The concept of taking food, cooking it, and having someone carry it to a table remains an odd business plan, if one considers it as such. Yet, there we all are, everyday, social animals.

"Senator," Preston yelled, the first to notice me. "Come have a drink."

Sobriety had obviously passed him by, but who could blame him? His brothers in the building trade had all doubted his ability to complete this job. They did not tell him that, of course, but jokes at his expense flew across my table like lightning bugs this summer. He had proved them wrong. For that he deserved respect and the right to drink his fill.

Upon Preston's gleeful shout, Jeremy gazed upon me with widening eyes. Yes, he was surprised. Everything must have been as he wanted it until my presence sent a fissure through the illusion. The self-absorbed create a world that others might not recognize. His face collapsed and then struggled to compose itself. While the cooks returned to their conversation, Jeremy's eyes did not leave my face. In the midst of his domain, the ceiling fans slowly turning, the splashes of color on the walls, and then the bar with its sparkling bottles and mirrors, so neatly arranged, he was worried. My presence provided the snap of a challenge. He rose from the table and slowly made his way over to me.

"What brings you here, Senator?" he asked. He did not offer his hand.

"I thought I would stop by and see the place. After all, it is town property. I know how busy you have been, and I did not wish to interfere during business hours."

"The funny thing is," Jeremy said, "this is normal business hours for us."

"Of course, and I'm aware that you've met code in every way, but I wanted to judge the aesthetic value for myself. It's an investment for all of us of in Laurel, is it not?"

"Get the man a drink," Preston said. Sophia ignored him, but watched me.

"Perhaps you could give me a tour anyway," I said, "if you are not so busy."

"We're having a meeting."

"I can wait."

"Fine. Let's get it over with."

A cursory walk-through revealed that the place looked like a restaurant. Imagine that. The walls in the dining room glossed and shined. White linen hung neatly over tables. Wine glasses sparkled. A promised bottle of Gosling's sat in a row on the back bar. Stools were lined up straight like soldiers. Freezers and refrigerators hummed quietly and efficiently in the kitchen. Gleaming stainless steel brightened the space there, which would probably never again be as clean as it now appeared. In a few days, bacteria would inevitably start multiplying, unseen and undeterred.

We climbed the stairs to the loft. I was shown a private dining room that overlooked the harbor. People would spend thousands for the privilege to perch there like peacocks, that was obvious. I entered; Jeremy waited a beat before he realized that I wished him to follow.

"I can understand why I wasn't invited to tonight's festivities," I said. "It might have looked inappropriate, and I assumed that was your reasoning. But I feel that an explanation is in order as to why when I phoned, I wasn't given a table for the grand opening on Friday."

"I'm sorry about that," Jeremy said. "We've been booked full for weeks." Lucky for him, a smile did not add to the smugness in his voice.

"Surely, there are tables saved for such special circumstances."

"Not for that night."

"I've got to admit, Jeremy, that this treatment confuses me. We've been friends for years. I helped you greatly and generously when you came to me. Was I not instrumental in helping you get this establishment off the ground?"

"You played a part," Jeremy said. "But it wasn't exactly the one offered up in our discussion. I think we were sold short on services provided. The reservation book is full for opening night."

"Didn't things go exactly as you wished? Aren't we standing here in your restaurant?"

"I've been around a bit myself, Senator, and I know a scam when I see one. I'm embarrassed that you have the balls to come in here, expecting something more than your free drinks. You didn't do shit for us that wouldn't have happened on its own. It must have taken less than a minute to convince Wilpon and Shannon, who own tourist-oriented businesses, that an establishment that would bring more tourists to the area was a good idea. How did you ever manage it? You let me be absolutely ridiculed at that meeting, then your code enforcement lackeys were up our asses the minute Preston started working. Do you call that help?"

"Yes, I would. Everything above board and legal. That's a reality."

"Like I said, it was going to happen anyway."

"What would you consider the negotiation of a favorable lease?"

"You were boxed into a corner by then. At first, I made a simple mistake and I appreciate how you let us correct that. But we were ready to move, and it would have cost the town money if you had waited for someone else. As for the lease, Rawley Harding doesn't think it's the greatest deal ever written."

I had to laugh.

"Without my help you would still be pushing papers from the town hall to the EPA offices in the state capitol. The beauty of how this played out is that conditions were created that left no one suspicious. There are many in this town and state who would claim that I significantly overlooked professional responsibilities to facilitate this for you. I acted out of friendship and now you treat me like I'm some sort of heel."

"You come in Saturday night, Senator, and bring three of your closest friends. I'll take good care of you and then that's it, we're even. But Friday, opening night, that's booked. I'm sorry, but that's the way it is in the restaurant business. All above board."

"Government often moves at a snail's pace," I said. "You do read the newspapers, don't you? Your experience was quite different." The blank look on his face revealed his failure to understand this simple concept.

"I'm well aware of how government works, because all I've done for the last two months is deal with one set of brainless inspectors after another. But it's over. You and I have been friends for a long time, and I can appreciate that. However, there's nothing I can do about Friday night. Like I said, Saturday you can have the best table in the house, and I'll take care of you personally."

He held out his hand, as if the pitiful gesture would rectify the matter. I shook it anyway.

When we emerged from the room, Sophia Harding was poised at the bottom of the stairs, her notable brow furrowed in rows. Perhaps she thought that she had reason to be concerned over her former paramour's bull-headedness.

"Hello, Sophia. How are you this evening?" I asked.

"Good." She looked confused. Jeremy stood beside her. I smiled at him.

"If something should open up for Friday evening, I would suggest that you notify me. I'd be glad to support a local business."

"Sure, Senator," Jeremy said, looking unappreciative of the face-saving opportunity I had just given him. I doubted his ability to realize it was even there, never mind my response should he fail to take it.

CHAPTER THIRTY-SEVEN

Two nights earlier, during the soft opening, they had fed forty people between six and eight o'clock. The servers had performed well, food had come out on time, and it had tasted great and looked good. Rawley had come in with Tia and gushed about it. Friends from Fore Street had thanked Jeremy for the invitation and were effusive in their praise. Preston and his crew of misfits had cleaned their plates as if they hadn't eaten in weeks. Even Marv Daniels had said that everything was wonderful. It had been wise to invite him, as he needed to realize that Jeremy's restaurant wasn't in direct competition with him—it was something far more substantial and elegant. Really, the night could not have gone better.

They had spent Thursday preparing for the true test, tonight. Steps of service were reiterated to the servers. Bus people were given further direction. Lamere tweaked some menu items that he deemed too labor intensive for an opening. It was better to scale back than be overwhelmed, he reasoned. Jeremy, Sophia, and Lamere had met in the private dining room, with the harbor below them. There had been none of short-sightedness and cover-your-ass mentality that disrupted so many other operations. They were working as a team. Now that Preston had been regulated to more or less of a maintenance man—albeit a well-invested one—much of the conflict and stress had been eliminated. They had all worked hard to get to this place. Doors would open in thirty minutes and they were ready.

He should have been exhausted, Jeremy reasoned. Just from the excitement, he hadn't been able to sleep more than six hours a night for a week. But as he stood at the end of the bar surveying his restaurant, Jeremy bounced on his toes as if he were back in college getting ready for a jump ball. He wanted to grab the Gran Marnier bottle and throw one down, something he could not do. There would be no missteps. He'd spent years working for people who didn't have the drive to make their places the best they could be. That was not going to be him.

The space was practically as he had imagined it. The nautical paneling that he had railed against and that Preston and Sophia guaranteed would deliver the look that they wanted had come out great. The tables, four tops and deuces that formed the middle of the dining room were pine, but covered with linen a shade darker than the walls. The booths and banquettes that ran along the outside of the room were lacquered a light walnut, a subtle contrast as the eye line ran from light to dark to the harbor.

Sophia had picked the colors and accents with artistry. On the wall behind the bar, between the two shelves holding the bottles, was a four-by-eight foot painting that she had done in college. He'd never seen it until she and Cam had driven it in, with her clutching it in the bed of his truck. It was a storm, with swirling blues from near black to royal. In the midst of the waves of color, a ghost of a sailboat persevered. In the upper corner was a flash of gold, as if something waited there, nearly in reach.

Sophia had sat there yesterday and gazed at it as Preston

had bullshitted, claiming to deconstruct its symbolism of color and shape, and what its placement meant above the backlit bottles, which he had likened to the stained glass of a church. Jeremy didn't know about the scheme any more than it looked like a fiendish reflection of the water that lay outside the windows. But more than anything save for the harbor behind them, it solidified the atmosphere. Not long after entering, one's eyes were drawn to it.

The lighting that came down from the ceiling on wires suspended at different heights covered the dining room in more waves. Jeremy looked down the bar, comprised of weathered wood that had its own stories to tell, even with its surface glistening and smooth. You could touch it and then you couldn't.

The servers sat at the round in the middle of the dining room, waiting for Lamere to come out with pre-service instructions. They were a good looking crew, with a few veterans thrown in, not so beautiful or handsome, but there to carry the load. A great restaurant had balance. He had known that and hired accordingly. By September, just in time for the fall season, they would be running on all cylinders. He congratulated himself on a job well done.

From his position at the end of the bar, he could command the restaurant like the captain of a ship. He had a straight shot down its twelve seats, and of Marybelle and Todd, filling juices and talking in quiet voices. To the left of the floor were the doors to the kitchen. He'd be able to follow service throughout the room and identify potential problems before they appeared at a table. Although the front desk was at the far end of the building, over the heads of his seated guests, he'd have a clear view there, too.

Sophia was all but hidden by the host desk, flipping pages on the reservation sheet. She wore her Victoria Secret little black dress. She'd had it for years and its sheen indicated that it probably needed replacement, but it still worked. He remembered times, there must have been more than one, when he ran his hands over her hips and it had seemed to vanish. Her hair was the gold of the flurry in the painting behind him. It could have been harder being around her, had not bringing this restaurant to life consumed him. He'd had so much to think of that her dalliance with Preston produced nothing more than an occasional dull ache in the back of his mind. That situation would take care of itself at some point. He couldn't waste time or energy thinking about it. Above all, there was the FishHouse.

Lamere and his sous chef, Hector Villareal, came out from the double doors and approached the service staff. Their white chef coats were spotless. Jeremy nodded at his bartenders and they walked over and sat at a deuce behind them. Sophia and Kim McIntire, the other hostess, moved over from their desk. The bus kids, former employees of the Squalor, stopped polishing glasses and joined them. Lamere welcomed everyone and reminded them that though they had done well on Wednesday, this would be different. The key would be communication. While Hector ran the line, Lamere would be expediting, and all food would pass through his hands. If they worked together, things would go smoothly. Lamere detailed the night's one special, a monkfish grilled and wrapped in bacon. Then, as they had planned, he invited Jeremy to say a few words.

Jeremy strode to the center of the restaurant with his back to the windows. All eyes were on him. He was sure that had the Queen Mary pulled into the small harbor, their gazes wouldn't have left his face. For the first time in months, activity inside the FishHouse had come to a stop.

"This is it folks," he said, careful to make contact with everyone. "You've been hired here because you are the best at what you do. Our goal is for The FishHouse to be the best restaurant not only in Laurel but the entire state. If we can achieve that, we'll all be happy. We're creating a destination here.   One that might pay for new cars or houses or a fine designer jacket." He brushed his lapel and everyone laughed. "Like Chef Lamere said, this will require us all to pull in the same direction. And please don't forget, I'm here for you. I'll be with you every step of the way. If you need a table bussed or have a question about the wine list or you're having trouble with the register, let me know and I'll help. Of course, if you need some drunk Neanderthal thrown out, that's when you grab Sophia."

Again, everyone laughed.

"I'm grateful you're all here," he said. "Let's do our jobs. An opening night is never easy, but it is the first step to being a success."

They gave him an ovation. He looked at his watch. They were to open in fifteen minutes.

He was at the host stand going over the seating plan one more time with Sophia and Kim. He tried not to stare down the substantial cleavage exposed by Kim's red dress—another bonus in greeting the customers. Seating would be the most critical factor these first weeks. How many times had he seen a kitchen get slammed and flame out due to over-booking? It was a typical rookie mistake. Even if there were empty tables in the dining room, he would hold them back and have people wait at the bar. A kitchen needed time to find its rhythm and pace. At the beginning, it was better to be modest and great, rather than try to cram the place and invite disaster.

With ten minutes to go, he went to the front door and surveyed the lot, currently empty but soon to be full. He waved for Sophia to follow him. The air was wet and hot and she looked up into his eyes.

"We did it," he said, bending down to hold her.

"Yes we did," she said, hugging back.

"Once you brought up this idea, I knew that it would get done. Now we just have to work it. Everything we hoped it would be, it is."

"You should thank him, too," Sophia said, as Preston's shitty little Ranger rolled over the hill.

To say that he had doubted Preston's ability would have been a more than considerable understatement. Sophia and her father practically strong-armed him to accept Cam as the builder. But goddamn, the putz had delivered. He'd gotten it done for less money and in less time than anyone had thought possible. Not even so-full-of-himself Brinkley—who had graced them with his presence a few nights before, as if to claim a piece of something he had wanted nothing to do with—could have pulled it off. There were those bastards from Portland, too, who thought it couldn't be built without doubling the GNP of the state. How wrong they were. The guy had worked himself into disrepair. Preston looked like an addict: pale and thin, scraggly and beat up. But Cam hadn't worked any harder than Jeremy, and he'd taken advantage of his position by leveraging his way in. So be it, Jeremy thought. He had kept to his agreement and remained a silent partner concerning restaurant operations. If he stayed out of the way, he would prosper, at least as far as the business went.

Back inside, Jeremy waited at the host desk. Precisely at five o'clock, two couples, the Macedos and the Strouts, owners of a pair of Laurel's B and B's, entered the building.

"Welcome to the FishHouse," Jeremy said, bowing. "My restaurant."

It was bad enough that Rawley and Tia were hawking him from table twelve, but Preston's stupid face, staring at him from two feet away, was too much to take. Jeremy hoped that the dolt wouldn't haunt the place every night from here until the end of time. It was as if he wanted to get under Jeremy's skin. Jeremy wiped his brow with a dinner napkin. The last thing he should be worrying about was Preston.

"What's the matter?" Cam asked.

"It's opening night," Jeremy said. "That's plenty." As a rule, nothing went as expected, although Jeremy had fully anticipated that the FishHouse would prove the exception. They had done everything possible to make sure that this wouldn't happen, and yet there it was—the floor was chaos.

"The other night was smooth, wasn't it?" Preston asked.

"Two different animals." Jeremy wanted to add, "you idiot," but did not. The kitchen was dead in the water. A plate hadn't come out in fifteen minutes. Five tables were currently waiting for entrees, and his trip to the line a minute earlier had discovered two sets of appetizers had been forgotten in the convection oven and burned. The front door had been overrun; an additional host should have been scheduled, at least for tonight. Just because Sophia had the money and was willing, it didn't mean that she was experienced. She had already pissed off two parties by telling them they were going to have to wait at the bar. One of them was the GM of 114 Commercial, a restaurant in Portland, who was here with five friends. Jeremy had immediately seated them in one of the banquettes. They were drinking a bottle of Veuve Cliquot that he had comped to soothe them. Greg Oliphant, now on a four top, had come in unannounced from Ogunquit, where he ran the biggest gay bar in the state. Jeremy wasn't going to make him wait, either. The kitchen was just going to have to suck it up and get its shit together.

He went back into the kitchen hoping things had been steered back on track. Lamere was soaked with sweat. He yelled for a salmon and Hector replied three minutes. The rest of the order sat under the lamp and Kelly stood waiting for it, her mascara starting to run. The two sirloins and a chicken accompanying the fish would likely be dried out before she got them to the table. Josie came bursting through the doors, a look of panic on her face. She had just brought table twenty-four's dinners to the deuce on fifty-one, which wasn't even in her station. After taking a bite of the chicken, the party, who Jeremy didn't know, was able to determine that it wasn't haddock, as if they couldn't have seen it and said something first. Of course, Josie could have brought the correct dishes to the correct fucking table. There was another re-cook.

Bruce came in looking for Oliphant's four top, which had been delayed because Hector had had to use a wolf fish for another table that had needed a filet replaced, as well. Bruce scrunched up his thin face, looking at Jeremy as if he expected him to wave a magic spatula and make everything better. Jeremy had been doing everything he could, that was the sad part. Besides taking care of the party from 114, he had talked to six other tables, reassuring them. He had bussed tables, ran cocktails, and ass-kissed from one end of the dining room to the other. What else could he be expected to do?

"These guys better get it together or we're fucked out there," Bruce whispered to him. "I've got Oliphant."

"I need pans," Hector yelled, presumably to the dishwasher.

"Lamere, we need thirty-seven," Jeremy said. "ASAP. VIP."

Lamere looked up from the yellow dupes lined up on his serving shelf and glared. "Every fucking time you come in here it's another fucking big shot. What the fuck happened to pacing the fucking night. Can you tell me that?"

"Just get the food out, for chrissakes. It's not that crowded."

Just as Lamere was going to reply, a crash came from the back of the kitchen.

"I'm on it," Jeremy told Lamere. "You cook."

He trotted around the corner. Tuna, the kid he had taken from the Port Tavern, was standing there looking at the shattered rack of wine glasses at his feet.

"What the hell, man?" Jeremy asked.

"Dropped it."

"Focus."

"Right."

Jeremy took two steps and stopped. Through the pungent sizzle of sirloin steak and the calming smell of the thyme and rosemary, he was stung by the rope-burning stench of cheap marijuana.

"Are you fucking stoned?" Jeremy snapped. Broom in hand, Tuna broke into a grin. Now that Jeremy stood still, he found that the kid reeked. At the height of dinner rush, this kid was taking out their knee caps with a baseball bat.

"Dude, I'm just washing dishes," Tuna said. "I ain't doing geometry."

"Get the fuck out of here," Jeremy said. "Now."

"What's the big deal?" He shook the hair off his forehead like a sheepdog. "No one said that we couldn't."

"Out," Jeremy screamed. The kid shrugged, took off his chef coat, and flung it on top of the broken glasses. He turned and walked out the kitchen door.

Jeremy ran back to the line. "I just fired your dishwasher." Finally, Lamere was plating Oliphant's table. "He was stoned off his ass."

"Then you better get back there and replace him," Lamere said, in a surprisingly calm voice. "Because you aren't pulling anyone from out here."

"We still need those sauté pans," Hector yelled. Jeremy ran back to the dish room and grabbed them from the rack. At least the kid had gotten that far. He brought them to the line and went back to the bar. He needed to think. No, what he needed was a fucking shot. And then a dishwasher. Who could he call? Should he just commandeer a bus boy? He couldn't do it himself, not with what was going on out here.

Though there were only fifteen people scattered across the bar, Todd and Marybelle were struggling as if it were a hundred. Marybelle was paralyzed in front of the wine cooler looking for who-knows-what. Todd was paused in mid-martini because he couldn't find the vermouth, which Jeremy had insisted they place in the speed rack, where anyone would have checked first.

"That was a hell of a crash," Preston said "What was it?"

Jeremy rolled his eyes and walked behind the bar. He grabbed the Gran Marnier bottle and a rocks glass and poured himself two fingers. Then he slugged it down. Regulars of his from the Dockside applauded as he snapped the empty glass onto the bar in front of the glass washer.

"What the hell was that?" Cam asked him.

"Gran Marnier."

"You think that's a good idea?"

"You ever wash dishes?"

"Sure. At home." Preston looked at him with his "I'm thick as shit" brow scrunched down.

"In a restaurant?" Jeremy asked.

"No."

"I had to fire the kid who was back there. He was baked, bad. Lamere needs another body. We can't afford to pull someone from anywhere else. Can you do it?"

"Sure," Preston said. Jeremy smiled. Preston had no idea that it was the most grueling job in the restaurant.

Jeremy took him back into the kitchen. Preston's eyes pinballed trying to follow the activity. Jeremy threw him an apron and put one on himself. He showed him where to scrape the plates and how to load the various racks. Then he got him the steel wool for the sauté pans that he'd have to take care of before they went into the machine. He pointed out the rack where he needed to stack the plates and throw the silverware and glasses once he'd finished with them.

"You think you've got it?" Jeremy asked.

"How hard can it be?" the slug replied.

Jeremy ran out to the line and told Lamere that he'd thrown a body back there. Lamere nodded and called for the meat for another table.

Back in the dining room, Jeremy ran over to Oliphant's party.

"How is everything, Mr. Oliphant?" he asked, looking magnanimously around the table.

"It was worth the wait," Oilphant said. "Blaise, what was that you said about the wolf fish?"

"De-licious." Jeremy smiled down at the happy round face topped with a blond crew cut.

"How is it going?" Oliphant asked, placing his fork down parallel to his plate.

"Busy."

"Who would have thought?" he replied. "Kidding."

"Well, I'm glad you're enjoying yourselves," Jeremy said, and retreated to his end of the bar. He looked over at the 114 table who had just received their entrees. After stopping by to see that everything was fine, he made his way to Sophia and Kim at the desk.

"Did you hear what happened?" he asked Sophia.

"No, but I saw you grab Cam."

"He's washing dishes right now."

Sophia looked at him as if he'd sent her precious Cam to Afghanistan.

"The kid from the Tavern was stoned," Jeremy said. "Totally."

"Does Cam know what he's doing?"

"He's learning."

"You could help him."

"He's a big boy, as we know." Jeremy nodded and went by some tables he had neglected. They had been lucky enough to get to their food on time. Before he had finished talking to them, he noticed Sophia running back and slipping into the kitchen. As if Cam—a fucking partner in the place—couldn't do a high school kid's work for a few hours without some encouragement. It made him sick. All of it made him sick.

The night was not the triumph he had envisioned. It was apparent that he was going to have to make some changes. Key people had let him down. Sophia had had no idea how to seat the dining room. She had crushed the kitchen right at the peak of regular business, so that when he needed to get certain people a table, the load was too much. Lamere should have better prepared his people, too. Of course, they were going to get slammed. That's what happened at good restaurants. Lamere should have overstaffed or tried to feed more guests at the soft opening. Jeremy would have to take a more active role in the strategic planning of the kitchen. Just because a chef could cook didn't mean that he could manage.

The wait staff, now doing their cash outs at tables in the center of the room, had run around with no clue for much of the night. But as he had led their training, he knew that was a result of the kitchen and hosts' poor performances. By the end of service, they had brought things under control. His people had done the best they could under the circumstances.

He was contemplating these matters while he sipped a Gran Marnier and watched Marybelle and Todd clean the bar. Sophia and Kim sat at the end near the wall, counting up the totals for the night and looking at the sheet for tomorrow. Maybe Jeremy would need to spend time at the host desk, too, until he could train them properly or find someone with more experience. It was going to be a hard road. He simply didn't have time to do everything. He was just about to go over and share his thoughts with Sophia and Kim when Lamere came out of the kitchen, his arm around Cam's shoulder.

"I was just saying," Lamere said, "this is the guy who saved our fucking ass tonight. Right when we were getting a grip on things, we lose the dishwasher and this hammerhead jumps in. Let me buy this man a beer."

Todd looked over to Jeremy, who nodded.

"Two Buds," Lamere said. "And I'll have a shot of Jack."

Preston looked like he had worked, at least. He'd sweat through his linen shirt, probably the only decent piece of clothing he owned and likely something that Sophia had bought for him. His hair was matted down as if he'd been swimming. Sophia got up and walked over to Cam and kissed him.

"Thank you," she said.

"Maybe I'll wash dishes tomorrow night if that's how we're paying off," Lamere said. He didn't wait long to down his whiskey.

"It was the least I could do after killing myself on the place for months."

"It'll be the rest of us who'll be killing ourselves from here on out," Lamere said.

"I'll drink to that," Cam said. "I really could live without being drafted like that again."

"Worst job in the entire restaurant," Jeremy said.

"You could have mentioned that when you grabbed me," he said, smiling.

"You've got to do what you've got to do," Jeremy said.

"Well, we survived," Lamere said, polishing off his beer and waving Todd over for another one.

"That's not how I would term success," Jeremy said, shaking his head.

"I know there were some fucking problems. But what did you expect on an opening night? There are always going to be kinks."

"I realize that. I just thought you, meaning the kitchen, would have an easier time keeping up. We tried to pace it steady and slow."

"Like hell," Lamere said, calmly. "Look at the sheet. We got slammed at seven-thirty. You put down three large parties that weren't on the books. A five top and a six top, and then another six top. With everything else going on, what did you think was going to happen? That sunk us for two hours. You girls have got to cut that shit out for a few weeks."

"Don't blame us," Kim said. "We were going to have two of those parties to wait at the bar, but—"

"All right everyone," Jeremy said. "We're certainly not going to break down the night now. We'll look at things and adjust for tomorrow."

Lamere looked from Kim to Sophia to Jeremy.

"I don't want to be blamed for something that I didn't do," Kim said.

"No one's blaming you," Sophia said.

"Actually," Lamere said, laughing. "I was blaming both of you. But I apologize if you were overruled."

"We could not have those parties wait," Jeremy said. "They were too important. Everyone needs to realize that I'm going to make decisions, and they're not always going to popular. That's just the way it is."

"But," Kim said, "you're the one who told us not to do what you went ahead and did."

"I think I know what's best for the place," Jeremy said, looking around the room. His voice had risen louder than he'd intended. The servers had stopped their counting. Lamere was shaking his head. Sophia was biting her bottom lip. Kim, the poor, stupid girl whose greatest assets were her tits, was bright red. Preston looked as if he wanted to punch him. He'd like to see that.

"Everyone calm down," Sophia said. "It will be easier tomorrow. We all worked really hard tonight. Let's everyone have a drink. I'm buying."

CHAPTER THIRTY-EIGHT

After three months of sixteen-plus hour days, Cam had never been as tired as he was at that moment. He'd been waiting at the bar for twenty minutes, listening to Lamere brag about how much Thai snapper soup they'd sold and how they had three stock pots going right now in the kitchen to prep for tomorrow. While Lamere started on a bottle of scotch, Cam turned down another beer. All he could think about was collapsing into their bed. That was provided Sophia and Jeremy ever finished their office work or whatever they needed to do to close down the restaurant. He'd hoped they were just going to throw the receipts in the safe and get out. Apparently, there was more to it than that. Likely, nothing was going any easier with the books than it had with the seating and cooking.

He stood up and crossed the floor. He crept up the stairs like an old man, pulling himself up by the railing. He wanted to tell her he was leaving. He'd wait at home, although he couldn't make any promises that he would be awake.

He ran his fingers over the faux bamboo along the loft, which really did look good. The office, a ten by twelve room at the parking lot end of the second floor, was as etched into his mind as every other part of the building. It had been finished with the remnants of the construction. Tan paint covered the walls and leftover wainscoting served as trim. He'd installed a small porthole as a window to let in some light. He'd also gotten Sophia to put up two of her paintings, one yellowish swirling thing that looked like a typhoon and then one of her cloudy seascapes. One metal desk sat on the far wall, and the other, a crooked wooden thing he'd shored up with shims, was perpendicular to it. He supposed it wasn't bad for what it was.

He swung open the door, a two-panel basic pine that they'd stained chestnut, and walked in without looking. It took an effort to lift his head, and he saw it before the word "Hey" left his mouth. Sophia, at the wooden desk, had spun her chair around so that she was poised to work on Jeremy's. Only they weren't working. Jeremy had his hands on her shoulders and he was kissing her. She was kissing him.

Cam's head dropped.

"What the fuck," he said to himself. He didn't bother to close the door, bolting down the stairs and out of the building. The Ranger's engine came to life. He didn't stop until the end of Pier road, where he pounded the steering wheel with both fists. 12:15 glowed at him in green. He went to the Tavern.

CHAPTER THIRTY-NINE

Cam had forgotten it was August and that the place would be crowded. He squeezed through some New Yorkers with their goddamn Yankees hats. A group of Bostonians sat at one end of the bar, the lack of "r's" in their speech already grating. Some of the Euro's that worked at the Hermit Crab Inn were huddled around the service station. At least they kept to themselves.

Janie smiled for him and came over to get his order. Before he could get it out, she said that she'd heard he'd done an awesome job on the FishHouse and that she was headed there on her next night off. Cam rolled his eyes, spit out a "thanks," and ordered a Bud and a shot of Jim Beam. He settled onto a stool and arranged his drinks, deciding which to pound first, then reached for the shot glass. Before he could get the bourbon to his lips, Horton materialized next to him, his face bloated in a smile and his chubby hand held out to be shaken. Cam returned the drink to the bar top, but didn't let go of it.

"Hey man, how're you doing?" Horton said, putting his ignored hand in his pocket. "I haven't seen you all summer."

"Some of us have to actually show up to our jobs."

"I heard you were building Jeremy's restaurant. See, things worked out for you after all."

"Like a dream," Cam said.

"I hope we can put that stuff behind us."

"What stuff?" Cam asked.

"You know," Horton said. "My little miscalculation. The finger you carved on my garage. Looking back, it's all pretty funny. Of course, we didn't think so at the time, right?"

"I told you it wasn't me," Cam said, deciding that Horton must be drunk.

"Come on," Horton said, grinning.

"If you think I did it and that I've been lying to you, why the hell are you talking to me? Why wouldn't it be: 'That Preston, he's an asshole. I wouldn't piss on him if he were on fire.' Instead, you're on me like we're long lost friends. What's wrong with you?"

"I guess I'm not full of myself like some people around here," Horton said. He shrugged and walked down the bar.

Cam supposed he deserved that crack. But he wouldn't have cared what Horton thought of him, even if his life hadn't imploded fifteen minutes earlier. Left alone, Cam downed his shot. He had two more before he let himself think about what he'd seen.

There was no doubting his vision. He'd been tired, not blind. Brinkley had been right about all of it. It was odd, though, that he'd never had an inkling of anything going on between she and Jeremy. But he'd proven himself obtuse before. Those two just had too much tied up in each other and that place for it not to happen. As always, he was the last to realize it. The world wouldn't start playing by different rules now just because he wanted it so, hadn't he learned that? It hadn't with Miranda. It hadn't with his grandmother. It hadn't with his parents and his uncle. It hadn't with Brinkley. Hope was no match for common sense. That shouldn't have come as a shock to him, either, but there was his hand, shaking as he lifted a bottle of beer to his mouth.

He tried to think of ways that could explain that he didn't see what he knew he had. Maybe he was afraid of commitment and his mind had imagined it. Maybe they were whispering. Maybe it was a friendly peck, congratulations for their accomplishment—something that wouldn't have existed if not for him. Perhaps she was thinking of him as she was kissing Jeremy. God, he was disgusting himself.

"Where's the rest of the crew?" Brinkley said, thumping him on the back. "Why isn't everyone out celebrating?"

"I think they went to the Brewery." That's what the staff had been talking about, anyway.

"Then why are you here?"

"I've had enough of them."

Brinkley waved forth a couple of drinks. Cam glanced around the bar. Some of the guys that Brinkley fished with, pavers by trade, were standing at one of the tall tables waiting for him.

"What the fuck did you do today?" Cam asked.

"Reynolds nailed a six hundred pound yellow fin, split three ways on the boat. You know how much that's worth?"

"Good for you."

"Are you going to tell me what's under your skin or should I just let you fucking sit here like a teenage girl?"

"I just want to drink," Cam said.

"Don't be a douche bag," Brinkley said. "This should be a big night for you."

"Really?" Cam said. "First, I washed dishes for four hours because Jeremy fired some kid in the middle of the dinner rush. Then I went to the office to grab Sophia and leave, and I found that asshole with his tongue down her throat. At least they hadn't got to the fucking yet. Look on the bright side, I always say."

"Shit," Brinkley said, patting his back.

"Don't say it," Cam said. "You want to do a shot with

me?"

"Sure."

"After all I did, that's what I get."

"One might not have anything to do with the other."

"Don't you be getting all logical. I don't know how much more I can take."

"You knew the deal."

"Well, fuck that. It doesn't make it right."

"Here we go again. What are you going to do?"

"I'm going to get as liquored up as I can between now and when Janie kicks me out. I'm not going back to Sophia's, that's for sure. I'll spend the night in the truck if I have to."

"You can crash on my couch. Just don't do anything stupid before I leave."

"It's too late for that," Cam said.

Brinkley nodded, squeezed his shoulder and returned to his fishing buddies.

Cam ordered another round. The twenty he pulled out of his pocket was crumbled into a ball. At least he thought it was a twenty when he threw it onto the bar as if rolling dice.

"Are you all right?" Janie asked.

"Dandy," he said, trying to pull her into focus. He attempted to smile.

"Are you sure?"

"I'll be right back." He hadn't pissed in what seemed like forever. He slid off the stool and stood on his feet. Then he was on his face. Something had tripped him.

He was in the parking lot and Brinkley had one hand under his arm, carrying him.

"What the hell just happened?" Cam said.

"Earthquake," Brinkley said. "So, I'm doing you and Janie a favor and getting you out of there."

"Thanks. But before we go anywhere, I got to piss."

Brinkley dragged him to over to edge of the parking lot, near a row of hemlocks. He maneuvered into the middle of the trees and propped himself against some branches, so he would remain upright. He pulled out his dick and let go. It was the best he'd felt all night. He climbed out of the tree and there was Brinkley.

"If you're on my couch, you better be able to hit the wastebasket when you puke. Or I can bring you back to the little tramp's and you can throw up all over the place, which might exact some measure of revenge."

"Take me home," he said.

"Mine or Sophia's?"

"Is my grandmother's house still standing?" he asked.

"Until Monday."

"I'll sleep there."

"Are you fucking kidding me? It's stripped bare. There's not even a door on it."

"Who cares?"

"You come with me," Brinkley said.

"Brinkley, take me to the beach house, please." Cam reached out to support himself on Brinkley's truck.

"Fine. You can piss and puke all over the place if you want. It doesn't matter. But you're going to have to find your way back tomorrow. I'm not playing taxi for twenty-four hours."

"Thanks, Brinkley."

"Don't mention it."

CHAPTER FORTY

"What the hell was that?" Lamere asked him before Jeremy reached the bottom of the stairs. "Cam goes running out, then Sophia races after him. She comes back in, goes up to the office, then runs out again."

"The star-crossed lovers had a bit of a problem," Jeremy said.

"Why, did he catch you fucking her?" Lamere was hunched over one of the tables in front of the bar. His left eye was three-quarters closed. A half-full snifter sat in front of him.

Jeremy walked past him. He pulled the Gran Marnier bottle from its spot and poured himself a short one. He was dizzy enough. He should have been happier about finally driving the stake through Sophia and Preston. He licked his lips and drank.

"Well?" Lamere asked.

"Don't be that guy," Jeremy said.

"You can't say you don't want to, the way you look at her, man."

"Shut up, Lamere. If I were you I'd be worrying about

your own shit." Jeremy nodded to the kitchen.

"We kicked ass," Lamere said.

"I wouldn't say that," Jeremy replied. "You did okay, but we'll need to be a lot better."

"We sold out of wolf fish. We sold thirty-seven bowls of the Thai soup. We sold sixteen New York strips. The only problem spots were when you overbooked the dining room. You got to cut that shit out."

"No, you've got to pick up the slack."

"No worries," Lamere said. "We will. Openings ain't easy."

"You're right about that."

"We're booked for the next three nights, Sophia said."

Sophia said, Jeremy thought. She said there was no chance they'd ever get back together. She'd said other things, too. That he was selfish and short-sighted and disrespectful. She'd been hurt by what he did. But she'd been right there before that, gazing at him with her grateful eyes. Maybe he was too full of himself. It would have only been a matter of time before she and Preston split up anyway, more than likely because of him. Instead of being overcome by the moment, he should have been patient. By blowing up her fairytale, he'd made himself the bad guy. He'd have to act as if he was sorry, too, and truthfully, he hadn't wanted to wound her like that. He'd have to wear his remorse when she was around or she'd stonewall him.

"Let's get the fuck out of here," Jeremy said. "Tomorrow's another long day. We've got a lot to discuss, front of the house and back. What time do you want to meet?"

"You've got to do something about Marybelle, the bartender. Every food order she took had some fucking instructions. Substitute mashed for the fingerlings. Wolf fish with the salmon prep. Well done frites with the steak. Over and over. We're not ready to handle that shit yet."

"I'll talk to her."

"The desk, whoever is running it, can't load up on the big parties all at once like that."

"Save it for the morning," Jeremy said.

"Yeah," Lamere said. "I've got to be here goddamn early. The stocks I've got on will be done around seven or eight, and then I've got a prep list a mile long."

"I'll show you how to lock up," Jeremy said.

Jeremy did a circuit through the building, Lamere stumbling behind him. They checked the windows over the harbor to make sure they were fastened. They shut down the lights behind the bar. In the kitchen, the delivery doors were locked. Jeremy inspected the cleanliness of the work stations. Lamere walked behind the line to make sure the ovens were off. He wiped down the cutting board, which should have been done before he let his crew hit the bar. He was adjusting the flames on the stock pots when Jeremy stepped in ankle-deep shredded romaine at the grande manger station.

"What the fuck?" Jeremy yelled.

"Hunh?" Lamere said, throwing down the rag he'd been wiping things with. He came around from the line.

"It's a fucking jungle down there." Jeremy pointed to the mess. "You motherfuckers didn't even sweep."

"I'll get on them," Lamere said. "The guys were in the middle of cleaning when I called them out for a beer. I guess we got a little happy."

"The party's over," Jeremy said. "It's real business from here out."

"No worries, Jeremy," Lamere said, nodding. "This place will look like an operating room tomorrow."

At the front door Jeremy tried to show Lamere how to set the alarm, but the Chef was too drunk to focus. He locked the door behind them and they walked to their cars, Lamere practically swaying. Jeremy would have to keep an eye on his chef's drinking. But it was their first night and they all had more than usual. Before he climbed into his MG, Jeremy took one last look at the place. He was sure he'd never forget how the gold lettering glistened against the gloss black of the sign.

CHAPTER FORTY-ONE

"I fucked up," she said, walking circles in front of her refrigerator with a wine glass in hand. The bottle sat sweating on the counter. "I fucked up. I fucked up. I fucked up."

When she had turned, his face wasn't even in the door. She never saw him; that's how fast it happened. Two seconds of weakness, a disgusting sentimental nostalgia. There was nothing in it for either of them and they should have both known it. Jeremy wouldn't even meet her eyes afterward. She hadn't known whether to slap him or scream or cry. For a second, she hoped she'd imagined it.

"I'm sorry," Jeremy had said. "I shouldn't have done that."

Those words kicked her over and she flew down the stairs. By the time she made it out the door, his truck was tearing from the parking lot. Her keys were at the host stand, but she knew that Cam wouldn't have stopped for anything, especially her.

"Let him go," Jeremy said when she returned to the office. "These last months have been the happiest of my life. Everything is coming together for us."

Sophia sat down in the chair at her desk. She put her

elbows on her knees and her head in her hands.

"You're a selfish son of a bitch," she said. "I've been your friend, but you can't even do that. I was happy, but not because of you."

"It couldn't have been with Preston the way it was with us, when it was good."

"It was better."

"I don't believe that."

"Believe that I'll never be with anyone who has so little respect for me, the way that you do."

She went home. She knew he wouldn't be there, but she hoped. Something shook loose in her chest when she realized that the image beneath the trees in front of the garage wasn't his truck, but a shadow. She sat in her Jeep and cried until she couldn't anymore. She left nine messages on his phone. He wasn't picking up. She didn't know what to do so she opened a bottle of Sonoma Cutrer that he'd bought for her. She was drinking alone, again.

"I fucked up. I fucked up. I fucked up."

Sophia knew how she was going to make this right to him; she was going to be honest. It had been a mistake. She could recognize it for what it was, a small disfigured flash of time, but Cam wouldn't see it like that. He could be emotionally stubborn. She hadn't experienced it herself, but she'd witnessed it with Horton and Brinkley and his family. He wasn't some wretched celebrity or stupid politician's wife who would go along because they imagined they had so much to lose. That's what they saw on TMZ. All Cam had was his own concept of himself. In some ways, she and Cam were the same. Whatever it took to explain that, wherever those words would have to come from, she would find a way.

CHAPTER FORTY-TWO

Brinkley dropped him in front of the beach house. He didn't
see the headlights disappear until he'd turned the corner to the
back porch where the door was missing, just as Brinkley said.
The place had been gutted; that was clear even in the dark. It
smelled like sawdust. He made his way to the steps and
crawled up into his room. Outside the window, it was black.
He couldn't see as far as the ocean. He curled into a fetal
position in the middle of the floor and slept.

Two hours later, he woke up, having to piss. As if on auto-
pilot he walked to the bathroom. He focused in the
moonlight. There was nothing there but a hole in the floor.
What the fuck, he thought. He couldn't bring himself to do it.

He inched back down the stairs and out to the end of his
lopsided deck. The neighbors' houses were dark. The beach
was gray, the water still. He exhaled and shot a stream into the
air and onto the lawn. He hoped the new owners liked the
brand new house that Brinkley was going to build them.

When he turned to go back to his room, he pivoted to the
south. At the edge of his vision, like the spot in the painting, a
glowing orange circle appeared on the edge of his vision. Why

couldn't she have just left him alone? Back in his bedroom, he curled into a ball and slept.

CHAPTER FORTY-THREE

Her phone woke her at three-thirty. She came to consciousness and grabbed for it. When she saw it was Jeremy, she put it back down. Two minutes later it rang again. She shut it off and went back to sleep.

The knocking on the door had force behind it. Her temples throbbed. It was still dark. If it was Jeremy she would kick him in the balls with all the force she had left.

"Sophia," her father yelled. She opened the door and one of the town's policemen was standing next to him. She thought the worst: Cam had crashed.

"Miss Harding," the cop said. "Your restaurant on the pier is on fire. Chief Turkington wants you down there."

"Come on, Sophia," Rawley said. "Where's Cam?"

"I don't know."

"He's not here?"

She shook her head.

"Let's go," Rawley said. "Quickly"

Sophia ran to the bathroom and threw some Advil down her throat. At least Cam hadn't run head-on into some tree thinking of nothing but strangling her. She went into her room and changed out of her black dress. She was shaking when her father put his arm around her and led her to his car. They followed the police cruiser, its blue lights careening off the trees, its siren silent.

"I can't believe this," Rawley said.

"Neither can I."

"So where's Cam?" he asked.

"I don't know, I said."

"Do you think he's already there?"

"I doubt it."

"Did something happen?"

"I fucked up," she said.

"Not with Jeremy?" Rawley said, disappointment drowning his voice.

"Cam walked in at the wrong moment, the only seconds when it ever would have mattered. It makes me sick."

CHAPTER FORTY-FOUR

They could see the glow a mile away at the head of Pier Road, and when she realized what it was her stomach lurched. There were fire trucks from every house in Laurel, as well as three from Milltowne, spread out over the pier. Smoke and flame poured from the kitchen windows, even as water from the fire hoses streamed against it. A noxious cloud of black smothered the pier. The building popped and hissed and crackled. The air was like kerosene, slippery and evil.

Her father held her as they walked closer to where Turk stood with Jeremy. Turk was in jeans and a Red Sox sweatshirt. His badge was tucked into his belt.

"Look at our restaurant," Jeremy said, crying. He stepped closer to her, arms outstretched, and she moved into her father.

"What's the story, Chief?" Rawley asked Turk.

"Alarm went off forty-five minutes ago. When they first got here it was central to the kitchen. They're trying to contain it. They're hoping it don't take down the whole fucking pier."

"Do they have any idea what caused it?"

"They won't know for sure until the fire marshal gets in

there when it's all said and done. But I don't know. Fucking kitchens. A lot can go wrong."

"We were careful," Jeremy said. "It was our first fucking night."

Turk shrugged and aimed his flashlight at the sign. "Looks to me like it's going to be a significant loss."

"What about the sprinklers?" Sophia asked. "Didn't they work?"

"They don't do shit to put it out, Schotzie, says. They'll work to contain it, but that's all you can hope."

"Where's Cam?" Jeremy said. "I called him, too."

"He wasn't at home," Sophia said.

"Preston's missing?" Turk asked, his voice raising. "Where the hell is he?"

"I don't know," she said.

Turk looked back and forth between them. "Is there something going on here?"

"Lover's quarrel," Jeremy said.

"Shut the fuck up," Sophia said.

"I'm sorry," Jeremy said. "All right?"

"No, it's not all right," she said. She saw Turk's eyes flare. It was obvious what he was thinking, even though he knew what kind of person Cam was.

"He probably fucked up the alarms or sprinklers or something," Jeremy said.

"Wrong," Turk said. "Schotzie checked it out himself and stamped it two weeks ago. Before you could even cook."

"He couldn't have been that pissed," Jeremy said.

"What are you talking about?" Turk asked.

"Nothing," Jeremy said. He noticed Sophia's glare. "We just had a little disagreement is all."

"About what?"

"Nothing important," Sophia said.

Lamere came running up to them in a pair of sweatpants and a t-shirt. Even in the storm of smoke, he smelled like booze.

"Holy shit," he said. "You've got to be fucking kidding me."

Jeremy hung a hand over his shoulder.

"I can't believe it, man."

"Who the fuck are you?" Turk asked, eyeing him.

"The fucking executive chef. Who the fuck are you?"

"The chief of police."

"He's cool, Turk," Jeremy said.

Turk raised his eyebrows. "No one," he said, waving his finger at the three of them, "leaves this scene until I clear them."

They nodded. Sophia squeezed her father's hand.

"You didn't leave those stock pots on, did you?" Jeremy asked.

"You know I did," Lamere said. "You were right there with me."

"I said earlier that you shouldn't do it."

"Like hell. They couldn't have caused this anyway."

"Wait a minute," Turk said. "You left something cooking overnight with no one in the goddamn restaurant?"

"Never in the history of restaurants has a stock pot caused a full-out fire like this," Lamere said.

"You've got to be kidding me," Rawley said.

"It's a stock pot," Lamere said. "You bring it to a boil, then turn it down to a simmer on barely a flame. It would take twenty-four hours for it to boil down."

"Schotzie is going to want to talk to both of you."

"Please tell me your insurance is in order," Rawley said.

"Of course it is," said Sophia. She felt ready to cry again as she looked at the two boys and her restaurant. She stepped away and called Cam again. He didn't answer and she didn't leave a message. He didn't have anyone left up here, she realized, except for maybe Brinkley.

"What do you want?" Brinkley's voice cracked over the

phone. "It's the middle of the fucking night."

"Is Cam there, Brinkley? He's not answering his phone."

"With you calling, I don't blame him. I warned him about this shit."

"You don't know anything. Put him on, please."

"He's not here."

"Wake him up. The restaurant is on fire."

"What?"

"Just what I said. We're at the pier. Jeremy, my father. Me. The entire fire department. Chief Turkington. Schotzenburg, the fire chief. Everyone but Cam. If you don't believe me, you can call Turk. But please give Cam the phone."

"He went out to his old place at the beach."

"What's he doing there?" she said.

"Ask yourself that question."

"I feel bad enough without having to explain to you. I need to talk to him. Will you call him and tell him what's going on."

"I could, but it won't do any good. Even if he were in condition to answer his phone, which I doubt that he is, he doesn't have a car. I dropped him there."

"He was drunk?"

"No thanks to you." Brinkley hung up.

"Father, I need to either borrow the car or have you take me home so I can get mine. Cam's out at his parent's old place at Gray Gull."

"What's he doing there?" Turk asked, stepping in.

"We had a fight.   No, we didn't. There was a misunderstanding."

"I can send a car for him," Turk said.

"No, I'll go and bring him right back," Sophia said.

"Be quick about it."

"You can drop me at home," Rawley said. "I'm not going to stand here with these two and watch our money burn."

"Where is that coming from?" Jeremy asked. "We worked our asses off."

"If I didn't think Turk would lock me up," Rawley said. "I'd take you two apart right now."

"I'm tempted to let you do it," Turk said, shaking his head. "Go on and get going. Sophia, you better had not be long. I'm going to need to talk to Cam."

"You should," she said. "He's a part owner, too."

"I wasn't aware of that," Turk said.

Rawley nodded in confirmation.

Jeremy scowled. "He's a silent partner. Sweat equity."

Rawley put his arm around Sophia and walked her to the car. The flames had been squelched but smoke poured from the building heavier than ever.

Her hands were shaking as she drove to Gray Gull. She thought she might throw up at every dip in the road. How could there have been a fire? If her one mistake was never made, she and Cam would have been there to the end and they wouldn't have allowed them to leave a pot on overnight, and everything would be fine. If that was even the cause. One stupid thing leads to another, and then everything is shit.

The front door of the cottage was nailed shut. Scrap lumber was heaped on the lawn. As she walked around the house, a spire of smoke rose on the western horizon. The sky was starting to lighten. The deck's pitch was more noticeable now that it had been. There wasn't a back door. She had to jump up to get inside.

"Cam," she called. The interior was bare. Walls had yellowed as if stained with a hundred years of cigarettes. The linoleum in the kitchen was streaked with black. Rust lines marked where appliances had stood. Even the ceiling seemed to be closing down over her. She expected the red eyes of a rat to peer out of open cupboards. She called his name again. The place itself was silent. The surf murmured from one side and a car passed on the street from the other.

She climbed the stairs. Her hand was coated with dirt as she gripped the rail. His old room was open and he lay in the middle of the floor curled into a ball where that little twin bed used to be. She knelt next to him and pushed the hair that had fallen across his face onto his forehead. She said his name softly and nudged his shoulder. He groaned and rubbed his hands across his eyes before opening them.

"You," he said. "Fucking Brinkley."

"I'm sorry."

"Right."

"Listen to me, please." He rolled over onto his stomach, away from her. She sat down next to him, her knees bent in front of her, her arms wrapped around them. A gull screeched.

"Whatever you saw, or thought you saw—"

"Do not tell me I was seeing things. I may be an idiot, but I'm not blind." He rolled himself over and sat with his back against the wall. His eyes went everywhere around the room except to her.

"I know this is going to sound foolish, but it was nothing. It was a moment. A stupid, non-existent flashpoint from all we had accomplished together and it was over the instant it started. It meant one thing to him and something different to me—something much different. Oh, fuck it." She started crying.

"So now you're the victim? Just like those fucking shows you watch?"

She needed to tell him about the restaurant. Which was going to be worse?

"Your day isn't going to get any better," she said.

"That's true, because I've got about five minutes before I puke."

"The restaurant caught on fire."

"Our restaurant?"

"That's the one."

"Fuck you."

"Look out the window." She stood up and went over to it. "You can see the smoke."

"How does this happen? Who?"

"They don't know yet."

"Is it bad?"

She nodded.

"We have to get going. Turk wants you over there."

"I'm a fucking suspect?" He stopped yelling and walked over to the corner of the room. He bent over and retched, his body convulsing as he spewed a rail of yellow bile.

"Let's get the fuck out of here," he said.

"They think that Lamere left a stock cooking or something. That might be the cause."

He could have torn apart the house right then and saved Brinkley the trouble. But why bother, he decided. It was over, all of it. When they stepped out of the kitchen he nearly fell. To the south, a nasty black contrail reached up into the just-blue sky.

"I remember seeing it," he said.

"What?"

"A glow. I was out here last night. I thought I was hallucinating. I could see the glow."

"I want you to come home," she said.

"Just take me to the restaurant."

He couldn't believe the number of fire trucks crowded on the pier, at least eight or nine. Lamere and Jeremy stood outside the lot behind the yellow police tape. Past them Turk was conferring with Harvey Schotzenburg. The smoke coming from his building was now gray and left in wisps. The place reeked of charcoal. Jeremy looked pale, as if in worse shape than the restaurant, which was plainly ruined.

"Look at it, man," Jeremy said, his voice cracking. He probably thought his anguish was so great that Cam would forget that there was something between them. Lamere stood there, too, his eyes red.

Turk was nodding and Schotzie was shaking his head and waving his arms.

"Did they find out anything yet?" Sophia asked.

"No," Jeremy said.

Turk and Schotzie walked over to the police chief's cruiser.

"You two, come here," Turk yelled. "No, all four of you."

Jeremy led the way. When Sophia fell into step beside Cam, he scuffled his feet so that he wouldn't be side by side with her. Lamere followed.

"Which of you is the idiot that Turk was telling me left a stock cooking?" Schotzie asked. Schotzie's gray beard was flaked with soot.

"It couldn't have been that," Lamere said. "We both checked it." He pointed to Jeremy.

"I told you not to do it," Jeremy said.

"What the fuck?" Lamere said. "You looked at it with me. The flame wasn't an inch high."

"Schotzie?" Turk said.

"I know the sprinklers and alarms were working, because I permitted them myself. They functioned. I know that the fire started in the kitchen. Anyone could figure that out. Your precious stock pot is melted to the stove top. So if it didn't boil down, maybe there was something next to it that caught, cooking oil, a wooden skewer, a rag, an apron. You might be aware that there's a lot of flammable material in a fucking kitchen. But the fire started on that goddamn stove. It's safe to say that's what the marshal's going to sign off on when he investigates."

"So, if they don't leave that pot on, probably nothing happens?" Sophia asked.

"Give the girl a prize, Turk," Schotzie said.

"If the gas on the pier caught, this whole end of town could've been leveled," Turk said. "Do you realize that?"

"It didn't," Jeremy said.

"It doesn't make any sense," Lamere said. "How does a giant pot over a tiny flame turn into this? It couldn't have been it."

"Maybe the flame was bigger than you thought," Schotzie said, shaking his head. "It's a goddamn unattended fire. Anything can happen."

"They simmer stocks overnight in every kitchen in the goddamn country." Lamere's chin quivered as he spoke.

"Jesus Christ." Schotzie spit on the ground. "To do what, make some fucking Campbell's soup? Big fucking deal."

"It was a long day and we were tired," Jeremy said, shaking his head. "We might not have been a hundred percent focused."

"Well, la-di-da," Schotzie said.

Cam launched himself linebacker-style into Jeremy's gut, taking him down with a ferocity he'd never approached in the three years he'd played Pop Warner football.

CHAPTER FORTY-FIVE
"Senator" Grimes

There are times a man does not wish to be disturbed. When a woman of beauty is spread-eagled across one's bed, that is one of them. To have a specimen like Brit so close that the heat from her skin makes the hair on the back of one's neck stand up is a reason to live. I had invited her here for the opening of the FishHouse, of which I should have held a position of honor. I was denied a table on opening night, presumably due to overbooking. We will dine there this evening, however, and as often occurs when Brit visits, Jeremy will be tripping over his tongue trying to impress her. Just this evening, the regulars from my table at the Dockside had pathetically and predictably fawned. Her jeans were cut short enough as to not have to imagine the curl of her bottom, which rolls like the hills of the promised land as she now lays next to me. Her breasts, full and prominent, had pushed the buttons of her fitted shirt to their limits. She would make a lesser man drool.

Brit reached over and put her hand in mine. It took great discipline to turn from her and answer the phone ringing on my night table. I was expecting a report, and if it were only a matter of business, I would have let it go all day. But pride was at stake. I had dispatched an associate to act on my behalf and was anxious to hear the results. I lay back with my head on the pillow and took the call. A successful outcome would make the rest of the morning and that evening even more satisfying.

"Hey, man," the voice said. "I didn't do it."

"You are joking," I replied, sitting up.

"Instead of treating me like a bitch, you should be thanking my ass."

"Why is that?"

"I hadn't heard from you, so I figured you don't know what happened. But when you do find out, I had nothing to do with the fucking thing. That's the lucky part."

"Try it one step at a time. What happened?"

"So, your honor hasn't heard?"

"Spill it, Boney."

"Place burned last night."

"Your place?"

"No, the dink's restaurant. Went up like a bonfire about three in the morning."

"The FishHouse?"

"If you give your dick a rest and look out the fucking window, you can probably still see the smoke."

I leapt from the bed. My room looked to the south, over the Shores. I ran across the hall to one of the guest rooms with a northern exposure. The sky was only dotted with cirrus clouds.

"I don't see anything, Boney," I said.

"Looked like a fucking coal plant out over the harbor last night. You didn't hear the sirens?"

"Obviously not. So what did you do, Boney? The truth."

"I didn't do anything. I didn't even go. I got preoccupied. But the word at the Beachcomber this morning, some of the fire guys were in there afterward, they said the dumbasses left something cooking overnight and it caught."

"You expect me to believe that?"

"Call, your public service officials, your honor.   Guy said that Schotzie wanted to kill the fucks. The whole pier could have gone up."

"Did anyone wonder what you were doing there?"

"I told you, I didn't even go. I don't like the prick, but if you had asked for that, I would have said, 'Screw.' Lighting a torch ain't throwing a brick through a picture window."

It then occurred to me just who I was talking to. Boney was not unintelligent, at least regarding limited aspects of common sense. He'd been supplying marijuana to residents here for the last fifteen years without detection or arrest. Even if he had a hand in it, he wouldn't have admitted it to anyone, including me.

"So how did you find out about this if you weren't actually there? Am I to believe a friendly sea gull stopped by and put a word in your ear?"

"I made a new friend last night, a little spinner who just hit town. We were up late and wide awake. We were over at the barn, went outside for some smoke.   I could hear the commotion and the sirens from out at my place. Then it's just a matter of turning on the scanner."

"I'm supposed to believe this?"

"What would've been the difference between last night and tonight anyway? It's just a brick through a window. You saved yourself a few C-notes, which I'm assuming you need."

"What makes you think a few hundred dollars means anything to me?"

"The Dockside boys were all buzzed up about that honey you brought back to town. They think all it runs you is a few nice dinners and a plane ticket, but I got an eye for these things, as you know."

"I find that your lack of commitment is exceeded only by your lack of knowledge."

"You can't bullshit me, your honor."

"Boney?"

"Yeah?"

"Go fuck yourself."

He was wrong about one thing—the money. The few hundred dollars I would have paid Boney to shatter one the FishHouse's harbor windows meant nothing to me. Pride, on the other hand, is everything. Knowing that Jeremy tried to take advantage and think that he got the better of me would have soured my time there. I couldn't have ever sat at that bar and enjoyed a Gosling's and tonic had I not made a statement. It wouldn't have mattered that Jeremy wouldn't have known that it was I who put the crack in his world. Turk would have told him it was some lobsterman's retaliation for a delivery truck blocking a parking space or some other pedestrian annoyance. That would have been fine. The only scoreboard that should matter is one's own.

Regardless, we had dodged the proverbial bullet. If Boney had gone to the pier as I had instructed, complications could have arisen. But luck usually visits those who deserve it. I would call Turk and get the details later. There was a lady looking at my figure from the bed. Her eyes, a sparkling blue, invited me to return. I lay down and assumed the position, a glorious start to the day.

CHAPTER FORTY-SIX

As she drove him to his truck, she tried again to explain what happened—not with the restaurant but between her and Jeremy. He sat on her father's leather seat and hung his face out the window like a dog. If she had been making sense about being trapped in a moment of time—the instant he happened to walk in the office—his mind was too clouded to understand. Causes and motivations were beyond him. What he wanted most was to not throw up again. When they reached the Ranger, parked crookedly across two spaces in the Tavern's faded lot, they got out of the car.

"Are you coming home?" she asked.

"No," he replied.

"Don't let a few seconds of stupidity on my part ruin everything."

"I can't deal now," he said and climbed into the truck. Tears were rolling down her face as he drove off. He made it to Brinkley's and then puked again in the man's driveway.

CHAPTER FORTY-SEVEN

For two days at Brinkley's, alternating between a hammock strung between oaks in the backyard and the Lazy Boy in the den, Cam read a copy of *The Bridges of Madison County* that he'd found amidst the fishing guides and furniture-making manuals. He was unable to remember what happened from one paragraph to the next. His mind kept backsliding to Sophia, searching for ways to rationalize a return to her. It was ironic, he thought. When they'd first started spending time together, he hadn't wanted to like her but had been unable to help himself. Now he was working at it, and it wasn't easy.

She had only kissed Jeremy, and briefly, at that. It was understandable. They had a history, and there was no denying the emotion they all had poured into the opening. That single action could be excused. However, he couldn't stop wondering what might have happened had he not walked in when he did. Would she have come to her senses and slapped him? Would he have hiked up her dress and ravaged her on top of the desk like in some Skinemax flick? The resulting phone messages indicated that something in her would have prevented it from happening. But that it might have had him uselessly flipping pages.

He also weighed his own actions.   He'd snapped after merely viewing Miranda and Mr. Chicken in matching spandex, riding bikes like kids.   Now he was trying to will himself into a bastion of compassion and trust.   He could consider himself the worst of the lot.   When he had cheated on Miranda with Sophia, Cam had been thoughtless and self-serving.   Not even at his most disgusted could he accuse Sophia of that.   On Monday afternoon he called her and told her he was ready to come home.

She was pacing the driveway when he pulled in.   Her face was more relieved than happy as she threw herself against him. They hugged and her thin body shuddered.   Side by side, they climbed the stairs to the apartment.   He changed out of the oversized clothes he'd borrowed from Brinkley.   His own shorts and t-shirt did not make him any more comfortable.

They rode in the Jeep out to the FishHouse.   The exterior could have looked worse.   Most of the lower clapboards remained intact and unstained.   There were clear indications of disaster, however.   The sign hung from one hook.   A ring of black covered the eaves like plaster.   The evergreens had been trampled and split.   Windows were again boarded shut with plywood.

They stepped over the police tape and approached the building.   A crack in the kitchen door revealed a goop of ash, fire retardant, and charcoaled stainless.   The stove top was a molten mess.   They walked around back and found the windows intact but coated with soot.   A hand had swiped a swath clean, allowing them to see into the dining room— which also gave them a view of the kitchen.   The wall separating the two had been reduced to a skeleton of blackened two-by-fours.   What hadn't burned was stained by smoke.   As soon as the building was declared safe, a salvage crew would be sent in.   Rawley had taken over dealing with the insurance company and assured her that everything would be replaced: Equipment, goods, food, linen, plates, silverware, booze, all of it. Some things, Cam knew, were a total loss: Her paintings, his sweat.

"We can get inside," Sophia said, "if you want."

"No," he said.

"It's not hard to imagine putting it back the way it was, is it?"

As if she had clicked on an icon, a critical path began forming in his head. He wondered how much of the framing had been damaged. Was it still structurally sound? How far was Ordway booked out? Where were Paine, Whitworth, and Scapa, and what were they doing? Logic dictated that piecing it together would be a more manageable task than its original construction, but something clawed at the notion. Suddenly woozy, he leaned back against the pier's rail to steady himself.

"We can do it," she said, wrapping her arms around him.

On their way home they got pizza and stopped at Bradley's for beer and wine. Just as they had so many nights that summer, they sank into the leather of the couch and let the day fall away from them. She turned on the Red Sox game for him. He searched for and couldn't find a conversation topic that wouldn't lead into a discussion of the previous four days. Sophia asked questions about baseball strategy. Cam explained the hit and run. They sat in the green light of the field, barely speaking, until the sixth inning.

"I'm sorry," she said. "For everything."

"Let's leave it behind us," he said. "We all took a beating."

"Some of us worse than others. You broke Jeremy's nose when you tackled him."

A scrap of justice.

The game ended, and they had nothing left but to go to bed. Sophia disappeared into the bathroom, and he started picking up the empty bottles. He threw their paper plates in the garbage and corked her wine and placed it in the refrigerator. Then he straightened the couch. The way the bedroom had always beckoned them like a ready-to-go carnival ride, cleaning had always been a morning activity.

He found her with the blankets pulled up to her neck. She watched him shed his clothes, save for his boxers, and he slid in next to her. He didn't know how close he could or should get. They lay with a pocket of air between them. He couldn't bring himself to pull her close. She rolled over to face him and placed her hand on his chest. He slid his arm beneath her neck. Neither of them moved. Eventually, they fell asleep.

They attempted life as they had known it. When she went running in the morning, Cam stared at the ceiling. He couldn't get back to sleep. With his bank account bled down to nothing and days of rehashing the weekend in front of him, he jumped out of bed. He drove to Gray Gull. In his old driveway was a box car-sized dumpster. A bulldozer had dropped the house into a jagged pyramid of splintered two-by-fours, plywood, and clapboards. Brinkley was doing his own demolition, running a front end loader. His new man, a kid that Cam didn't know, was throwing armfuls of the wreckage into the scoop on top of what Brinkley had picked up. The wood that would comprise the forms for a new foundation was stacked next to the sidewalk. When Brinkley saw Cam, he shut down his machine.

"Need any help?" Cam asked.

"On this job?" Brinkley asked. "You sure?"

"I am." He couldn't imagine anything sinking him lower than he already was. All he'd have to do is show up, shut off his mind, and do the work he'd started as a teenager. It would be a relief.

"I've got gloves in the truck if you need them. We'll deal with the rest later."

Over the course of the week, they cleared the debris, excavated, and fabricated the forms for the foundation. The new house would stand on rectangular concrete pilings set sideways to the ocean, so that when the storm-to-end-all-storms came to punish the beach, the structure would have a chance. As Cam sweat through the late-summer days, his gaze often found the sea wall and white sand and shoals that he'd known his entire life. He never consciously thought of them as being "his." This was a job site that happened to be on the coast. Cam simply enjoyed the view.

He and Sophia tried to regain their rhythm. They met at the Dockside after work on Friday. By the time she joined him, he'd had a head start drinking with Lenny, Trouper, the Senator, and Brink. They'd felt compelled to tell him that the fire was a tough break after all he'd done, especially considering the nature of the blaze, which Cam was surprised to find was general knowledge. When Cam nodded and answered with a one-word, "Thanks," they let it rest. He was happy to listen to Trouper regale them with the success of his Lobster Cruises. The Senator mourned that his lady friend had flown back to Dallas. Perkins bragged about putting up ten condos at a development in Wellport, and then argued with Brinkley over who would pull in the biggest striper that weekend. He supposed that this night was not so different than any other of the summer.

When Sophia arrived, they moved to the bar. Surrounded by tourists, they got shitfaced on beer, wine, and shots of Jaegermeister. At home, they only had to let their instincts take over. Clothes were strewn from the doorway to the couch. But instead of waking twisted into a pretzel as they had so often in the morning, Cam found himself on the opposite side of the bed. She leaned over and kissed him before she got up.

"I'm relieved that's out of the way," Sophia said, as she put on her dri-fit shorts.

"We were awful drunk," he said. "Neither of us should have driven."

"Sometimes it's a rough road back to normal," she said, smiling.

"Here we are," he replied. Since walking onto the pier the

morning after the fire, he'd had to measure his every word and
action. He found his vocabulary dwindling. When he heard
the door close and her sneakers hit the stairs, his head fell deep
into the pillow and his limbs slackened.

Sophia and Jeremy had started planning the FishHouse's
resurrection. There had never been a question that they would
soldier on as partners. She described their progress to Cam
over dinner each night. On certain issues, they had come to
quick agreement. Lamere would not be back. There would be
no overnight stocks. Their next opening night would be paced
more reasonably with fewer tables, no matter who showed up.
But what brought life to her eyes was their deciding that every
possible detail in the original FishHouse would be replicated.
Cam tried to listen without grimacing. The ease at which
Sophia was able to forgive Jeremy astounded him. She hadn't
blamed him for any of it, but instead acknowledged her own
responsibility. That didn't stop Cam from finding Jeremy
culpable. In another month, they would be thrown together
again. Cam doubted his ability to accept an apology, or that
one would suffice.

When the fire marshal's report came in on a Tuesday
afternoon, a meeting was scheduled for that evening in
Rawley's office. Jeremy's MG was in the driveway when Cam
and Sophia came out of their garage. Sophia held his hand as
they walked over. Cam wiped his palms on his jeans before
entering the house. In the office, Rawley was behind his desk.
Three chairs were spread out in front of him. Jeremy stood
when they came in.

"Hey," Jeremy said, shaking Cam's hand. Unfortunately,
his nose showed no sign of fracture.

"Hey," Cam replied. Sophia sat in the chair between them.

"If we're going to move forward," Rawley said. "Personal

issues have to be dead and buried. Are we all on board?"

"Absolutely," Jeremy said. He sat with his head up, his hair perfect, a serious, eager expression on his face. He'd either refused to examine his role in bringing them here or lacked the ability to do so. Rawley had to be sucking it up for Sophia's sake; otherwise why he wouldn't he have had Jeremy's legs broken?

"Cam?" Rawley asked.

"All business," Cam said.

"Good," Rawley said. "We've received some great news. The report definitively states that the fire was determined to be of an accidental origin starting in the kitchen, which is what we suspected. They've also declared that the building remains structurally viable. We can get in as of today, and we'll have a salvage crew hit it by the end of the week. One other thing has fallen our way, as well. I've gained approval to have Cam head the rebuilding, this despite the insurance company's usual policy prohibiting owner-contractors."

Sophia bounced in her seat and clutched his arm.

"To get things rolling," Rawley said, "we're going to meet with the adjuster to make some preliminary determinations. We're doing that tomorrow at nine."

"I've got to work in the morning," Cam said.

"You're joking, right?" Jeremy said.

"Of course, he is," Sophia said, her fingers digging into his wrist.

Rawley's eyebrows were raised and his smile uneven, as if he knew something that Cam did not. Cam didn't doubt that to be true.

Cam and Sophia followed Rawley over in the morning, as Cam planned on going to Gray Gull as soon as it was over. Jeremy drove in right behind them. They waited at the start of the walkway without speaking. Neal Farmington, the adjuster, wore Dockers, a short sleeved white shirt, and rubber boots. He also possessed an iron grip when shaking hands. Cam feared it would be the least painful part of the day.

Farmington passed out hardhats and they entered the restaurant through the kitchen. Cam had expected it to look as bad as it did. What he hadn't anticipated was the smell, worse now than the morning of the fire. It was a combination of charcoal, burnt iron, rotting meat, and chemicals. He didn't know what napalm smelled like, but he imagined it was like this. Just breathing made him wonder if it would ever leave his nose.

"Of course, this area is a total loss," Farmington said. "Everything not damaged by fire got it with the hoses. You know, there's thousands of gallons shot into a blaze like this. But that's what kept it contained." They walked to the dish area. "Perhaps some of the minor appliances in the prep station might be saved. My guess, the interior walls will need reframing. You win some, lose some, and this could have been much worse. We'll need figures on building costs, from soup to nuts, no pun intended."

"This sucks," Jeremy said, as they stepped through the walkway, over the dining room doors which had been knocked down either by the fire or the attempt to extinguish it. Sophia stood apart as they looked over the devastation. Cam followed her eyes. They went from the painting behind the bar, which had seemingly melted, to where others placed on the wall opposite the kitchen were now ashes. She bit down on her bottom lip. She was trying not to cry. Cam put his arm around her.

Three bottles remained on the liquor shelves. At the spot where Jeremy had planted himself at the end of the bar, a pile of shattered glass as high as their knees rose from the floor. The bar top itself had survived, although the poly had melted and the pine charred at the end near the kitchen. That repair would be a project in itself.

"You might actually be able to save some of the furniture," Farmington said. The tables and banquettes on the far side of the restaurant seemed intact. However, most of the chairs and stools were on their sides. Tablecloths had either been scorched or blackened. A layer of sludge coated the floor near the windows, where the force of the hoses had thrust everything. Glasses, bottles, silverware, menus, and candle holders were mired in fallout against the baseboard, the flood tide of the apocalypse.

"What about that stench?" Jeremy said. "That's not something that will be covered up with paint, right?"

"No shit," Cam said.

"All the drywall will have to be replaced," Farmington said. "That's fairly obvious."

"I'd hate to see what this place would've looked like if the fire had spread," Jeremy said.

"I'd have loved to see what the place would've looked like had you and your chef been sober and watching what the fuck you were doing," Cam said.

"What was that?" Farmington said.

"Needless to say, there are some hard feelings stemming from the disappointment," Rawley said, glaring at Cam.

"We've got a lot of work to do," Farmington said. "Let's start by going over the construction materials used here."

Farmington asked construction questions and Cam supplied answers. He could have been filling in ovals with a number two pencil on the LSAT's. Jeremy's input, given as if it wasn't his fat-headedness that had brought them here, ceased to spark a reaction. When they had reached the end of Farmington's list, Sophia, Rawley, and Jeremy smiled as if real progress had been made.

"Of course, we'll need to inventory the financials in the office and examine the loft, as well," Farmington said. "Smoke damage could be an issue."

They proceeded upstairs without Cam.

He went outside behind the restaurant and sat in the sun, hanging his legs off the end of the pier. Most of the lobster boats were out, their moorings solitary circles on the blue. At the far end of the pier, a few men cast lines into the water. He looked down at his construction boots. They were coated with muck up to the ankle. When he raised his head, he was staring across the bay at Horton's. A black square—a tarp, he guessed—covered his and Sophia's handiwork on the garage. He hadn't noticed it before and wondered how long it had been there. He returned his gaze to the harbor. An ache passed through his entire body. He tried to clear his head.

He heard them come down the stairs and lock the front door. A few minutes later, Sophia found him. She sat next to him, her thigh against his. He didn't move.

"That was encouraging," Sophia said. "Don't you think?"

"Not exactly," he said, surprised he could voice it.

"What do you mean?" she said.

"I can't do it," he said. "I don't have it in me."

It killed him to watch her face collapse.

CHAPTER FORTY-EIGHT

There was always a morning at the end of August when the heavy, humid atmosphere of Laurel broke. A crisp coolness enveloped the town. The two-month sprint was over. Vacationers packed their SUV's. Tourists vanished. The town returned to its residents. In those ways, the weeks after Labor Day were as sweet as the beginning of summer. It was Cam's favorite time of year.

But that wasn't going to stop him. The window in the Ranger was rolled down and his left arm hung out in the sun. The green fields off the turnpike streamed past.

Cam flew onto the Piscataqua River Bridge into New Hampshire. As he crossed the state line his cell went off. He glanced at the caller ID, then slowed down to pick up the phone and answer the call.

"I'm sorry," he said.

"I knew you were going to leave early," Sophia said.

"How?"

"You packed two days ago. Planning like that is unlike you, unless it's something big. Building a dog house, for example."

"I was afraid if I waited I'd have said some things that I

wouldn't be able to back up."

"I know. I read your note. I understand."

"Will you come visit?"

"I don't think so," she said.

"You're the only reason I'm able to go in the first place." She'd lent him five hundred dollars to get there and given him a GPS. She'd already programmed the garage as "home."

"You were going anyway," she said. "I just made it comfortable."

"I wouldn't call this comfortable. I had to sneak out."

"I know you'll come back to me," she said.

"I'm planning on it," he said.

"This is where you belong."

While he had always believed that, thinking about it now dropped him under the surface where his vision blurred and he struggled to hold the air inside him. Cam said goodbye to Sophia as he passed through the Hampton toll booth. It was only three thousand miles to Dan's in Long Beach. He would spend his winter at some movie studio building illusions for people he didn't know. In a few weeks maybe he'd check in with Brinkley, who was rebuilding the restaurant. Cam had chosen to remain a partner, turning down Rawley's offer to buy out his share. He hoped that at some point he'd start feeling like his old self again.

Cam programmed the cruise control and sat back. Wind whipped through the cab. All he had to do was keep pointed in the right direction.

ABOUT THE AUTHOR

Albert Waitt is a long time resident of Maine. His short fiction has appeared in *The Literary Review*, *Third Coast*, *The Beloit Fiction Journal*, *Words and Images*, *Stymie: A journal of sport and literature*, and other places. Waitt is a graduate of Bates College and the Creative Writing Program at Boston University. He teaches Creative Writing for the University of Phoenix. He also coaches youth basketball and softball when not putting in the miles around Kennebunkport.

Made in the USA
Lexington, KY
17 June 2013